ALSO B

WARPATH: JACK'S FAITH IS TESTED

WARPATH: JACK'S FAITH IS TESTED

THE FRONTIER CHRONICLES
BOOK 4

MARK GREATHOUSE

WISE WOLF
BOOKS

WISE WOLF BOOKS
An Imprint of Wolfpack Publishing
wisewolfbooks.com
1707 E. Diana Street
Tampa, FL 33610

WARPATH: JACK'S FAITH IS TESTED.
Text copyright © 2024 Mark Greathouse

Paperback ISBN 979-8-9908171-8-0
eBook ISBN 979-8-9908171-7-3
LCCN: 2024946316

Dedicated with love to my wife Carolyn, our two sons Mike and Matt, and the memory of my father John F. Jack Greathouse

Pay your obligations to everyone: taxes to those you owe taxes,

tolls to those you owe tolls, respect to those you owe respect,

and honor to those you owe honor.

MATTHEW 13:7

THE CAST

Jack O'Toole – Seventeen-year-old son of Joseph and Kate O'Toole. He strives to carve a life from the Texas frontier on the easternmost reaches of the Comancheria.

Mukwooru (aka, Spirit Talker) – Seventeen-year-old son of a Penateka Comanche chief camped within the heart of the Comancheria. The warrior name bestowed upon teen Wild Horse in recognition of his apparent connection with Taa Narumi (the Comanche Great Father) whom they confused with God.

Blue Flower – Young sister to Spirit Talker and daughter to Buffalo Hump, she's married o Jack.

George Freeman – A Black cowboy driving cattle north; later an Army scout. He establishes a ranch on the North Platte River in Wyoming.

Running Waters – George Freeman's Pawnee wife.

Kate – Jack's twelve-year-old sister.

Buck – Jack's seven-year-old brother.

Mato (aka Bear) – An Oglala Lakota warrior.

Otaktay (aka Kills Many) – An Oglala Lakota war chief.

Isaac Fisher – An Amish farmer from Pennsylvania seeking new opportunity on the frontier.

Sarah Fisher – Isaac Fisher's wife and mother to baby son named for Jack.

Topsannah (aka, Prairie Flower) – Young Comanche girl captured and enslaved by Arapaho Tribe and living with George Freeman.

Sam Collins – Owner of the Circle C Ranch located near Jack's spread.

Hank Johnson – Drover on Jack's cattle drive to Fort Laramie. He carries deep prejudice against Indians.

Juan Perez – Creative, hard-nosed Mexican cook on Jack's trail drive.

Shorty McBride – Drover on Jack's cattle drive who lives up to his nickname.

Willard *Will* Smith—First hired hand on the Rising Cross Ranch.

Stella Klappenbach—August Klappenbach's wife.

Tosahwi (a.k.a. White Knife)—Nokoni Comanche warrior.

Mupitsukupu (a.k.a. Old Owl)—Ambitious Comanche seeking to become the shaman of Buffalo Hump's Penateka Comanche village.

Hardy Sullivan—Grizzled Texas Ranger who becomes friends with Jack and finds God.

William McGregor—A Scottish immigrant who serves as a blacksmith and pastor in Austin, TX.

Zeb—A wolf that Jack believes is a gift from God. They develop an ever-closer bond as the Frontier Chronicles evolve.

HISTORICAL CHARACTERS

Buffalo Hump – War chief of the Penateka Comanche, the southernmost band of the Comanche people in the Comancheria. In the famous Council House Fight of 1840, he led roughly a thousand Comanche across Texas to the Gulf Coast where they ransacked Victoria and burned Linnville.

Captain Nathan Benton – Texas Ranger captain assigned to protect settlers from Indians in the Leona River region northwest of Fort Inge. (Benton eventually would serve as a lieutenant colonel in the Confederate Army, 36th Texas Cavalry.)

Makhpia-Luta (aka Red Cloud) – Chief of Oglala Lakota of the Sioux Nation.

Tasunke Witko (aka Crazy Horse) – Future chief of Oglala Lakota of the Sioux Nation. He is about 19 years old at the time of this story, but already gaining attention of tribal leaders. He will go on to lead the massacre of General Custer's troops at Little Big Horn (aka, Greasy Grass).

Tatanka Iyotake (aka Sitting Bull) – Chief and medicine man of Hunkpapa band of Lakota Sioux.

August Klappenbach – Early settler of Bandera, TX and owner of first general store and post office.

Thomas Twiss – Indian agent assigned to Fort Laramie region.

Major William Hoffman – Officer-in-Charge at Fort Laramie in 1857.

John Salmon *Rip* Ford—*Texas Ranger, Confederate colonel, doctor, lawyer, journalist, newspaper owner, and legislator.*

Quanah Parker—*Chief of the Quahadi band of the Comanche. Son of Comanche chief Peta Nocona and Cynthia Ann Parker.*

Po-bish-e-quash-o (a.k.a. Iron Jacket)—*Tenawa Comanche chief at Battle of Little Robe Creek.*

Hardin Richard Runnels—*Sixth governor of the state of Texas.*

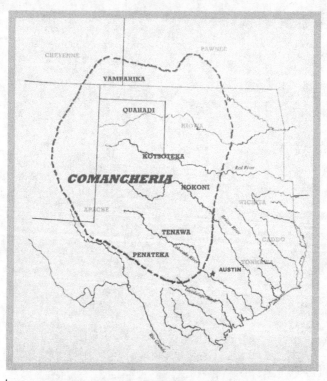

The Comancheria features six of thirteen recognized Comanche tribes: Yamparika, Quahadi, Kotsoteka, Nokoni, Tenawa, and Penateka. Other tribes are identified in gray typeface, all caps, including Apache, Cheyenne, and Kiowa. Note that the Sante Fe Trail followed the northern border of the Comancheria. (Map by Mark Greathouse)

YOU ARE INVITED

Dear Reader,

If you've read *Perilous Trails, Wyoming Calls,* and *Longhorns North,* it's likely my story has fully grabbed you. This fourth part of my tale begins in 1857 but mostly occurs in 1858. In 1855, I had been thrown alone and vulnerable onto the vast Comancheria, the most dangerous part of the frontier. I am now eighteen years old. The Comanche made the Comancheria a no-man's-land for White settlers. I journeyed twice to Wyoming, first exploring the trail northward and then driving a herd of longhorns to my friend George Freeman's ranch on the North Platte. Hostilities between White man and Red man were about to explode, and I was driven to quench the fires.

Warpath: Jack's Faith is Tested continues the tales of my frontier adventures, further testing my courage, faith, endurance, and pure grit. In this chronicle, we must take on the feared Comanche tribes of the ever-dangerous Comancheria. It turns out to be a test of my faith, my strong medicine—the Indians now call me Walks With

Wolves—and it sure teaches me a ton of life lessons. Do keep in mind that my story incorporates history not found in most school history books. This book relates my tale as driven by fate and guided by God.

I have met up plenty with Indians, especially Comanche and Lakota Sioux, so you'll find me using some of their language throughout *Warpath*. I have provided a handy glossary of Comanche and Lakota words toward the back of this book.

I'm a devout Christian, but I tried to grasp the Comanche and Lakota religions to better understand them. The Indian religion is based upon what is referred to as animism, in which every common natural item, from fish and animals to plants, trees, waterways, and mountains, was believed to have souls or spirits. The spirits and traditions connected with them guided the Comanche and Lakota. Their passion for their spirits no doubt gave them their fearlessness as fed by the belief that they were protected in everything they did. Would they kill to defend their beliefs? Theirs was not a religion of love and forgiveness.

Could Indians like the Comanche or Lakota become Christians? My story in *Warpath* continues at evolution at the intersection of faith and culture. Historically, it was not unlike Saint Patrick's conversion of the Irish to Christianity by folding many of their less-offensive heathen rites into the Catholic faith. The British thereafter derisively referred to the Irish as *Black Catholics*. Would this work with the Indians? Well, it's part of the story I'm sharing with y'all.

As you follow my adventures, ask yourself whether you might be up to meeting the challenges I take on. Dangers? Privations? Hmmm. How might you have fared? Through it all, I first relied on the teachings of my family, then went on to learn from the raw and risky experiences I faced. I learned to trust in instincts forged from my biblical lessons.

To be straight here, I had no idea that my story was going to fill multiple volumes until I began to write it all down. I invite you to follow my adventures on America's western frontier.

Kindest regards,
John *Jack* O'Toole

WARPATH: JACK'S FAITH IS TESTED

PROLOGUE

WE HAD PUSHED HARD on our return from driving
longhorns to Wyoming. As we finally drew within sight
of Rising Cross Ranch, our stomachs were turned upside
down at the sight of billowing smoke. It brought back
horrible memories for me of the massacre of my family
by Comanche three years back at the very spot from
where the column of smoke now swirled to the heavens.
Were my hopes of witnessing the birth of my first child
to be dashed? Would tragedy once again strike me?

Our horses were dead tired from having pushed on
through the night, but I nevertheless pulled my revolver
and dug my spurs into Big Red's flanks. He quickly rose
to the call with a full gallop. The rest of my *little army*
was caught off guard by my reaction but quickly unlim-
bered weapons and followed at my heels. This was now a
full-scale charge toward my home, come hell or high
water!

The pounding of our horses' hooves joined with
plenty of sweat, lather, and battle whoops. Combined
with our veritable arsenal of weaponry, we made for a

terrifying sight engaging any enemy daring to cross our path. What mayhem lay ahead? Comanche? Kiowa? Would anyone still be alive? Was God testing Jack O'Toole? Would the *sunipu* of Walks With Wolves prevail again?

ONE
GOD'S PROVIDENCE!

AS WE PULLED CLOSER to the cabin with all our whooping and hollering, the cold, hard truth of reality set in. There was a roaring fire but—blessedly—no Indians. It was a big fire, but one that had been set on purpose to burn off a considerable pile of debris. It was in full fury and giving off hide-blistering heat. We reined back our cayuses in clouds of prairie dust. Me? I was just a tad embarrassed at having jumped to a conclusion. I hadn't realized how strongly I still carried vivid memories of the past.

My little brother Buck stood at the door of the barn and gave me a decidedly curious look before bursting with joy at our arrival. My sister Kate heard our noisy arrival and dashed from the house to see what the commotion was about.

A sweat-coated Isaac leaned on his pitchfork as he paused from tending to the fire and gave me a nonplussed look that said, *it's about time you returned*. He stuck his pitchfork into the ground and smiled at me.

Our hearts were just about ready to burst from our chests. We had feared the worst.

Buck and Kate came running.

I slid from my saddle and swept them into my arms.

Just then, Isaac's wife Sarah came around the corner of the cabin with baby Jack in some sort of contraption on her back. She stood for a moment with her jaw dropped and hands on hips just watching the aftermath of our arrival.

"Dang, but you're dirty, Jack," were the first words from Buck as he found himself trapped in my sweaty arms and dust-covered buckskins.

Kate pulled herself free and gave me the once-over. "Wow, brother! You've grown a piece."

I suppose I had added some muscle onto my better-than-six-foot frame since leaving nearly six months back on the trail drive to Wyoming. I returned the once-over. Kate was now thirteen years old, but she'd filled out a bit herself. She was fast becoming a woman. "Glad to be home, sis," I said with a broad smile.

The world seemed to be in suspension for a brief moment as the reality of our return sunk in.

Spirit Talker scanned the homestead. "Big attack, Jack," he said with uncharacteristic sarcasm. He laughed and helped Prairie Flower from her pony.

The rest of our little army proceeded to dismount and head for the barn and water trough. Shaking off the trail dust and tending horses was the first priority.

I released my grip on Buck and urged him to follow Collins and the other men. I felt her eyes before I even turned to look.

Blue Flower stood in the cabin doorway.

I bounded to her as fast as my saddle-worn legs could carry me.

There must be something to what folks say about the physical impact that surprise, that something unexpected, can cause. I was nearly to her when I stopped. We both looked down. There was water on the porch floorboards beneath where she stood.

Sarah's jaw dropped, and she sprang into action. "Stand back Jack O'Toole, your wife's about to birth a baby!" She dashed past me and helped Blue Flower to our bed. "Kate, get some warm water and some of those cotton cloths!" she barked. She was like a military commander directing a battle. "Jack, you stand by out yonder," she ordered, pointing toward the barn.

I stood fast and looked firmly at her. I then did something that simply wasn't accepted practice in most good Christian homes. I stalked determinedly past Sarah and stood beside the bed. I took Blue Flower's hand in mine. I was not about to budge from the spot. "We are doing this together," I stated flatly but in a loving way. "Dear Lord, please help Blue Flower through this birth of our first child. May he or she be healthy and grow to enjoy your bounty. By God's grace, Amen." The little prayer just spewed out unexpectedly.

"Amen," responded Sarah reflexively. She found herself momentarily embarrassed by my presence over my half-clothed wife but knew that I wasn't about to move a muscle from where I stood.

Zeb appeared in the doorway to our bedroom, peered around, and sniffed the air as only a wolf might do.

Sarah gave him a look that was as strong a command as any that might be spoken, and Zeb strode over to a spot just outside the cabin's front door and sat with a regal demeanor. He likely saw the look of awe that had swept across Buck's face at a real live wild wolf sitting on the front porch. I didn't realize it at that moment of focus on childbirth, but it was as though Zeb was patiently and purposefully waiting for something.

Meanwhile, Sarah sought to keep everything inside the cabin in some semblance of order.

Kate paused awkwardly with the bucket of warm water and cotton cloths occupying both hands before setting them on the table beside the bed. She stood with hands fidgeting, awaiting Sarah's next command.

Sarah shrugged resignedly and began to softly coax Blue Flower through the beginnings of the delivery of our child.

I was already sweating bullets in the July heat. With a coating of trail dust and rivulets of sweat, I didn't present an especially attractive picture. But I was resolute in trying to offer comfort to my beautiful wife.

Despite my disheveled appearance, Blue Flower cast loving eyes between paroxysms of pain. God had indeed smiled upon us and brought me home just in time.

Prairie Flower instinctively realized what was happening and left Spirit Talker's side to see what she could do to help the womenfolk. I gave her an appreciative look as she entered the bedroom. She was even younger than Blue Flower, but seemed to possess some instinct born especially to the Indian women of the frontier plains. Like many young folks, she had become an adult far younger than her years might typically permit.

It was tight and hot in the room as Blue Flower struggled and pushed with all she had in her. I felt sure she would squeeze my hand off. Yet her eyes stayed glued to mine.

Outside, I could hear the fire dying down and the voices of Collins and the others helping Isaac while patiently awaiting the outcome of the goings-on in the cabin.

"One more time, Blue Flower," urged Sarah. "Push hard!"

Blue Flower's face scrunched up with the pain as she gave a mighty final push.

Tears rolled down my cheeks as I heard a small but plaintive murmur, then a true earth-rattling cry. George O'Toole greeted the world. Yes, we named him after my good friend up on the North Platte country.

I was about to kiss Blue Flower when Sarah's arm reached out to stop me.

"Blue Flower isn't finished, Jack," she said gently but firmly. "Another is coming. Y'all are blessed with twins."

Sure enough, an exhausted Blue Flower was instantly back to pushing. The blood flow had barely returned to my hand, but now she held it even tighter. Pain and love lit her eyes, and her gaze locked on mine. Frontier woman? Indeed. She was the measure of any woman on the frontier.

As our second child was brought into the world, I realized that we hadn't considered the possibility of two. I was at a loss for a name. But that could wait, or would have to wait.

Blue Flower lay with two baby boys clinging to her chest. She was totally spent but beaming with joy.

I sat beside her. A six-foot-three tower of lean muscle, crying my eyes out with joy over these miracles of life. God had fulfilled my prayer to be here for the birth of my first children. The O'Toole legacy would fully take root on the Texas Comancheria.

Sarah, Kate, and Prairie Flower went to work cleaning up the bed and making Blue Flower comfortable.

Blue Flower looked up at me with love writ large across her face. The pain of childbirth had been quickly forgotten in the sheer exhilaration of this moment. "I love you, Jack."

I lovingly stroked her hair and caressed her cheek. "I love you. God has blessed us."

Zeb sensed that it was time and came trotting in to investigate. He'd waited patiently. He eased over and placed his muzzle on my lap, whimpering softly at the twins. After permitting me to briefly stroke his head, he nuzzled me again, turned, and ran from the cabin. He stopped and looked back at me, apparently satisfied that all was well. He locked his blue eyes on mine for a moment and took off at a run. A bit of a chill swept through me at Zeb's departure. Was he leaving? Had he said goodbye?

Blue Flower had caught the obvious bond between me and the wolf. She wasn't yet aware of the frontier name that I'd been given. "*Isa?*" she said with a nod to the second twin.

George and Isa? Now, that would be a pair of names special to the Texas frontier. "Isa it is," I agreed. I never could have imagined naming my children after a Black cowboy and a wild wolf.

Blue Flower smiled. I could see her eyelids growing heavy.

Sarah placed the twins in a cradle that Isaac had gifted us with. "She needs rest, Jack," she gently advised.

I nodded, took a loving look at Blue Flower, and strode to the front door.

"Jack walk like Comanche," were Blue Flower's words following me from the room.

I glanced back at her as her smile faded and her eyelids closed in sleep. I wasn't sure what to make of her observation. I suppose that hanging around Comanche and cowboys and switching back and forth from moccasins to boots had caused my gait to hang somewhere between a horseman and a woodsman. I couldn't linger on the thought. As I walked out the front door, a lineup of men with expectant expressions on their faces greeted me. I smiled broadly and raised two fingers. "Two boys!" I exclaimed.

The entire crew took to jumping and shouting with relief at the news and joy over the outcome.

———

LOOKING into the lively eyes of our tiny twins, stroking their soft skin, and watching Blue Flower nurse them combined to give life a new perspective for me. My days of being a carefree teen on the wide-open prairies of Texas had ended with the Comanche attack on our home three years back. Since then, I have been growing up right quickly by necessity. The frontier didn't truck with children doing adult work. It would eat you alive and spit out your bones to bleach in the sun. Here I was, seventeen years old and the father of twin boys, the husband of a beautiful Comanche wife, and the chief family breadwinner by virtue of building a cattle business.

"You must go to Bandera," reminded Blue Flower.

I gave her my "I don't want to leave" look. Taking in the tender sight of her cradling George and Isa in her arms had the effect of breaking down any rough edges from my risk-filled frontier travels or rough-and-tumble cowboying around Rising Cross Ranch. I had to nevertheless resign myself to leaving with Collins and the others to give our partner August Klappenbach his due. It seemed that I had no sooner arrived than I had to go bid goodbye and head to Bandera. It wouldn't be a long visit, but my heart nagged at me to enjoy these early moments with my new sons. Plus, Spirit Talker and Prairie Flower were anxious to be reconnecting with their Comanche *numunuu*.

She smiled. "You must go, Jack."

I gave a reluctant nod.

"Where dog?", she teased.

I laughed. She knew Zeb was a wolf.. "Zeb? Now, you know he's a dog. He is *isa*, a wolf."

She shook her head playfully as though trying to free cobwebs. "Wolf?"

I figured to play along. "You know it's a long story. I named him Zeb, which means gift from God. I saved the life of his mate, and when he lost her, he became loyal to me. Just about every time I seemed threatened in my journeys, Zeb appeared. *Isa* is a strong spirit with the *numunuu*, and his appearance kept the Lakota and Cheyenne and Arapaho from attacking."

"Lakota...Cheyenne...Arapaho?" she gibed.

"Tribes up north near George Freeman's ranch."

Blue Flower nodded. She pretended to shake off her feigned stupor.

"Spirit Talker gave me a Comanche name."

She looked at me playfully, as though with anticipation.

I reckoned she was hiding her concern about my trip to Bandera. I smiled, teasing her just a bit. "My name is Walks With Wolves."

Just as a broad smile creased her lips, baby Isa let out a tiny hunger cry. George quickly followed suit.

"I really must get ready to ride to Bandera."

Blue Flower nodded and began nursing the twins. "We be here, Jack." Her eyes smiled tenderly at me.

I gave her a loving look and headed out.

———

WHERE HAD Zeb run off to? I surveyed the area as I walked to the barn. Zeb was likely hunting. In any case, he had a mind of his own. It wasn't as though he was some pet dog craving my affections. Still, I very much appreciated having him near.

Collins and the others were gathered at the barn door, awaiting my arrival.

"Think yuh can tear yerself away, boss?" teased Shorty.

I blushed in the face of the general chuckling. Everyone seemed in good spirits.

"Walks With Wolves?" Spirit Talker's words were spoken softly but firmly. His pinto, Prairie Flower astride a buckskin mare, and a packhorse stood behind him. His intentions were clear. "We go home, Jack."

I wanted to say that Rising Cross Ranch would always be home for them, but all I could do was nod. A lump had somehow found its way into my throat. Despite his having ridden point for most of our travels to and from Wyoming, we shared a special bond of faith and brotherhood. Shucks, we'd fought together, been baptized together, and he'd married me to his sister. It was hard to imagine two men being any closer. We enjoyed a special bond. Little could I know at this moment that it would be tested.

"We said goodbye to Blue Flower and others."

Buck emerged from the barn with Big Red saddled and ready to ride. He handed me the reins and then realized he'd interrupted something special. "Sorry, Jack," he whispered.

I smiled. "We come visit," I said, gripping Spirit Talker's hand and drawing him near for what I figured to be a man hug. I nodded to Prairie Flower who responded with a smile that said she'd appreciated all the good that had fallen to her after we saved her from enslavement.

As Spirit Talker vaulted into the saddle, I glanced beyond him to see Zeb way off in the distance, observing. "Go with God, Mukwooru," I prayed. With that, I reached into my saddle bag, drew out a New Testament, and handed it to my Comanche brother. I had taught him the rudiments of reading during lonely nights on the trail. "Remember, one of these saved my life."

Spirit Talker nodded. How could he forget the bullet lodged in the pages of the New Testament that I had carried in my breast pocket? He proceeded to lay a very serious look on me. "Beware Noconi and Tenawa," he said, intoning a clear warning.

We had heard about the predations of the Noconi Comanche from Captain Benton. Apparently, the Tenawa Comanche a bit farther to the north had seen fit to mimic their tribal brothers. I looked up at Prairie Flower. She seemed torn between staying a tad longer to get better acquainted with Blue Flower and the inbred desire to be among her own people with her new husband. "We will visit soon," I assured her.

With that, Spirit Talker smiled at Buck and Kate. It wasn't but a couple of years back that he'd helped me rescue them from his very own Penateka Comanche *numunuu*.

Kate offered a tearful little goodbye wave while Buck laid an admiring gaze on his brother's Comanche friend. I could see the adventure in his eyes. Another inch or two in height and a year of mostly helping the women around the ranch, and he'd be just about ready for what folks considered more manly chores.

Blue Flower appeared in the cabin doorway and gave

her departing brother a great smile. All was well…so far as we could tell. A cry from one of the twins drew her back inside.

As I stood taking this all in, I found myself overwhelmed by how truly blessed we were. From time to time, I'd lapsed into thoughts of what I called *couldabeens*. What if the Comanche had not killed most of my family? What if I had not met and become friends with Spirit Talker? And what of George Freeman? Kate and Buck would have been Comanche slaves with no hope of conventional lives. I likely never would have met Blue Flower and begun a life on the vast prairies of the Comancheria. These thoughts rolled through my young brain. Through it all, my faith, my trust in God saw me through.

I went to the cabin door and put my arm around Blue Flower, who had reemerged with a twin in each arm. We watched Spirit Talker and Prairie Flower ride away until they faded from sight. Spirit Talker made one final stop to look back just before disappearing from sight.

Collins and the others had been waiting patiently while we'd said our goodbyes. Now, it was time to head to Bandera. It would only be for a couple of days, though it would seem to last forever. I was home and not enthused about having to leave right away. But I was the trail boss, and that carried weighty responsibilities. I had to respect the needs of the loyal men who'd worked so hard on the trail drive. Surely, Collins was anxious to return to his Circle C spread, and any delays from me were downright selfish on my part. Besides, I admired that he was committed to seeing the venture through to the end.

I kissed Blue Flower and each of the boys before taking Big Red's reins and vaulting up into the saddle.

Blue Flower offered up a great smile. "Go with God, Walks With Wolves," she said with a come-hither tone that said I could not return too soon.

What could I do? The men were looking at me expectantly. I took a deep breath, waved to Blue Flower, and turned Big Red southward. "Head 'em out, men," I said, finding a confident, decisive timbre in my voice.

TWO
BANDERA BUSINESS

THE RIDE to Bandera was easy compared to our recent travels from Fort Laramie. Other than a cowboy or two tending cattle or an errant maverick or mustang, we encountered nary another human or beast. Our senses nevertheless remained on high alert for lurking threats. We would alternate riding a couple of hours and walking an hour until the sun had dropped beneath the hilly horizon to our right. We cold-camped just shy of the second crossing of the Medina River so we could arrive fresh at Klappenbach's store in Bandera the next morning.

We awoke to what promised from the start to be an exceptionally hot day.

"Mornin', boss. We headin' for Klappenbach's store?" Collins asked the obvious.

I laughed. "Thought we might take a swim first." That got everyone in a good humor.

It didn't take long until we reined up in front of August Klappenbach's fine establishment. I put my finger to my lips as a signal for everyone to stay quiet. I dismounted, climbed the stairs, removed my bandana, and wrapped it around the clapper to the bell at the store's entrance. Everyone was smiling at the deviousness of my prank. I expect they were a tad surprised, too, that I had a sense of humor.

I eased the door open and strode on tiptoes to a table where Klappenbach was folding some shirts. I stood behind him. "Where's the owner of this infernal place?" I demanded.

Klappenbach's shoulders hunched just a tad as though he was considering whether he was hearing a vaguely familiar voice. "Who wants to know?" he said as he turned around with a Colt revolver in hand.

I hadn't anticipated his having a weapon, much less finding myself looking down its barrel.

Fortunately for me, his jaw nearly dropped to the floor with surprise. "Well...I'll be goldarned," he spit out, lowering the gun and grabbing my hand in a fearsome handshake. "Welcome back, boy! Heard you made the delivery."

Word seemed to travel faster than a *little army* of drovers and a couple of Comanche journeying by horseback from Wyoming to the heart of Texas. Apparently, some new-fangled invention called a telegraph had hastened the delivery of the news. "Sure did, August. We sure did."

"Well, y'all come on back, and we'll toast to it," he said with a great smile, pointing to his newly outfitted saloon addition to the store. He right quickly had a bunch of chairs drawn up around a big round table and was pressing his barkeep to serve beverages.

"Welcome back," offered Stella Klappenbach as she peeked into the saloon. "Y'all stayin' for dinner?"

We collectively nodded. There was no way we would pass up another one of Stella's feasts.

"Harumph!" guffawed Klappenbach to return our attentions to the matters at hand. Clearly, he figured to get business out of the way before socializing.

I was ready for the good fellow. "We lost eighteen beeves on the trail and ate a half-dozen. Sold a hundred and fifty head and left three hundred twenty-four to graze on George Freeman's pasture. He'll broker their sale with the Indian agency, the military, and surrounding ranches. We cleared two hundred dollars in profit." With that, I laid a pouch containing one hundred dollars in gold on the table in front of Klappenbach.

"You made a profit?" he observed with genuine surprise.

"Should be more as George sells the remaining beeves," I said with a satisfied smile.

By this time, glasses had been filled and everyone was smiling.

"Here's to more successes," offered Klappenbach, and we proceeded to clink glasses together as a toast to the modest success of our venture. It seemed clear that Klappenbach was enthused for another drive.

I gave him an inquisitive gaze.

"Next year?" he asked.

"Let's see what happens with George's herd," I responded. "We've sort of planted seeds for cattle trade in the North Platte country."

Klappenbach nodded.

We spent the next couple of hours regaling our business benefactor with tales from the trail drive, helping the wagon train in its battle with the Indians, and the adventures of our return journey. Unlike my companions, I did have the foresight to back away from the alcoholic spirits or what the Indians called firewater. The men were getting just a bit shy of rowdy when Stella poked her head in and offered us an early dinner. I think it was partially aimed at heading off any trouble stemming from loosened inhibitions.

As we gathered around a long table and Stella and a young Mexican girl began serving a scrumptious feast, she leaned toward me. "Any word on more O'Tooles, Jack?"

"I smiled broadly. Twin boys, Mrs. Klappenbach."

"I have a small gift for the new mother. I'll be sure you have it before y'all head back," she said with a joyful smile. Seemed my news had made her day.

———

THE MEAL HAD BEEN beyond delicious, especially after weeks of trail dining on jerky, pemmican, and whatever could be shot and cooked. Among plentiful belching and much laughing, the men eventually eased away from Klappenbach's store to walk off a combination of too much liquor and much too much food.

Me? I eased over to a small table and absentmindedly picked up a copy of the *State Times*. I couldn't for the life of me recall when I had last seen a newspaper. This was a current issue, so I figured to soak it up like a dry bandana. There was a lot happening in the world, and I had been clueless about it.

Well, the newspaper was indeed filled with news, most of it concerning slavery. It caused me to search for whom the publisher was, as the opinions expressed were downright strongly felt. Turned out that the *State Times* was run by a Texas state senator and former Texas Ranger named John Salmon Ford.

Just then, Klappenbach strolled in.

"August, you know anything about this Ford fellow?" I asked.

"You never heard of him, Jack?" he replied with surprise.

"Been spending most of my time between here and Wyoming," I reminded him.

"Well, Ford's nickname is Rip, as he'd been an adjutant to General Taylor in the Mexican American War and used to have to send letters to the homes of soldiers killed in action. He would sign them RIP, as an abbreviation for *rest in peace*, he related with a thoughtful scratch of his chin as though thinking on what more to say.

"But he's a politician and runs a newspaper," I offered. "Convenient way to get your opinions out to the folks."

Klappenbach was not to be deterred. "I understand he's got his ear to the ground about rumblings back east about states' rights and abolishing slavery. As I hear tell, Texas has nearly two hundred thousand slaves mostly working cotton from here to the Louisiana border."

I shook my head and thought back to how my friend George had escaped slavery, lived with the Pawnee, and drove cattle before establishing his own ranch in Wyoming as a free man. It didn't seem right to enslave another person, but the Bible described the Egyptians and other nations as having slaves. We knew the Comanche and other tribes on the frontier held slaves, and we had bought Spirit Talker's wife, Prairie Flower, out of slavery. It seemed all too common and all too wrong. "You think this Ford fellow is trying to stir up trouble?" I asked.

"Hard to tell, Jack. There's rumor that he could be

appointed to gather a passel of Texas Rangers to deal with Indian problems up north."

"I'm surprised that he hasn't written more about the way the Comanche are stirring up trouble. They're burning homesteads, killing settlers, and worse. Yep, worse." I paused at that fact. "Folks are even being advised to save a bullet for themselves rather than be captured and tortured by the savages."

"Well, we've all managed to keep our scalps around here," observed Klappenbach as he swept his hand over his thinning hair. "I do expect that if Rip Ford goes after the Comanche, the hostiles will pay dearly. He sure cleaned things up a might down on the Rio Grande a few years back."

I folded the newspaper, put it aside, and took a long sip of coffee. I savored its taste before swallowing. I wondered whether Captain Benton had any inkling of the goings on in Austin toward quelling the Indian attacks. That also got me thinking about Spirit Talker and whether he and Prairie Flower had made it safely back to the Penateka Comanche village. I then came back to the present with the realization that Klappenbach was quietly standing opposite me with a strange expression across his face.

"They taking to calling you Walks With Wolves?" he finally blurted.

I smiled broadly. "Seems a wolf adopted me, August. He tended to appear most any time there was trouble. The tribes thought I must have strong medicine. My Comanche friend Spirit Talker gave me the name, and it's been racing around the tribes faster than a prairie fire with a tail wind."

Klappenbach thought on that for a Texas minute. "You ever think of scouting for the Rangers?"

I shook my head. "August, my friend, I've got a wife, two young children, and a ranch to work. I think I'll leave Indian fighting and politics to other folks."

"There's going to come a time when you can't avoid those sorts of life complications, Jack. You already dealt with Comanche killing your family. Crises are parts of the snags of life that must be faced," he said insistently. He took a deep breath. "I know you're a man of deep faith, Jack. But even Christ couldn't avoid involvement in the realities of the world of His times. Shucks, from what I've heard, you've already proven your mettle many times, whether against Indians or bandits."

I knew in my heart that Klappenbach was right. When it came to defending the lives of my family and friends, I'd proven myself up to the task. Did I have the sense of patriotism to do the same for my community, for my country?

Klappenbach must have been reading my mind. He grabbed a stick from the fireplace and broke it in two quite easily. Then, he grabbed six sticks bunched together and, try as he might, was unable to break them. "You understand?" he asked.

I nodded. "Better a community to fight off threats than try to do it by yourself," I responded.

"When the call comes, I expect we'll all step up, Jack."

Klappenbach made perfect sense. "I ought to be heading back to the Rising Cross, August. I've appreciated your advice." I stood and paused. "I reckon you're right."

He offered a satisfied smile. "If not a trail drive in '58, then '59 for sure."

"Count on it," I said and shook his hand.

———

AFTER THANKING STELLA, I headed to the stable. Collins and the others were gathered about, each with their own thoughts as to what they might be up to next. Collins and Johnson figured to head back to the Circle C, and Juan had been talking about setting up a modest dining establishment just up the main street from Klappenbach's store. Juan was a great cook, though he couldn't hold a candle to Stella Klappenbach's cooking. That left Shorty. He was a tough old cowpoke who had toughened himself as a cavalry man in two wars. I'd witnessed his enduring a wound from a poisoned arrow, a true measure of his toughness. One of our drovers described him as being so tough that he'd cuddle with rattlesnakes. As I approached, he stood leaning against a corral post and chewing on a piece of prairie grass. His hat hung low on his forehead, and a Colt Peacemaker set precariously in its holster on his hip.

"You headin' back to the Risin' Cross, boss?" asked Shorty, tipping up the front brim of his hat.

I stopped. "What are you looking to do next, Shorty?"

"Ain't goin' back to them camels," he said with a wry smile, referring to the Army's ill-fated experiment at Camp Verde.

I can't say that I blamed him for that. "You want to come work up at the Rising Cross?" I asked. I recognized that good cowboys were hard to find. Shorty now had trail drive experience and was reliable. Even though Isaac was a hard worker and we had just hired Will, I reckoned we'd be growing our herds fast enough to be needing more hands soon. There was no shortage of chores needing to be done.

Shorty shuffled his feet. "Thought you'd never ask, boss."

"Well, time is wasting. Saddle your horse, and let's head home."

"I don't own a horse."

It occurred to me that Shorty had been riding my horses. He didn't have one that was his. I looked at my string in the corral. We'd be bringing them all back to the Rising Cross with us. "What do you think, Shorty? The chestnut or the buckskin?"

"You're giving me one?"

"Seems like," I responded. "Figure my cowboys will take better care of what cayuses they own." I saw that questioning *what about* look in his eyes. "Yes, the tack, too." What good was giving a cowboy a horse if it had no saddle and bridle?

Shorty wasted no time as he opened the gate and threw a bridle on the chestnut gelding. He looked back over his shoulder. "Be ready fast as I can cinch a saddle, boss."

I headed into the barn and soon emerged with Big Red in tow. Collins and Johnson were waiting over at Klappenbach's store. We'd all ride back together until we reached Rising Cross Ranch, where we'd part company.

Everything in Bandera had gone smoothly. What could possibly go wrong?

THREE
VENDETTA

THE RIDE northward tended to pass mostly in silence, as each of us was left in our own thoughts. We'd be an attractive target for hostiles, given the half-dozen horses and a pack mule we were driving with us. We held to the hope that any Indians would be occupied further north or west.

For reason that escapes me, I got to thinking about the trouble Bart Toliver had made for us. I'd learned long ago from my pa that vengeance or any sort of vendetta made for a sparse meal for our souls. Revenge rings hollow, simply unfulfilling by most any measure. That's not to say that bad behavior ought to go unpunished, but by my account, forgiveness and mercy offer far greater reward to our lives. I thought about how the very essence of the battles between the Whites and Indians boiled down to the one side getting back at the other for perceived or actual sins.

Call it revenge. Call it vengeance. Similar battles were going on in the minds of folks for and against slavery. Was it a state issue or a national issue? Did the common good of a nation trump the laws of a state? That seemed to be at the root of the problem in my mere mortal mind. Were two sides to any strong belief ever able to compromise, to meet in the middle, so to speak? Could basic moral values be compromised? And from where did those moral values or truths come? Whose were they? The Bible? Some concoction of mankind? Who decided? Who was the ultimate arbiter? For me, it was God...but for others...who knows? I was deep in considering these matters when Collins rode up beside me.

"We're bein' watched, Jack."

I shook my head from my ruminations on vendettas. "Who?"

"Ain't seen 'em. Just feel them," he responded.

I reined in Big Red and surveilled our surroundings. Pulling up and gazing around was a move that tended to exact a response from anyone who might be watching. Guess it was a fear that they'd been discovered. "Nope. Don't think so, Sam."

Just then, a bullet ricochetted off my saddle horn. Big Red needed no further urging as he leaped forward with me hanging on for dear life.

Collins and the others spurred their mounts to a nearby tree line, then grabbed rifles and dove for cover as bullets buzzed by like stirred-up hornets.

Blessedly, whoever was shooting was a poor marksman.

I managed to bring Big Red under control, grab my carbine, and join my companions behind a cluster of cypress trees along the Medina River. There were four of us, and we as yet had no idea how many we were fighting, much less who they were. "What do you think, Sam? Whites? Indians?"

"Ain't see a one yet, Jack."

"Can't shoot worth a hoot," I responded thankfully. I peeked out from the cypress trunk and pointed my carbine in the general direction from which the shots had been fired. Pulling back the hammer, I squeezed off a round. I heard it ricochet from a rock. No response.

Hank Johnson and Shorty each fired off a round. Nothing.

We heard a bit of squeaking leather, jingling spurs, and the thud of horse hooves fading away from us.

I pondered our situation. "Someone's playing with us, Sam," I said with concern. They hadn't meant to kill us... at least, not yet. "Let's ride on...but stay alert. We should spread out." I reckoned it wouldn't do to ride in a cluster where we'd be easy targets for whomever the cowards were.

We rode on for about an hour, leaving the Medina River behind us. The trail took us through hills and ravines and dried-up creeks. It was perfect country for ambushing. While I had become fairly adept at scouting for trail signs, I found myself wishing that Spirit Talker was with us.

An especially deep ravine carved by a now-dried-up creek lay ahead. I pulled up and considered whether to chance riding through. I had just about figured to ride eastward to avoid the looming threat when a hail of bullets zinged over our heads. Again, we put spurs to horse flanks and rode for cover. We pulled up among some live oak trees.

"Ain't this fun, Jack O'Toole?" boomed a voice from the ravine.

That got my attention. Where had I heard that voice before? Yep, it came to me: Bart Toliver. With the perversity of his ego-driven vendetta, he'd tracked me all the way to Bandera. Now, the questions were how many men were with him and what were his ultimate intentions? I looked questioningly over at Collins. "How many do you think there are? I whispered.

"From the gunfire, can't be more than three or four, Jack. If they outnumbered us, I reckon they'd attack in force," he responded as more shots rang out over our heads.

A couple of more shots zeroed in lower, hitting trees and rocks around us. I feared for our horses. "We're easy targets here, Sam. Let's surround them."

Collins looked at me as though I was stark raving crazy.

"You and Hank go around to the right. Shorty and I will approach from the left and draw fire."

"You're serious?"

"They'll never expect it," I said with a devious grin. "Oh, and get rid of those spurs."

We drew our revolvers, as this wouldn't be a job for rifles.

A couple of more bullets whizzed overhead...a tad closer this time.

I checked the load in my gun, then took a deep breath, mumbled a couple of words of prayer, and nodded to Shorty. "Let's go." I headed toward a live oak roughly twenty yards away, firing as I ran. Shorty followed with fire bellowing from his own Colt.

Meanwhile, Collins and Johnson moved as quietly as possible in the opposite direction with the objective of eventually flanking Toliver's position.

Shorty and I reloaded and laid down more covering fire.

A hail of bullets buzzed past us from Toliver's position. "Splittin' up ain't gonna help yuh none, O'Toole!" hollered Toliver.

Just then, a slug took a slice from the side of my head, knocking my hat clean off. It dizzied me for a moment. It had grazed me, but I bled profusely. That's apparently the way it was with head wounds. I grabbed my bandanna and wrapped it around my head so as to cover the wound. It pretty much stopped the bleeding.

"Ain't gonna miss again, Jack!" came Toliver's refrain.

Shorty and I exchanged glances. We figured that Collins and Johnson had enough time to get around behind Toliver's hiding place.

"You okay, boss?"

I wiped away blood with my sleeve. "Just getting started, Shorty. Let's go!"

We bolted toward Toliver's position just as Collins and Johnson opened fire.

I heard a terrible cry of pain from our attackers.

"You okay, Hawk?" It was Toliver calling out. There was no response.

More shots from behind Toliver, and now we were pouring lead into them.

Another yelp of pain. "Bart! Bart! They kilt me!" came a gasping cry.

I stopped behind a live oak that I reckoned was twenty feet from where Toliver was dug in. "Had enough, Bart Toliver?" I called out.

Silence. The shooting had stopped.

"You okay, Hank? Sam?"

"Good here," came the response.

I cautiously moved from behind the tree. Nothing. With Shorty covering me, I took a half-dozen steps toward the spot where I figured Toliver hid. Still nothing. I glanced back at Shorty before taking a couple of more steps. Finally, I parted some grass to see Bart Toliver lying flat on his back, pale as a ghost. He wasn't breathing. I nudged his boot just to be sure that he was no longer a threat. "Looks like it's over," I announced.

There were sighs of relief as everyone moved toward me. Looking down at Toliver, I was taken by how peaceful he appeared in death. His rough-hewn face was relaxed as though he hadn't a care in the world. I pondered but a moment as to whether he might have ever known his Maker. I reckoned his pride likely kept him from a faith that preached love and selflessness. What an unhappy existence he must have led. Nevertheless, Bart Toliver had indeed finally found a contentment of sorts.

Collins appeared first from among the trees. "There's one back yonder, Jack. Looks like the feller you stripped to his skivvies and let return to Toliver," he said, shaking his head ruefully. "Dummy shoulda quit while he had the chance. Guess he was jus' born a sorry sort."

"I expect we should bury these poor souls," I suggested.

"Seems like the Christian thing to do, Jack," offered up Johnson.

"Shorty, kindly grab the shovel from the packhorse." There was a part of me that was inclined to leave the bushwhackers' bones for the buzzards and coyotes, but that feeling was short-lived. Faith aside, the vision of a bird tearing apart dead human flesh seemed wrong. "Hank, see what you can do to fashion three crosses." The dead men didn't act like they had an ounce of God-believing blood in their earthly bodies, but I figured that they might have gotten some churching at some time in their lives.

I appreciated that Shorty fetched a clean bandana from my possibles bag and cleaned my head wound. It was now properly hurting, but I gritted my teeth as

Shorty did his doctoring. He finally figured it was clean enough and tied the bandana around my head. I was going to be presenting a not-so-pretty vision to Blue Flower. It wasn't so much the wound but the thought that I came close to pushing up daisies from an early grave.

With the bushwhackers buried, I uttered a few prayers over each of their villainous souls. Naturally, I asked God to forgive their sins.

There was still plenty of daylight, so we wasted no further time resuming our journey homeward. As we rode out, I was left wondering what it was in Bart Toliver's life that led him down the wayward path he'd taken. Life had struck him crossways, and he never found a way to peace while he lived. So sad. It reinforced my thinking of how unfulfilling vengeance was. The only peace a vendetta could find was death.

———

WITH A FULL MOON and a sky brimming with stars to guide our way, we decided to ride on through the night. It was nearly midday when we pulled up a couple of miles shy of Rising Cross Ranch.

"Where you headed, Sam?" I asked. "You and Hank are welcome to join us in a home-cooked meal before you finish your ride."

Collins gave a broad grin. "Jus' about had enough of yer company, Jack," he said with a laugh dripping in sarcasm. "Thanks for the invite, but we'll be headed home. Lookin' forward to sackin' in my own bed this night."

"Thanks for all your help with the trail drive, Sam.

From what Klappenbach is saying, looks as though we'll be doing it again soon enough."

"We'll be ready, Jack...Shorty."

Collins and Johnson tipped their hats and turned their cayuses east toward the Circle C Ranch.

Shorty and I held our ground and watched until they rode from sight. We had all made a great team on the trail drive with all its challenges. And on the journey home, we'd been like a little army doing whatever it took to reach home. As we turned our horses, I found myself scanning our surroundings. It occurred to me that Zeb was nowhere to be seen. Had he abandoned me? Had God decided that I no longer needed him? It sort of hurt my feelings, as I had grown some affection for my wolf companion.

———

SOON ENOUGH, Shorty and I reined in at the newly installed hitching rail in front of my cabin. The place was eerily quiet for midday. Not a soul in sight.

I was growing concerned when I heard a squeal from Buck. Apparently, everyone went into hiding as a prank when they saw us coming. However, young Buck couldn't contain his joy over the family's little joke.

As we dismounted, a hungry baby's cry was joined in perfect harmony by that of a second. Blue Flower emerged with a smile despite two wailing baby boys cradled in her arms.

Now, noises came from just about every direction. It was wonderful. I was home. "Shorty, tend the horses, then come on up for dinner," I directed as I headed straight for Blue Flower. Big Red snorted after me, as if to say *thanks for nothing*.

I swept mother and children into my arms. Doggone, but it felt good. The very feeling that we might actually have some months of family time ahead was at the forefront of my mind. God had indeed been good.

As I removed my hat with its fresh bullet hole and stepped back to gaze lovingly at my wife and children, I couldn't miss a concerned look in Blue Flower's eyes. She was staring at the bloodied bandana wrapped around my head. "Jack?" she inquired.

"What?"

If the boys hadn't occupied her arms, she'd likely have had her hands placed firmly on her hips. "You hurt?"

"Oh, that," I said off-handedly. "Nothing really."

She shook her head, then smiled and gave me a kiss. She looked again at my bloodied bandanna and smiled. "Get cleaned up. We eat," she said resignedly. "Then, we rest."

The light in her eyes told me what *rest* would involve. I got to thinking that she'd just birthed our boys a week ago, so put certain thoughts from my mind. Shucks, just holding her close would be wonderful after months on the trail drive. I looked into her beautiful eyes, smiled, and half-stumbled away to go get cleaned up. I heard her laugh behind me.

FOUR
COMANCHE!

HOW HOT WAS IT? We feared Isaac's and Sarah's hens might start laying hard-boiled eggs. Seriously, the humidity combined with the heat gave the atmosphere a leaden feel. No sooner was a bandanna wrung out than it would get soggy again. The normal cooling effect of the evaporation of moisture from our clothes failed in the oppressive dampness.

It had been three days since my return from meeting with Klappenbach in Bandera. We were establishing routines around the ranch while Blue Flower and Kate did those things that frontier women did. They made soap from lye, ashes, and water, spun wool into thread, cooked, sewed, and repaired clothes, tended the garden that we shared with Isaac and Sarah, churned butter, ground flour, and even occasionally chopped wood. Blue Flower now had the added primary responsibility for the twins. Her Comanche heritage taught her that the children were her charges until they were ten or eleven years old. It was part of the matriarchal tribal governance she'd grown up with.

Us men? We cared for the cattle, including branding, doctoring, castrating, and birthing, mucked stalls in the barn, repaired fences, made certain living quarters were kept in repair, such as making sure the cabin roof didn't leak, protected the ranch from predators, gathered fire-wood, and put meat and fish on the table. I had the added burden of managing the financial side of ranch operations.

In the midst of all of our frontier duties, we stayed alert for threats from savage hostiles and White lawbreakers. After reading the newspaper back in Bandera, I now found myself thinking about the political issues stirring things up at the state capital in Austin. I figured that one day, I'd like to meet this Rip Ford fellow and have a conversation. It occurred to me that states' rights were a smoke-screen for the slavery issue.

I wondered how Spirit Talker was making out rein-serting himself among his people. I prayed that his faith would be strong enough to withstand the influences of the Comanche religion. Thinking about my Comanche brother led me to cogitate on whether Captain Benton caught up with any of the Nokoni Comanche savages that were attacking up north of us. The Comancheria remained a dreadfully dangerous place, although we were determined to live peacefully within its vast boundaries. Maybe Klappenbach's rumor about Ford heading up a company or two of Texas Rangers to stop the Indian predations had merit. I was under no illusions as to our safety despite my reputation of having strong *sunipu*, friendship with Spirit Talker, and marriage to a famous-but-aging chief's daughter.

I sat on a bench sipping coffee on the gallery that now ran the width of the front of our cabin. Blue Flower sat beside me, nursing George and Isa. Early morning chores had been completed, and I savored the opportunity to spend a few quiet moments with loved ones. With autumn and winter soon to arrive, we'd learn to fully enjoy every chance to share peaceful moments. I had a premonition that 1858 was going to bring serious new challenges to our lives on the Comancheria. For now? Well, I was determined to enjoy my family.

Shorty and Will worked hard and were fitting right well into ranching routines. Three-dozen mustangs and about twice as many beeves roamed at leisure on our pastures. Atlas, our breeder bull, was thoroughly enjoying helping us build our herd. I reckoned we'd be ready for another trail drive the year after next. I chuckled to myself as I thought on working to replace those camels at Camp Verde with some of my horses.

Yep, it was sure peaceful. Perhaps, too peaceful.

———

I DIDN'T EXPECT Collins and Johnson to come riding in hard on well-lathered horses. Their somber expressions didn't bode well. They pulled up in a cloud of dust, jingling of spurs, and squeaking of leather, and quickly slid from their saddles. The commotion set the twins to crying, so Blue Flower headed inside. "Comanche, Jack!" hollered Collins.

Just as I stood and was about to respond, I spotted Captain Benton heading our way with a couple of dozen Texas Rangers.

Collins and Johnson turned and spotted Benton's approach. "Too late!"

"What happened?" I desperately sought to know what had happened.

Blue Flower reappeared, having settled the boys in their cradles. "What happened?" she asked.

Johnson cast a judgmental eye toward Blue Flower. Memories of losing his family to Indians likely were returning to his thinking, but he spoke nary a word of it.

"We were lucky to escape. Cabin's burning. Everyone else killed or worse," blurted Collins. "They may still be there."

A vision of what Collins meant by *worse* flashed through my mind. It left me momentarily speechless.

Just as Shorty and Will emerged from the barn to see what the commotion was about, Benton's Texas Rangers came thundering in. More dust.

Collins looked ruefully at Benton. The Rangers were too late, far too late.

Blue Flower and I exchanged glances. She nodded.

"Shorty, Will, saddle up! Get your guns! Buck, saddle Big Red for me." There was no mistaking my intentions. "Let's see whether we can save a life or two at the Circle C."

"What do y'all think yer doin'?" hollered Benton. "This is Texas Ranger business."

I gave him a hard look as only a trail-toughened seventeen-year-old can, "Nuts, Captain, this is Texas business!" I replied. "You're welcome to join us."

Benton was startled by my determination but decided not to challenge me. Time was wasting.

Shorty and Will appeared outfitted and ready with Big Red in tow. We were armed to the teeth and ready to ride. Off we went in a clatter of hooves and a grand swirl of prairie dust.

They were headed out before I could climb into the saddle. I took a moment to ease over to the gallery and give Blue Flower a kiss before spurring the big stallion into action. Kate appeared behind Blue Flower and gave me a wave goodbye. Poor Buck stood and watched longingly as I galloped away.

————

THE CIRCLE C was about a two-hour ride from the Rising Cross Ranch, and we likely near killed our cayuses getting there.

Collins brought us to a halt on the crest of a hill a couple of hundred yards from the ranch house. We could see the hostiles still picking the place clean of anything of value to them. There appeared to be about thirty warriors. A few were busy carrying off a handful of warriors killed or wounded in the attack.

"Comanche for sure, Sam...Captain," I said just loud enough for Collins and Benton to hear. "Looks as though they're not expecting company," I added with a devious smile. "Shall we teach them not to mess with Texans?"

Benton gave me a look as though about to challenge my authority. Perhaps he was tired or wasn't up to arguing with me, but he held his tongue.

"Sam, you head to the right with Hank, Will, and Shorty. Make them think all the Texas Rangers in the state are attacking. Captain, we'll go left and head off any escape." I patted Big Red's well-lathered neck. "Here we go, big fella." With that, I let out a holler and charged toward the totally surprised Comanche.

No sooner did they find themselves under heavy fire from Collins's party than they felt the sting of Texas Ranger bullets whizzing at them from behind. Caught in a murderous crossfire, they bolted for their ponies and tried to make their escape.

Our assault likely endured for no more than two

minutes. At least a dozen Comanche fell to our death-dealing attack. The rest managed to escape, carrying a few of their wounded brothers with them.

We pulled up before the still-smoldering cabin. Two women and two men were lying just outside the cabin with multiple arrows announcing their painful demise. All had been scalped. Two cowboys lay at death's door, having been tied down and endured horrific tortures. We'd be doing a bit of burying.

Collins scanned the surrounding hills. "Devils din't git hardly no livestock," he observed. It was a small consolation.

Shorty rode into our midst with a Comanche in tow. The savage was kicking and snarling to free himself from the cowboy's lasso. Every time the warrior stood, Shorty would give the rope a yank and pull him over. The Comanche's skin was scraped up badly from cactus and mesquite, and our bullets had taken a chunk of his upper arm and grazed his chest. He tried to act defiant despite the blood and dirt.

Shorty dragged him over to me.

"*Tabu*," I said, calling him a coward in his own tongue.

He flashed his black eyes at me. "Nokoni Comanche," he hissed, trying to be prideful in his moment of vulnerability.

I pointed to myself. "Walks With Wolves, *peeka* Comanche. Strong *sunipu*." I let him know who I was, that I killed Comanche and possessed strong medicine.

The savage gave me the most defiantly hateful look he could muster.

Once again, I pointed to myself. "Me *kuhmabai* daughter of Buffalo Hump. My brother Spirit Talker of Penateka Comanche." I was striving to get the heathen to comprehend that I held all the cards in this game. I raised a finger skyward. "My God strong. Stronger than *taa narumi*."

The warrior's eyes widened as he weighed my words. His demeanor was beginning to soften in the face of my strong *sunipu*.

"Nokoni *peeka tosa aitu*," I said, trying to get him to understand that killing Whites was not good.

What happened next might be described as a miracle. Seemingly out of nowhere, Zeb appeared. He walked past the Texas Rangers and others and nuzzled my hand. He gazed for what seemed forever at the Comanche and nuzzled me again. Zeb then turned and walked away.

The savage's eyes nearly popped from his head.

I turned to Shorty. "Release him. Let him tell his people, his *numunuu*, what happened here."

Benton was taken aback. "What the...what are you doing, O'Toole?"

I sighed. I could see the vengeance still brewing in the eyes of Collins and Johnson. The Texas Rangers remained caught-up in the excitement from the battle. I had to exercise control of the situation to protect the wounded warrior. My size and deep maturing voice served my physical dominance, plus Collins and Johnson still looked upon me as trail boss, short had my back, and I had long ago cowed Benton into backing down. "Anyone lay a hand on this Comanche, and I'll tear his hide apart," I threatened. "Now, free him."

Benton's face was a deep red. "I'm gonna tell the folks in Austin about you, O'Toole. It won't be pretty."

I didn't see any point in taking on Benton, so I let his threat pass. I nodded to Shorty, and he removed the lasso.

The savage looked at me with prideful eyes. "Quenah-evah," he said, pointing to himself. The name translated to Eagle Drink.

I told him with a sign to go, and he didn't hesitate. Eagle Drink never looked back.

Johnson shuffled his feet. "Yer a brave man, boss."

"Where'd that dang wolf come from, O'Toole? Consarnit, who or what are yuh?" asked Benton, trying to calm down.

I shrugged and, ignoring Benton, sought to change the subject. "Sam, it looks like you still have most of your livestock. We'll help rebuild the cabin."

Benton persisted. "You some kind of medicine man with that Comanche friend of yours? An' that wolf?"

I reckoned I had to face up to the medicine, so to speak. "The wolf chose me, Captain. I don't understand it. I figure it must be the Lord's doing."

"What did yuh call yerself?"

"Comanche call me Walks With Wolves," I said as though challenging him to question how I got the name.

"O'Toole not good nuf fer yuh?" Benton persisted.

I pretty much lost hope of Benton understanding. I managed a laugh in hopes of lightening the mood. "If it keeps hair on my head, I'm good with it, Captain." I wanted to tell him to go chase the Comanche but figured not to push my luck.

"Let's get back to the Rising Cross, boss," suggested Shorty. "Them savages might double back."

I could see Will nodding in agreement behind him. Poor Will. I expect he'd never been in a battle before. Shooting humans, even savage Comanche, likely wasn't in his heart. Whether he hit any Comanche or not, I hadn't a clue. His presence had helped. I could see that he'd understandably turned a tad green in the face at the sight of the two cowboys staked out and horribly tortured.

I reckoned the Comanche were done fighting for this day, and we need not worry about the Rising Cross. "We'll go after we clean up here," I counseled, nodding to both Shorty and Will. Action was the salve for overcoming the sheer horror of the scene. "Sam, you and Hank untie those two poor souls and wrap them in blankets." I turned back to Benton. "If you Texas Rangers aren't going to chase after those Comanche savages, how about lending a hand? We have brave souls to bury, and there's likely valuables we can salvage from the cabin." The fire had mostly died down, though it would be a couple of hours before cooling off enough to retrieve what we could. At least the barn was still standing. I scanned the bodies lying about the area around the cabin. They had apparently been killed escaping the flames. I turned to Collins. "Sam, who were these folks? Do they have next of kin?"

Collins nodded. "They had families back east. I'll reach out to them," Sam assured me as he reached for a shovel. He glanced back at me. "The big man that they tortured was Riley Collins, a cousin of mine. He owned this place. Guess it'll be mine now."

"Sorry, Sam."

He began to dig, then paused. "Ya know, Jack…yuh got a talent. Yer a natural leader. Must say, yuh sprised me on the trail drive. Yer genrus, hard workin', show mercy, an encourage folks."

I blushed. Leader? I'd never thought about it. "Er… thanks, Sam." It was as though Collins was quoting the Bible. I think it was in Romans. What could I say? Distracted, I grabbed a couple of blankets. We figured to wrap the bodies, since we hadn't enough wood for coffins. It gave me time to think on Collins's compliment. "I think we all stepped up when we had to, Sam. My pa told me from the Good Book...third chapter of James, I think...that where envy and selfish ambitions exist, we'll find plenty of evil. You call me a leader. If true, a leader can't lead without strong men as followers. You've been solid, Sam...a rock. I'm grateful."

Collins lifted a shovel full of dirt and smiled at me. "Glad to be yer neighbor, Jack O'Toole."

Shorty strode up. "What about them dead Injuns, boss?"

I found myself confronted with a choice. I knew that the Comanche would sneak back at night to recover the bodies of their fallen warriors. If we scalped them, we would keep their souls from their spirit world. If we didn't, the Comanche might see us as either weak or naïve. They figure that we didn't know any better and be encouraged to attack again and again. Shorty impatiently shifted his weight from one side to the other. I gave him about as hard a look as I could muster. "Scalp them and leave them to rot, Shorty." A twinge of guilt coursed through me, but we had to play tough with the Nokoni Comanche. I felt certain that Spirit Talker would have agreed.

"You sure, boss?" Shorty questioned.

"We have to send a message that attacking our families won't be tolerated. I don't like it either, Shorty."

Benton had overheard our conversation. His unremorseless smile was less than comforting. "Yuh can collect bounties on them scalps, Jack."

I resented his cold-blooded, barbaric tone. But then, nothing from Captain Benton surprised me. I gave him a look aimed at boring through to his very soul, if he had one. "Help yourself, Captain. Enjoy the blood money," I added with a sarcastic tone. "Maybe it's time you got to what they pay y'all for and go after those Comanche." I was angry and not inclined to hold my tongue.

Benton shrugged and signaled to his men to mount up.

I had to admit that they'd helped a little with salvaging goods from the burned-out cabin. We could handle the burials and the remaining cleanup. I looked over at Collins. "Guess the Comanche are safe for now," I said with even greater sarcasm.

Collins kept digging.

"We will outlast them, Sam."

He smiled. "Let's get these folks buried and get to rebuilding, Jack."

Soon enough, I was conducting a brief funeral ceremony for the six settlers who'd lost their lives. Death had been their final arbiter, and I prayed that their souls would find their way to heaven.

———

IT WAS dusk when we rode into Rising Cross Ranch. All was at peace. Collins and Johnson had remained back at the Circle C as much to continue cleanup as to protect what remained. It was unlikely that the Comanche would return except to gather their bodies. We'd dragged them to an outlying live oak motte and marked the location with a Comanche lance. Benton's Texas Rangers had scalped each of them. The act reeked of its own sense of raw brutality.

Buck greeted us as we rode up. He looked up expectantly at me.

"It was bad, Buck." I wasn't going to sugar-coat the

attack. I dismounted and handed him Big Red's reins. "You help Shorty and Will take care of the horses."

"I think Kate's got some grub ready, Jack. Blue Flower is sleeping."

I appreciated the heads up. Blue Flower had her hands full with chores and the twins, so rest was important. I washed trail dust off as best I could with the warm water in the basin beside the door. It served to remind me how hot the day had been in far too many respects. It struck me that the Comanche hadn't wounded or killed any of us. Before opening the door, I took a look off across the prairie. The sun was just dropping below the distant horizon. We had been kept safe from harm, though six souls had paid the ultimate price defending their home. "Got dinner," I announced in a low voice upon entering.

Kate spun about. "Jack! You're back!" She ran into my arms.

Blue Flower appeared at the bedroom door.

I broke away from Kate and strode over to my wife, who buried herself in my arms.

"Jack safe," she whispered.

"It was Nokoni," I said. I could feel her shudder. The Nokoni Comanche could be extremely savage in their attacks.

"We chased them away. We're safe for now," I reassured her.

Blue Flower stepped back, held my hands, and stared into my eyes as though for stronger reassurance. "Jack hungry," she stated flatly.

"How are George and Isa?"

"Jack sit...eat," she commanded.

"Shorty and Will are hungry, too."

Kate laughed as much from relief as an effort to

lighten the atmosphere. "We'll get y'all fed, brother." She went to work whipping up a late dinner. She pushed Blue Flower off, indicating that she should attend to me.

Blue Flower took the strong hint and joined me at the table. "George and Isa good," she assured me. Her eyes took me in with allure that had captivated me from the time we had first met. She brought life to the depths of my soul.

"God protected us today." I proceeded to tell her about Eagle Drink, the Comanche we had released, and how Zeb had shown up.

Blue Flower groped for the proper English word. "Walks With Wolves brave. Give Comanche warrior life. *Tumhyokenu.*" The Comanche word translated to trust, but she was unable to articulate mercy or forgiveness. "God good," she stated firmly.

"Whites and Comanche must live in peace," I added. "I pray Quenah-evah will share with Nokoni *numunuu.*"

Blue Flower shook her head. "Nokoni no peace," she said firmly. It was decidedly a reality, a hard fact of life and death. Her own Penateka Comanche rarely found peace with the Nokoni. So it was with the Comanche. One day allies, another enemies.

She pulled an envelope from a shelf beside the table. "This come today," she said and handed it to me. Her eyes spoke of curiosity.

George had sent me a letter. I slipped my Bowie knife from its scabbard. The knife was over-kill so far as a letter opener, but it was what I had handy. I opened the letter. George's scrawl was hard to read. He wasn't exactly a product of some highfalutin university back east.

It was hard to concentrate with Blue Flower's eyes affixed to mine from inches away.

Just then, Shorty, Will, and Buck walked in. "What's to eat, boss?" asked Shorty.

"It's coming, boys," called out Kate with a smile at young Will.

"Hang on, boys, I've got a letter here from George Freeman. Just sit and settle down."

I won't quote George's letter here, but suffice to say that he assured us that all was well in Wyoming. He had sold forty head of beeves, Running Waters was ever closer to birthing their first child, and he looked forward to another trail drive. He prayed that I had been with Blue Flower for the childbirth. I reckoned he'd be quite surprised when he learned that I was a father to twins.

By the time I had summarized the letter, Kate had a feast set before us. We dug into the chow like hungry, raving beasts.

All seemed well for now. I wondered how Spirit Talker and Prairie Flower were making out at their people's village.

FIVE
CAPTURE!

SUMMER TURNED to autumn and thence to early winter. The Comancheria remained a threat, but its rolling hills and vast prairies didn't prevent us from rounding up the wild horses and maverick longhorns that grazed our pastures. We'd managed to put away a good supply of hay and feed for the upcoming season. Texas winters were best characterized as ever-changing, so we knew to expect the unexpected. As to the lingering threats, I reckoned the seemingly endless reaches of the territory was a protection of sorts. Still, the beeves and especially the horses had to be a considerable temptation to the Comanches and Kiowas that surely prowled about. I prayed that my deep ties with Spirit Talker's Penateka Comanche *numunuu* and my perceived strong *sunipu* held any hostiles at bay. I kept an eye out for Zeb, but he remained nowhere to be seen.

"It's time," I said gently to Blue Flower.

She nodded with the demure smile that always grabbed my heart.

I had promised a visit to her *numunuu*, her people. It

hinged on the boys being able to travel the rough trails to the village. As a White man, I naturally underestimated my Comanche wife's determination to make the boys ready for travel. Frontier life had caused me to grow up fast, but I neglected to transfer that reality to four-month-old twins being nurtured by a woman of the land.

"We ready fast," she said with a broad smile.

The twins would travel in a rig draped over and tied behind the saddle cantle. It was far preferable over rough trails than a travois and would enable us to be more nimble in avoiding threats.

The winds of November were already beginning to nibble at our doorstep. Livestock had grown their winter coats when we were finally ready. Blue Flower and I wore buckskins for the trail and brought buffalo robes to wrap in if temperatures plummeted downward. Oh, and I also wore my wolf vest, lovingly crafted from the pelt of Zeb's mate. We had one pack horse, mostly loaded with gifts, and another packed with necessities for the trail. In addition to my bow and arrows, I carried the Sharps carbine in a saddle scabbard, two Colt 1851 Navy revolvers, and my Bowie knife. Blue Flower was armed with a revolver and knife, as well. We had an arsenal that would likely serve us well if needed, though I reckoned that Indians encountered at this time of year would mostly be with small hunting parties.

We departed Rising Cross Ranch in mid-November with little fanfare. I think my little brother Buck and sister Kate were comfortable now and held on to some sense of safety. They had survived so very much in their young lives, not the least of which had been the Comanche attack that killed most of our family and their subsequent kidnapping by the hostiles. With Isaac and Sarah nearby and our two ranch hands ever at the ready, a sense of guarded safety prevailed. A mist enveloped the terrain so far as we could see, as I nickered to Big Red and we rode out from the ranch. I gave a look toward Atlas, enjoying hay in the corral. He'd been doing his part in expanding our herd of longhorns. Between Atlas's blessings with our cows and the mavericks we managed to round up and put the Rising Cross brand on, we'd likely be ready for another trail drive in about a year.

I must admit to being excited at the prospect of visiting my Comanche brother. He'd been in my prayers regularly, as I imagined him dealing with his Christian faith among followers of a religion that worshipped gods representing most everything. I thought about what I had learned from Spirit Talker. The Comanche had no creator god, having figured that they'd originated from animals, possibly wolves. Their faith was manifest in worshipping anything perceived to hold supernatural powers, appeasing them however they might. Comanche religion was personal.

There were few group religious ceremonies and no religious leaders per se other than a medicine man or shaman. The Comanche concept of life after death entailed living through eternity in a land where everyone was youthful and had access to plenty of game to hunt and horses to ride. Warriors scalped in battle were denied this afterlife. As I pondered the Comanche religion, I had little trouble understanding how Christianity appealed to Spirit Talker and now to my beloved Blue Flower.

As with Christianity, sins like adultery, murder, theft, and covetousness were frowned upon and often dealt with harshly. Yet, God's great commandment of loving your neighbor didn't fare so well in the Comanche religion. It thus concerned me that he faced spiritual challenges among his people. That his father had named him Spirit Talker and recognized that his visions for the Penateka Comanche rose above their traditional culture. I think that Buffalo Hump saw the future of his people resident in the warrior and philosopher that was his only son. These thoughts tumbled through my mind as we headed westward toward the Penateka Comanche village —or at least where we hoped the village still lay. Like most Indians, the Comanche moved with the availability of game. The herds of buffalo were beginning to thin a bit.

———

THE PINTA TRAIL hadn't changed a lick since our little army traipsed along it on our way back from the trail drive. It was perhaps a tad more worn as more travelers discovered it. Still, it was as rough and tough as ever.

Blue Flower nursed the boys as we rode. She impressed me, not so much with her love and commitment to our sons, as her resourcefulness and mothering skills that had been inculcated within her as part of her Comanche upbringing. She was frontier tough but motherly gentle. And the luster had definitely not worn off our relationship, as we enthusiastically endeavored to grow our family.

The first day on the trail had gone without incident. We encountered nary a soul. I wasn't sure why, as there was an occasional fresh trail sign. I reckoned the sign was left by hunting parties that would tend to enter and leave the trail as necessary.

Blue Flower and I talked of the coming visit and the future of the Comanche in particular and Indians in general.

"White father in Washington not understand," she offered during our conversation over coffee on the morning of our second day on the trail.

"True," I responded. "But Comanche *numunuu* not understand Whites."

She nodded. "*Aitu* make *kaahaniitu*. Make *tumhyokenu*," she said, mixing Comanche and English. Loosely translated, she was saying that it wasn't good, bred deception, and broke trust. It was certainly complicated by humans and their cultural frailties.

"There is hope. Our children will bring peace," I suggested. I tried to be convincing.

Blue Flower smiled winsomely. "Hope," she repeated.

We reached the Pedernales River and began heading westward along its southern banks. The day was chilly, but nowhere near freezing. I wore the wolf vest while Blue Flower wrapped a buffalo hide blanket around her shoulders. I began to sense eyes watching us. I considered that by this time, we might be seen by Penateka Comanche, perhaps a hunting party. Were this so, I would have expected them to reveal themselves, given that we were of them. No, this feeling in my bones was different. These were enemy eyes. We were being stalked.

I glanced at Blue Flower. Blessedly, the twins were sleeping, thanks in part to the rocking motion of the horse. I slowed to allow her pony to move up alongside mine and gave her a nearly imperceptible nod.

Ever so slowly, Blue Flower's hand slipped over the butt of the revolver in its scabbard beside the saddle horn.

I calculated that fetching my carbine would be too obvious. My bow and arrows also were not a viable choice. I wasn't ready to have our stalkers know that we were aware of them. My right hand grasped the revolver holstered at my waist. My keen vision had caught sight of at least two hidden in bushes perhaps a hundred feet off our trail. "Nokoni," I mouthed.

Blue Flower nodded.

I saw a rock outcropping ahead. It would be a perfect spot to ambush us. I stole a glance at the river. It was shallow enough, but we'd be exposed. I found myself breathing shallowly to better hear. My eyes slowly surveilled our surroundings as I strove to not reveal our awareness of the Nokoni presence. There was no point in risking a ride into an ambush. I pulled up. "Nokoni *kuya akatu* Isa Pohya *sunipu*," I said, telling them that they must be afraid of Walks With Wolves's medicine.

Silence.

"Nokoni *kuya akatu* Walks With Wolves *sunipu*," I repeated and drew my revolver.

There was a rustling in the brush, and a lone Nokoni Comanche warrior emerged. "*Isa Pohya*," he growled my Comanche name, Walks With Wolves. He knew with whom he was dealing and surely recognized that I was in a vulnerable position in the open with my wife and children. "Tosahwi *peeka!*" He threatened to kill me as he shook his war lance at me for emphasis. Tosahwi was decked out in full battle regalia, from the five feathers tied in his braided hair to the beaded moccasins on his feet.

I sat tall in my saddle and sought to stare him down. Tosahwi translated to White Knife, and he was figuring to make a name for himself by killing Walks With Wolves and thereby assuming my strong *sunipu*. In but a moment, five Nokoni warriors moved in behind him. All held bows with arrows nocked.

"*Tabu!*" spat out Blue Flower. A woman calling a

Comanche warrior a coward was a strong insult. Her words especially carried weight, given that the culture was by nature matriarchal.

"Tosahwi *tabu!*" I said, reinforcing my wife's words. "Attacking women and babies is cowardly," I accused in the Comanche tongue.

If a Redman's face could get redder and angrier, White Knife's would have set a high bar. The veins were popping out on his neck as he glared at me. He looked to be getting up the nerve to attack.

"Buffalo Hump *onaa*," blurted Blue Flower. As the words left her mouth, she regretted them. She had revealed herself as a prize, a chief's daughter.

One of the warriors behind White Knife whispered something that suddenly caused him to sit back on his pony, flash devious eyes, and relax. "Tosahwi capture *onaa*," he hissed with about as evil a smile as could be imagined.

What was I to do? To open fire would likely mean certain death for us or worse. We were likely a half-day ride to the safety of the Penateka Comanche village. If we tried to make a break for it, we'd likely be cut down right quickly. Despite the chill air, I felt a trickle of sweat run down my back.

White Knife motioned at me to dismount, and I reluctantly obliged.

Three Comanche warriors ran forward and relieved me of my guns and knife.

Our captor rode forward and dismounted. He stood before me, his nose roughly at the level of my chest. His hot breath in the cool air hinted at peyote. He'd gotten himself just a tad high to boost his spirit. White Knife glared intensely with coal-black eyes set between two bands of black warpaint. Strong, sinewy hands went to my shoulders as he stripped off my wolf vest and threw it aside as though he'd weakened my powers. My buckskin shirt came next. Two warriors bound my hands tightly behind my back with wet rawhide strips. I quickly realized the rawhide binding would tighten when it dried and likely cut my wrists. A long rope was tied to my bindings. Now, White Knife pushed me to the ground as a show of his control.

All Comanche eyes were on me as Blue Flower drew her revolver. There was the tell-tale click, the squeeze of her finger, and a warrior took a .36 caliber lead ball straight through his heart. Before she could fire another round, she froze.

White Knife had quickly placed the point of his knife blade at my throat.

Blue Flower dropped the gun.

Two Nokoni warriors strode over and ensured that she had no other weapons.

"*Isa Pohya tabu,* no *peeka,*" said White Knife firmly. He called me a coward but said I was not to be killed.

I managed to stand up. I breathed a tentative sigh of relief as I had the sense that the savage was relishing the idea of negotiating hostages for plenty of horses. I stole a look at Blue Flower and nodded ever so slightly. It seemed we were safe for now.

———

LIFE'S RULES HAD CHANGED. I was no longer an unencumbered teen roaming the frontier alone or with male companions. I had new responsibilities not the least of which was a wife and children. Family sure changed the life perspective. I reckoned to be a reasonably intelligent soul, had my faith, and was a seasoned frontiersman. By all I could figure, I was in full possession of faculties and, combined with my faith, the present would yet end well.

White Knife was no fool. He had the skills, the cunning, the instincts bred into every Comanche warrior. That he did no harm to Blue Flower spoke of his deeply embedded cultural roots. Comanche were raised by their mothers and grandmothers through the early years of their lives, before being turned over to the men around age twelve to learn the hunting and fighting skills upon which the very existence of the tribe depended.

I found myself staggering along in front of the assemblage.

Now and then, White Knife would give a hard tug on the rope as a reminder that he was in charge. The others in his war party laughed derisively each time he brought me to nearly falling.

Despite the Comanche warrior's show of power, I sensed an uncertainty among him and his band. They exhibited a lack of confidence in having blunted my powers. I remained Walks With Wolves in their minds. My *sunipu* remained, and they seemed fearful that I might yet exercise it.

Blue Flower rode stoically in their midst. As we slowly moved along the Pedernales, the Nokoni Comanche warriors only became flustered when she demanded they stop to permit her to answer nature's call or pause for her to nurse the twins. They treated her with respect, befitting a chief's daughter, and were perhaps more fearful of her than Walks With Wolves.

I wouldn't know until later that she left a sign at each stop. A piece of buckskin fringe...hair from her braids... all messages to be found by possible rescuers.

Hunger set in a bit, and my bindings tightened as

they dried. The hostiles seemed in no hurry. They seemed intent on spending the night short of the Penateka Comanche village and heading in fully refreshed come morning. I was grateful that our captors had allowed me to keep my moccasins, as the trail was extraordinarily rough. As it was, thorns and branches tore at my exposed flesh.

As we made camp for the night, White Knife made certain I was secured. To that end, he wrapped the lead rope around me and the tree they propped me against. Bare from the waist up, it was going to be a cold November night for his prisoner. For good measure, he spit on me before striding to the campfire and making a show of chowing down on a piece of roasted rabbit. In a show of utter contempt, White Knife donned my wolf vest and pranced around the campfire, mocking the *sunipu* of Walks With Wolves. His band of savages laughed heartily. Their revelry soon ended as they tired of making fun at my expense.

Thoughts of revenge crept into my thinking. It was a decidedly un-Christian reasoning, but I couldn't help myself. Somehow, I'd make White Knife regret his arrogance. I knew in the deepest recesses of my soul that revenge made for a sparse meal, never fully satisfying. I prayed for the strength to clear my mind and come up with a plan to turn the tables on the Nokoni. A breeze picked up and sent a chill over my bare chest.

White Knife saw me shiver. He walked over and laughingly emptied a bota bag of water over me.

I strove to remain calm, though the water caused more shivering. I watched White Knife whisper to one of his band. He pointed to the blanket-wrapped body of the warrior Blue Flower had killed as though warning that their captives were dangerous. He apparently figured to rotate sentries on shifts through the night to watch me and the horses.

Thus far, the Nokoni seemed disinclined to dispose of me. It seemed as though they were uncertain as to my fate. That could change. What was I worth? Was the combination of my being married to a chief's daughter and my strong *sunipu* keeping me alive? The tales of my exploits and bonding with wolves had certainly reached them. I prayed nearly constantly for a plan to escape this terrible situation. Importantly, any plan must include saving Blue Flower and the babies.

White Knife sat on the opposite side of the campfire from me. Now and then, he would glance up from the knife he was sharpening and give me an appraising eye. He occasionally made some unintelligible comment to a nearby warrior. He put on an air of smug nonchalance, but I sensed a growing tenseness in his overall demeanor. He strove to put up a brave appearance. He'd need to make a confident impression in any negotiation with Buffalo Hump. He slipped a peyote button into his mouth and began to chew.

They had permitted Blue Flower to lie near a cypress tree under a buffalo hide blanket with our boys. She'd proven her mettle in killing one of them, so they kept especially watchful eyes on her.

The moon was but a sliver, and a thin cloud cover shielded the stars. The combination made for a pitch-black night. In the reflected light from the campfire, I could see my carbine, Bowie knife, and revolvers dangling on a tree limb to White Knife's left. I heard an owl hoot. It was definitely an owl, not an Indian. A distant coyote joined in the evening's chorus. Soon, the entire camp was dozing save for the sentries that came on duty every couple of hours.

I wondered where the Penateka were. By my reckoning, we were well within their hunting grounds.

DID I hear what I thought I heard? There was a faint rustling sound behind the tree. There was a low growl and a gnawing sound. I felt the lead rope tying me to the tree begin to slack. I didn't dare pull away lest the sentry be alerted even in the darkness. Was it a Penateka Comanche? Had they found me? There was still nary a sound.

All of a sudden, I came fully alert. A cold nose was at my wrists, and sharp teeth were chewing at the rawhide bindings. Zeb had arrived! His hot breath on my hands was exceedingly welcome.

I still dared not move. I kept my hands behind my back, rubbing them to return circulation. From what I could make out in the darkness, the sentry remained alert. Soon enough, he'd be replaced. I stole a glance at Blue Flower. She lay awake, but I couldn't catch her eyes.

One of our twins—likely George—awakened, but before he could cry, Blue Flower's hand muffled any sound. She quickly turned to feeding him, and he returned to sleep.

The crescent moon had moved higher in the night sky, and the cloud cover was dissipating. The air was teetering on freezing, and I felt as though my heart and lungs might freeze within my bare chest. If I was going to make any move, the time had become ripe. "*Ana o'a hi'it,*" I whispered to the sentry. I figured that telling him I was hungry would seem unthreatening. Just as I hoped, he arose and walked over to within a couple of feet of me. Now, the question was whether my legs, drawn under me for at least four hours, could muster the strength to spring. Zeb stood just out of sight behind the tree.

The sentry looked down at me with a derisive smile. "*Tabu*," he said with clenched teeth, seething out the Comanche word for coward.

"*Kuya akatu tumah tuyai*," I retorted, suggesting that he was afraid of the afterlife.

He gave me a curious look, then his eyes grew wide as Zeb emerged from behind the tree. The sight of the great gray wolf caused the sentry to step back and lose his balance.

The moment had arrived. As I sprang upward, I grabbed a piece of the rope the Nokoni had used to tie me to the tree. I was quickly on top of the sentry before he could utter a sound and was tightening the rope around his neck. He flailed a moment, then was still. I stood up from his lifeless form. White Knife and the remaining three warriors remained asleep. My motion had caught Blue Flower's eyes, but she didn't move for fear of awakening the twins and causing them to cry out.

I stealthily made my way to the Bowie knife. I decided not to chance the sound of squeaking leather that freeing my carbine or revolvers might make. Knife in hand, I retrieved my bow and arrows from behind the cantle of Big Red's saddle.

As I looked past the dwindling embers of the campfire, I spotted a warrior awakening. He likely aimed either to answer nature's call or replace the sentry I had killed or both. He paused as though sensing something was amiss. I nocked an arrow. The warrior never got up.

Now there was only White Knife and two warriors remaining. I silently walked over to one of the sleeping warriors, knelt beside him, and stuffed a fist-sized chunk of rabbit in his open mouth while placing the sharp point of my Bowie knife at his throat. Zeb appeared with bared fangs not six inches from the Nokoni's face. The savage willingly submitted to being gagged and trussed like a hogtied calf. I did the same to the other warrior, leaving only White Knife sleeping all too comfortably on his back. He appeared so peaceful it almost seemed a shame to ruin his fun.

A low growl from Zeb began the process of awakening our remaining captor. White Knife snorted as Zeb nudged his cheek. Finally, his eyes flitted open to lock onto a pair of crystal-blue wolf eyes. He blinked dimly, likely the effect of the peyote combined with the surprise of staring into Zeb's eyes.

I quickly sat astride his chest with my knees pinning his arms. "*Tabu*," I said with a triumphant smile.

His wild-eyed gaze, first at me and then at Zeb, was indeed a triumph of the moment. Soon enough, tales of his succumbing to the strong *sunipu* of Isa Pohya would travel across the Comancheria. His worth as a feared warrior would plummet into infamy.

He said not a word as I relieved him of my wolf vest and bound him securely with the rope that had been used to tie me to the tree.

Despite having slipped into the wolfskin vest, I found myself shivering. The morning chill continued to flirt with freezing. Blue Flower wrapped her buffalo hide blanket over my shoulders, looking at me with fully admiring eyes. My strong *sunipu* had saved us, though I was sure that God had once again intervened.

I looked to the east. The early pinkish glow across the sky signaled the beginning of sunrise and told me that it was time to renew our journey. I secured White Knife and then the other two warriors to their ponies while stringing their mounts together to prevent escape. The two dead warriors were wrapped in their blankets and tied over their ponies.

I looked around for Zeb, but he was nowhere to be seen. Once again, he had saved my hide.

With our prisoners secured, Blue Flower and I resumed our journey along the Pedernales River. We likely made for quite a sight: a White man, a Comanche woman with twin babies, two pack horses, and a string of prisoners, including three dead Nokoni Comanche. It was a caravan that might go down in legend.

We hadn't ridden but a couple of hours when shards of sunlight basked upon a fierce-looking trio of Penateka Comanche warriors setting astride the trail ahead of us. They quickly recognized us and smiled broadly. It took but another moment for them to realize that Walks With Wolves had some prisoners. *"Natsuitu sunipu,"* exclaimed the lead warrior as he admired the strong medicine that was on display. One warrior immediately turned and headed westward toward the village to alert them of our coming. The other two would escort us. It was a very good morning. Indeed, we'd been blessed.

SIX
SHAMAN?

"MUKWOORU TABU," spat the black-eyed warrior through tight lips set in a chiseled jaw. His aquiline nose nearly touched Spirit Talker's chest. "Mupitsukupu shaman!" Old Owl said, invoking himself as shaman or medicine man of the village.

Spirit Talker felt the spittle run down his chest. "Mupitsukupu *kaahaniitu* Buffalo Hump," responded Spirit Talker, accusing Old Owl of deceiving the chief.

Old Owl's hand angrily reached for his knife, gripping its handle with ever-whitening knuckles.

"Mukwooru!" shouted a voice from the edge of the encampment. "Isa Pohya!"

Old Owl relaxed for the moment. There would be no fight this day.

Spirit Talker gave Old Owl a derisive glare before turning to greet the warrior riding in on a well-lathered pony. This challenge would yet be played out. "Mountain Bear, what is this news?" asked Spirit Talker.

"Walks With Wolves come with Blue Flower. Many captives," responded the warrior excitedly.

Spirit Talker shook his head as if to clear his thinking. "Captives?"

The warrior nodded vigorously.

Old Owl slinked quietly away toward his teepee, likely to conjure some potion or ease his problems with peyote.

Spirit Talker watched Old Owl and shook his head resignedly. The warrior had been naught but trouble ever since he'd returned to camp from the trail drive with Jack. Using outright deceitful tales of his accomplishments to convince the aging Buffalo Hump, he'd asserted a claim as shaman. Spirit Talker was challenging that claim when interrupted by the news of the arrival of Jack and family. At the news of captives, his head spun a bit.

It didn't take long for the entire village to be alerted to the news of our visit.

WE MOSEYED into the Penateka Comanche village around midday. Our arrival caused quite a commotion. Our escorts were beaming at having encountered us on the trail and having the honor of leading us in.

The chill of the morning had worn off, and Blue Flower and I were far more caught up in the excitement of our visit than the wildness of our early morning drama with White Knife's band.

Speaking of White Knife, he tried to sit as proudly erect as possible, bound upon his paint-bedecked pony. He suffered the derisive name-calling and stone-slinging of the Comanche women. A cordon of Penateka warriors ensured that no undue harm would come to the prisoners.

At last, we found ourselves approaching Buffalo

Hump's teepee. Spirit Talker and Prairie Flower stood beside him. All were decked out in their very best bead-decorated buckskins. Buffalo Hump's eagle-feather head-dress trailed to the ground, while my Comanche brother Spirit Talker chose simple braids with no feathers. I was sure that by now, he could have rightly worn a chief's headdress. He still wore the mountain lion necklace with the cross dangling from its center.

The entire village had turned out, so there were more than a hundred warriors and three times that of women and children. The welcoming spirit was strong.

I made the universal Indian sign for peace. *"Ana o'a hi'it,"* I said with a broad smile. The desire to eat was among the first Comanche words I had learned.

Buffalo Hump instantly caught the humor and laughed. *"Onaa kamakuna,"* he said. Indeed, his *tosa* son and beloved daughter were welcome.

Spirit Talker and Prairie Flower simply stood by admiringly, allowing the aging chief to fully relish the moment.

We dismounted, and Blue Flower lifted George and Isa from their decorated board cradles. With a twin in each arm, she slowly approached Buffalo Hump.

The chief could not hold back his emotions as he smiled broadly and tiny droplets of tearful joy ran down his wrinkled cheeks.

"Isa and George, meet grandfather," said Blue Flower.

A cheer welled up from the gathering.

Finally, Spirit Talker stepped forward and embraced me and Blue Flower. "Now time," he said. *"Ana o'a hi'it,"* he added, punctuated with a knowing smile. There would be a feast. My brother paused, looked over at White Knife, and gave me a questioning look.

"They attacked us. When they learned that Blue

Flower was a chief's daughter, they decided to ransom us. They are *tabu kaahaniitu*." The Comanche words for deceitful cowards rang out over the gathering. More derisive shouts and stones were pelted at the Nokoni Comanche prisoners. Blessedly, a cordon of Buffalo Hump's warriors freed the hostiles from their ponies, tied them together, and led them forward.

Buffalo Hump stood menacingly with arms crossed over his chest.

White Knife now did his best to appear contrite.

Unknowingly, I was about to witness a very un-Comanche act.

The chief deferred to Spirit Talker.

"*Tabu kaahaniitu*," said Spirit Talker, echoing my words. He shook his head. Apparently, the fate of the trio of prisoners was fully in his hands. We made eye contact. My brother looked skyward for a second, and I nodded in recognition of his thinking.

White Knife cleared his throat as if to speak but was waved to silence by a swift motion of Spirit Talker's hand.

"Mukwooru *peeka* Tosahwi or *tumhyokenu* Tosahwi," Spirit Talker shrugged his choice between death or trusting the Nokoni. "Tosahwi dishonor Isa Pohya, like *wutsutsuki*," he said, reminding the prisoners that they had dishonored a Penateka Comanche brother and behaved like a rattlesnake. He shook his head resignedly, then turned to me. "Isa Pohya strong *sunipu*," he stated firmly. "Punish Tosahwi." He stepped back and motioned me to act.

Did I hear what I thought I had heard? Was Spirit Talker going to have me punish White Knife?

I glared hard at White Knife. His life, his *kahni*, was in my hands. He could be turned over to the women and beaten or tortured until he died or enslaved. I sought some hint of contrition in his demeanor. It had been slow in coming, but there was a hint of it beneath his prideful exterior. He had already felt the strength of my *sunipu*, and two of his warriors had paid the ultimate price. Walks With Wolves would now determine his fate.

I looked at Blue Flower with our twins. Their lives had been threatened. It would be easy to punish the Nokoni with death for that alone. By Comanche tradition, I could have five scalps plus one for the warrior that Blue Flower killed. There was an uncomfortably long silence.

White Knife was holding his breath as he awaited his fate.

"*Tumhyokenu* Tosahwi," I said firmly.

A bewildered expression swept across White Knife's face. By my words, he was to be trusted, he was to go free. His eyes swept the gathering. No more derisive shouts...no more stones thrown.

Buffalo Hump nodded agreement, and a half-dozen warriors came forward to untie the Nokoni Comanche prisoners. "Go to Nokoni *numunuu*. Tell of Isa Pohya strong *sunipu* and Penateka *numunuu*," he advised. Basically, he was telling White Knife to return to his people and not mess with Walks With Wolves and the Penateka Comanche people. The Nokoni were returned to their ponies, given jerky and pemmican, and escorted out of the encampment.

With this behind us, a smiling Spirit Talker once again invited, "*Ana o'a hi'it*." The feast would begin. He placed an arm of brotherhood over my shoulder and escorted all of us into Buffalo Hump's teepee.

The feasting went on for hours. The Penateka certainly had no fear of starving for the present. Every time a dish was consumed, another replaced it. As to the future of the tribe, that might be another matter. I thought back to Thomas Twiss's challenges as the Indian agent up at Fort Laramie. I sensed that troubles yet brewed on the trail ahead of us.

While I hoped for the best in having released the Nokoni, I sensed that their predations across the Comancheria would continue. Perhaps there was something to the rumor that Klappenbach shared back in Bandera about Rip Ford becoming involved in what was viewed as the Indian problem.

———

BLUE FLOWER and I awakened early. The drink must have been laced with peyote, as we both had splitting headaches. Coupled with the uncomfortable tightness of over-stuffed bellies, it appeared that a much-needed and well-earned day of relaxation and recovery lay ahead. The village women would surely dote over Blue Flower and our babies.

I stepped from the teepee barefoot and felt the frozen grass crackle underfoot. I gingerly stepped back into the teepee and donned my moccasins. As I reemerged, I saw Spirit Talker standing silently among his ponies. It was as though he was communing with them. As I took him in, I thought it odd that he wore only breechcloth and moccasins. He held a knife close by his side. In the chill air, the scars from the mountain lion fight a couple of years back reddened. It had a sort of spiritual effect, as surviving so ruthless an attack was thought to be big *sunipu* in itself. It was no matter that I had saved him from the beast.

My curiosity at this break-of-dawn hour was especially aroused when a stealthily moving figure caught my eye as it moved toward the pony remuda. It was an older warrior, and he too wore only breechcloth and moccasins. It seemed obvious that a fight was brewing. What brought it on was a mystery to me. In our conversations during yesterday's feast, Spirit Talker made no mention of any troubles within the village. Neither did Buffalo Hump give a hint of any problems.

The two were soon facing each other roughly six feet apart.

"Mukwooru *tabu*," the older warrior stated, once again taunting him as a coward. He spat at Spirit Talker.

Spirit Talker remained stoically calm, not flinching at the least at being called a coward or being spit at. He stood perhaps a half head taller than the older warrior and sported a well-muscled body. "Mupitsukupu no shaman," said Spirit Talker firmly.

So, that's what this was about. The older warrior, Old Owl, had apparently been nearly successful in persuading Buffalo Hump to acknowledge him as medicine man to the village. He must have seen Spirit Talker as a challenger to that role. I knew that the shaman position was more symbolic, as the Comanche really had no such priesthood. It was more of an honorific, though the shamans were often sought after to dispense wise advice. I knew better than to step in. This was Spirit Talker's fight.

Old Owl appeared about to spit again, but Spirit Talker's strong hand flashed upward, wrapped around the older warrior's throat, and pushed him away. It was a well-timed shove as Old Owl's knife slashed through thin air.

"Mupitsukupu *tabu*," snarled Spirit Talker as he took a

fighting position. *"Peeka!"* he said through clenched teeth. This would be a fight to the death.

For the first time, I sensed self-doubt in the older warrior. He had figured to make quick work with his knife at close quarters, but Spirit Talker had retaliated swiftly.

The two Comanche circled warily, each looking for an opening in their opponent's guard. Now and again, Old Owl took a swipe, but Spirit Talker easily parried the attempts.

I felt a soft hand on my shoulder. Blue Flower appeared alongside me. I motioned her to be quiet, but her eyes said that she already knew not to speak. So far as I could tell, the combatants were unaware that they had an audience. We could only watch, transfixed by the live play before us. I said a prayer for Spirit Talker's protection. Blue Flower clung to my arm. I could feel her hands tighten with each knife swipe as her brother easily fended off Old Owl.

The older warrior was showing signs of tiring. A desperate move was becoming ever more likely. I wasn't to be disappointed. A thrust by Old Owl brought him slightly off balance, and Spirit Talker was able to grasp his knife wrist in an iron grip. Veins popped out on the warrior's neck as he struggled to free himself. My Comanche brother twisted Old Owl's arm and brought his own knife to the older warrior's throat. Old Owl dropped his knife. Resignation as to his fate swept across his face.

Spirit Talker saw me in his peripheral vision. He smiled. With a firm grip on Old Owl's throat, he pushed him to the ground and sat menacingly on his chest. He replaced his deadly grip with the point of his knife. Spirit Talker stole a glance my way, as though to say, *watch me.*

Old Owl dared not move a muscle. He was defeated. A trickle of blood appeared on his throat where Spirit Talker's knife tip lay.

It was all Blue Flower and I could do to hold back as the scene unfolded before us.

"Mukwooru no *peeka*." Spirit Talker's eyes riveted into the very depths of the defeated warrior just as his words were meant to penetrate the fallen warrior's inner conscience. He was not going to kill Old Owl or shame him. He was giving him a chance to leave with his masculinity intact.

Old Owl stared up with wonder. He could feel the pressure of the tip of Spirit Talker's knife at his throat. Spirit Talker pulled the knife back but still sat astride his chest. He croaked out a surrender, "Mupitsukupu *kwakuru*." He gasped for air and stifled a cough for fear of Spirit Talker's knife tip.

"Mukwooru *tumhyokenu* Taa Narumi. *Natsuitu sunipu*." Spirit Talker told Old Owl that he trusted in one God who had strong medicine. Slowly, he arose from the would-be shaman. "Mupitsukupu go," he said firmly.

Old Owl strove to get up, but my Comanche brother's weight on his chest had enough residual effect that he lost his balance and fell back.

Spirit Talker reached down and helped him up.

The two combatants gazed at each other in silence for a moment.

"Mukwooru *natsuitu sunipu*," intoned Old Owl. "*Natsuitu* Taa Narumi." He was recognizing the strong medicine Spirit Talker possessed and his strong God.

Spirit Talker had won the battle and, apparently, both the physical and spiritual wars.

Old Owl bowed his head ever so slightly to Spirit Talker as he picked up his knife and departed.

Spirit Talker finally turned and looked over at us full-on. "God wins," he said with a triumphant smile.

If ever I had doubt as to my Comanche brother's faith, it was cast aside at that moment. He was a hundred percent Comanche, but also a man of God. Somehow, he'd found a way to mix the two together.

"Mukwooru *natsuitu sunipu*," I offered with a touch of pride at having brought him to faith in Christ. Indeed, Spirit Talker had strong medicine and was rooted in his trust in God. "Fight good, too," I added with a smile.

Blue Flower ran forward and embraced her brother. "Mukwooru *natsuitu*," she said as though not wanting Spirit Talker's physical victory to be overlooked. After all, Spirit Talker stood as a Penateka Comanche warrior. She stood back and took him in from head to toe admiringly. "*Natsuitu sunipu*," she added for emphasis and returned to my side. I expect it was somewhere in the Comanche code that sisters did not display affection in public for their warrior kin.

"*Ana o'a hi'it*," I said, releasing any tension by laughingly suggesting that we eat. I figured that Spirit Talker must have worked up at least as much appetite as I had by just watching him fight.

Spirit Talker nodded. "We must talk," he added with a slightly more serious expression. His words weighed heavily in the morning chill. With that, he headed toward his teepee to clean up.

A few whimpers followed by a plaintive chorus of wails from our teepee let us know that George and Isa were hungry. Blue Flower flashed a loving look at me before scrambling into our teepee to feed the twins.

BLUE FLOWER and I readied George and Isa and headed for Buffalo Hump's teepee to enjoy breakfast. We had not as yet fully accommodated the tense scene we had witnessed at sunrise.

Spirit Talker and Prairie Flower followed us. To look at my Comanche brother, no one could ever have guessed that he'd partaken of a life and death struggle but an hour before.

We entered the teepee. The women busied themselves, helping to prepare and serve breakfast.

"Where Mupitsukupu?" asked Buffalo Hump as we sat around the fire. "No see this morning." Buffalo Hump's English had improved remarkably since I'd last seen him.

Old Owl apparently had a habit of early morning meditation at a place where Buffalo Hump could see him and be deceived by his feigned spirituality.

Spirit Talker glanced at me with a smile of resignation. He would not tell the entire story of the morning's encounter unless pressed to do so by his father. "Mupitsukupu go," he said flatly.

Buffalo Hump nodded.

Spirit Talker could see that the chief wasn't satisfied. "Join Nokoni. Taa Narumi say fight *tosas*." It was a plausible reason. Old Owl had departed the village to join the Nokoni Comanche in fighting Whites.

"Mupitsukupu *natsuitu*," observed Buffalo Hump. Perhaps it was just as well that the chief had respectful memories of Old Owl.

Spirit Talker opened his mouth to speak but was interrupted by the women serving a feast of buffalo cutlets, prairie turnips, potatoes, and berries, along with a steaming brew that tasted vaguely like coffee. I think the latter may have been an accommodation to me.

As the meal wore on, I sensed that Buffalo Hump and Spirit Talker were anxious to discuss something important with me.

With the meal finally finished, the women continued busying themselves about the teepee. Buffalo Hump emitted a frustrated sigh and signaled Spirit Talker that we should adjourn to someplace beyond the range of prying ears.

The three of us bid a brief farewell to the women, along with profuse thanks for their cooking prowess. They had perfected the art of just the right mix of herbs and spices to add zest to a meal.

———

I SOON FOUND myself seated with Chief and son on a blanket laid upon a jagged rock outcropping overlooking the Pedernales River. We were roughly twenty feet above the water and had a clear view of our surroundings. No one could approach within earshot.

Buffalo Hump had brought a pipe and took his time stuffing it with tobacco and lighting it. He took a long pull and passed it to me as a guest.

I put the pipe to my lips and breathed in the fragrance then passed it to Spirit Talker.

"Potsunakwahipu worry," ventured Buffalo Hump. It was one of the few times I had heard his Comanche name, so I immediately reckoned this to be a very serious conversation. "Mukwooru Penateka shaman," he added. Recognition of Spirit Talker as shaman was critically important, as it reflected the deep respect with which my Comanche brother was regarded.

A questioning look creased the sunbaked crevices of my young face.

"Nokoni...Quahadi...Kotsoteka...Tenawa...Yampar-ika...Tanima...all Comanche talk kill Whites." He articu-lated the name of each band slowly for emphasis. They included the five bands of what was called the Comanche Confederacy as led by the Quahadi chief Iron Jacket. "Kiowa and Apache," he added even more emphatically to give a sense of the forces being arrayed.

I glanced at Spirit Talker, but he sat stoically.

Buffalo Hump gave me a look that was surprisingly sorrowful. This was the chief who had led nearly a thou-sand warriors on a devastating raid through the guts of Texas from the hills to the gulf. He sighed resignedly. "Penateka must join."

It made perfect sense. The Penateka were regarded as one of the five bands comprising the Confederacy. It would not do for them to opt out. I looked at Spirit Talker.

My Comanche brother sighed deeply. "We must join." He looked at me as if asking where I stood.

Here I was, married to a Comanche princess, father to twin boys who were half Comanche, and blood brother to a tribal shaman. Yet, my position was not as clear as it seemed. My heart and my faith sided with the Indians who had been wronged for decades. Settlers came in wave after wave. They over-hunted the land, brought diseases for which the tribes had no defense, and broke treaty after treaty. Then again, the tribes had not held up their end of the treaties. They would not accept the White man's ways. Their deadly raids, featuring the torturing, killing, burning, and enslaving of Whites, were notorious. My own family had suffered at the hands of the Comanche. Yet, here I was seated with a Comanche chief and a shaman. My children were half White and half Redman. I deeply loved my Comanche wife. We had a wonderful life ahead. Why couldn't all the *numunuu*, all the people, simply get along?

By now, the pipe had passed through our small circle three times. Buffalo Hump had just passed it to me to begin a fourth round, and I found myself frozen. I held it horizontally before me and followed its ornate carvings from bowl to stem. My mind was a jumble. I may have been White, but I felt that the past three years had molded me into nearly as much a Comanche as Spirit Talker. I ceremoniously held the pipe aloft, put it to my lips, and took a long pull. I blew smoke upward. I wanted to say that I must pray, but somehow, in the pregnant weight of this moment, that seemed disingenuous. Before passing the pipe to Spirit Talker, I looked off across the Pedernales. On the north bank—plain as day—sat Zeb. He'd followed us from Rising Cross Ranch. If he was a gift from God, as I believed. What message was the Lord conveying? A peace swept over me. I shifted my gaze to Buffalo Hump and then Spirit Talker. "Penateka Comanche must fight." I passed the pipe.

Spirit Talker took a long, thoughtful pull. "Penateka protect Rising Cross. Where Isa Pohya fight?"

I stared into my Comanche brother's eyes. Why would he ask me such a question? My mind was a jumble. What to do when you're not sure what to do? "I hear that a great chief named Rip Ford will lead many Texas Rangers against the Comanche." My eyes remained locked on those of Spirit Talker. I paused and looked out at Zeb still seated on the far river bank. "Many Comanche will die," I added sadly.

Buffalo Hump took a long pull on the pipe. He followed my eyes to where Zeb sat and nodded. "*Nasuitu sunipu,*" he observed.

Yes, my medicine was strong.

The chief's gaze returned to me, and he echoed Spirit Talker's question. "Where Isa Pohya fight?"

I sighed. Could I fight against people of my own race? I took the pipe from Buffalo Hump and took a pull. The delay in my response was getting just a tad uncomfortable. I sent silent prayers to God for the wisdom to fashion an answer to my dilemma. It began to come to me. Seems wisdom creates awareness, and I reckoned I was getting a pretty fair handle on this situation. I thought back to the story of King Solomon deciding between two women who claimed to be mother to a child. My decision here seemed just about as momentous. I was working up the strength to make a blood decision. I'd heard folks refer to it as having plenty of sand, as in courage or backbone. I strove to look as confident as possible. "Isa Pohya fight with Comanche. Jack O'Toole fight with Whites."

Both Buffalo Hump's and Spirit Talker's jaw dropped. What was I saying? How could I fight for both sides?

My heart beat furiously. I lofted as earnest a silent prayer to God as I could muster.

All of a sudden, Zeb was beside us. I had not seen him cross the Pedernales River. With his presence, I felt a peace come over me.

Buffalo Hump looked on in amazement as Zeb nuzzled me. God's timing? Spirit Talker simply nodded. He knew that there was *nasuitu sunipu*, strong medicine, at work. There was far more to my response than seemed at first blush. He realized that I had been called by Taa Narumi to find some way to bring peace.

I passed the pipe to Spirit Talker. He took a pull and turned to Buffalo Hump. "This good *sunipu Ap*."

Buffalo Hump was still staring in awe of Zeb. The wolf was revered by many of the frontier tribes, especially so among the Comanche. That a wolf, an *isa*, would be so intimate with me fully bewildered him. But he was beginning to understand why I had been given the Comanche name Isa Pohya. He looked at Spirit Talker as though weighing his words of advice. Indeed, my medicine was strong.

Spirit Talker passed the pipe to his father.

Buffalo Hump gazed at me, then at Zeb, and back at me. With a near-toothless smile, he snuffed the pipe. "Isa Pohya *nasuitu sunipu*. Good for Penateka Comanche." His smile broadened. "Jack make more children," he reflected in near-perfect English.

I breathed a great sigh of relief. My position in the matter at hand had been fully accepted.

Spirit Talker gathered the blanket, and he gave me a wink. We began to head back to the village.

I hadn't taken but a few steps when I found myself pausing. Zeb remained at the spot we'd been sitting. He cocked his head curiously, as animals often do. I signed Spirit Talker and Buffalo Hump a message that I'd join them shortly and walked back to Zeb. "What is it?" I asked as though expecting him to tell me in spoken English.

Zeb turned his head toward the river and eyed the far side. There sat a female wolf and three pups. He had found a new mate.

"This is good, Zeb," I said, still conversing as though he'd understand. I stroked his head.

He nuzzled me and trotted off. He looked back as if calling me to accompany him.

I followed him to the river's edge.

He jumped into the river, and I waded across behind him.

Upon reaching the opposite riverbank, he led me to

his family. The female wolf, what was referred to as a luna wolf, stood guardedly over her pups. Zeb went over and nuzzled her. She had obviously become his mate. With his urging, she backed off and permitted the pups to frolic a bit in front of me. Zeb nudged them toward me, and each got a fill of the scent of Jack O'Toole with plenty of licking and play biting worked in. This apparent ritual over, Zeb spoke up with a soft bark, gave me a confident look, and led his new pack away. He glanced back once as I watched him fade from sight.

What message was being sent? What was God telling me? Was it family? I suspected that was it. It was about making a future for all people. A future where all lived in peace. I could only hope and pray. Where it might lead me, I knew not? It wasn't for me to decide yet God had gifted his human creations with free will. Dare I plan anything?

As I waded back across the Pedernales and walked toward the village, I reflected upon all that had transpired that morning: the fight with Old Owl and his banishment, Spirit Talker assuming the role of shaman, and my counsel with Buffalo Hump and Spirit Talker. For the moment, all was good, but it was all too clear that the future looked challenging. The road ahead would be rough. My role was akin to taking an oxen's yoke and pulling two cultures to some peaceful solution. I'd come to the realization that God must have a sense of humor. As man plans, He often laughs at those plans. Nevertheless, I reckoned to give plenty of heavy-duty thought into how I might fashion some sort of peace. The task was prodigious.

I found myself reflecting upon who I had been and what I had become. It occurred to me that it was likely that most men did not always recognize themselves.

Some lived lives disguised to their true selves. I didn't think that I was one of those folks. Far as I could tell, I stayed true to my faith, to my trust in God. While I could likely be right proud of what I had accomplished in these couple of years of growing up faster than anyone might expect, I strove to remain humbled by it all.

My pa had always told me to be proud but not prideful. So, here I was at a life crossroads of sorts. My faith was being tested...or was it? If I stayed true, it was no test at all. I determined to find some way to bring peace between the Redmen and the Whites. It led me to think back on my good friend George Freeman and all he had endured because of his race. Yet, George had escaped his chains and built a wonderful life in Wyoming that most men would envy. He would surely tell me to pray and do the best that I could to achieve peace. Yet, I intuitively knew that there would be violence before any peace. Seems my faith would be tested.

SEVEN

TALK OF WAR

"GO TO QUAHADI CAMP," urged Buffalo Hump as we sat around the fire. Apparently, all of the Comanche tribes were going to gather and lay out the strategy for stopping the onslaught of Whites. Messengers, mostly Nokoni and Tenawa Comanche, had passed through several times to report on their attacks on ranches and homesteads across the Comancheria. Many scalps had been taken, as well as a few prisoners.

I reflected back on the desperation I had experienced when Kate and Buck had been kidnapped and how fortunate I was to have rescued them. At the time, rescuing them had transcended life itself.

With each visit, the Penateka Comanche warriors felt increasingly compelled to join in the attacks. The younger warriors were especially excited by the prospect of counting coups and taking scalps. They worked diligently at practicing their fighting skills. Arrows filled quivers, lance points were made sharper, and ponies were prepared for war.

Blue Flower and I seemed to be existing in a cultural

wilderness. She heard the talk among the women, the fear for their own safety when the feared White soldiers retaliated. They recalled the men, women, and children killed at the Council House massacre and the Red Fork raid. Buffalo Hump's subsequent raids on Linnville and Victoria were small solace to them.

"*Wa'ipu* are afraid," Blue Flower shared with me as we sat in our teepee and she nursed our boys. "Many *numunuu* die."

Normally, I'd find her mix of English and Comanche endearing. However, the blend of language seemed a tad conflicted at the moment. That may have been a reflection of our standing in both worlds. "Rising Cross safe," I assured her. "We cannot help Penateka *wa'ipu*." Doggone, but I had just gone and done the same mixing.

She placed the boys in their cradleboards, and they quickly fell asleep. She sighed deeply and turned her eyes on me. "We must leave."

I had no idea that Blue Flower had even been considering cutting our visit short. I gave her an inquisitive expression.

"Much trouble here," she replied.

Again, I gave her an inquiring eye.

"No say." She didn't seem inclined to elaborate. "Danger," she stated emphatically.

Far as I could figure, somebody in the village had it in for me as a *tosa*, a White man. I pointed to myself.

Blue Flower nodded.

"Do you know who?" I asked.

She nodded. "No say," she repeated.

I gathered it must be someone important, perhaps a subchief. I looked over at the boys, sleeping so innocently, so peacefully. Buffalo Hump had spoken of growing our family. I slid over and gave Blue Flower a hug. We sat in our embrace until voices from outside stirred us to investigate.

The talk of war was beginning to metamorphose into action. As we emerged from our teepee, I caught the accusatory eyes of two warriors passing by. To their thinking, every White man was the enemy—even the husband of the chief's daughter. I thought back to Hank Johnson's view that the only good Indian was a dead one. I had turned his thinking with an appeal to God and forgiveness, but convincing a bunch of fearful, hate-crazed warriors to accept peace and love was too great a challenge to my mind. Fearful? Yep. They feared for the end of their way of life. Such thinking turns folks to desperate actions, like war.

I stared into Blue Flower's eyes. "We must tell Buffalo Hump," I said. As we prepared to head to Buffalo Hump's teepee, Spirit Talker and Prairie Flower appeared in our path.

Spirit Talker wore a sad expression. "Isa Pohya must go," he said softly. So, he had seen the growing hostility as well. He placed his hand on my shoulder. "Mukwooru visit Rising Cross soon."

I felt that he was trying to reassure me yet feared for me and my family.

"Penateka no attack Rising Cross," he assured me, then put on a rueful grimace. "No stop Nokoni, Tenawa, or others."

I nodded my full understanding. He and Buffalo Hump would not be able to control the other Comanche bands.

We approached Buffalo Hump's teepee.

He must have sensed our approach, for he emerged just as we arrived. He nodded ruefully. "Pot-sunakwahipu not happy. Isa Pohya and Blue Flower must live many moons. Must make *numunuu*, must make peace."

I nodded. "Isa Pohya natsuitu sunipu," I said, trying to sound reassuring. Would my supposedly strong medicine matter in God's total plan for us. "We go to Rising Cross Ranch." I purposely did not say *home*, as I didn't want the chief to think that we didn't consider the Penateka Comanche village home.

Buffalo Hump nodded. "Heart heavy," he said. It was as though he recognized that he might not have many years of life left yet was resigned to his fate—whatever that might be.

Blue Flower stepped forward and gave her father a hug.

Buffalo Hump, great warrior that he was, couldn't quite hold back a tear.

Blue Flower moved to my side and grasped my arm. "Make more *numunuu* at Rising Cross," she said as though to reassure her father.

Buffalo Hump nodded.

"Must leave today," urged Spirit Talker. "Send best warriors with you. Keep my brother and sister safe."

Spirit Talker and I clasped each other's forearms. It was as intimate a goodbye as we dared with half the Penateka village looking on. I felt a mix of emotions from those warriors who deigned to see us off. The younger brave had a touch of savage fury in their eyes. The older warriors were more reserved and held back any overt display of hostility to the White man whom Buffalo Hump had accepted into the tribal fold. Perhaps we had overstayed our welcome...or at least mine. We had gotten just a tad comfortable, and Blue Flower had reconnected with her friends, some of whom, like her, had borne children. We nevertheless had to leave. It was mid-December, and the winter had not fully set in. I'd already learned just how unpredictable and changeable winters on the Comancheria could be.

Blue Flower wasted no time gathering our few belongings. Nevertheless, we decided to use two pack horses to keep our loads light. I figured the horses would appreciate it. The boys would once again ride in cradleboards draped behind the cantle of Blue Flower's pony. We had plenty of grub and carried the same weapons we'd brought with us. With five Comanche warriors accompanying us, we'd likely be seen as far too formidable a target for hostiles.

———

WE TRAVELED SLOWLY in deference to the boys in their cradleboards. Roughly a half day along, we came to the spot where the Nokoni warrior White Knife had attacked us. Our five escorts talked among themselves, and I could understand enough to be aware that they were impressed that I had overcome the Nokoni.

The going was a tad rough as we made our way along the south bank of the Pedernales River. Blue Flower and I were grateful that we'd decided to lighten the load on the pack horses, as negotiating certain portions of the terrain required a nimbleness afoot. Even the Penateka Comanche warriors, with their best ponies, found some places especially challenging. They rode proudly, even in traversing difficult portions of the trail. In fact, we were mostly making our own trail.

I must admit that being accompanied by fierce Comanche warriors was very much appreciated.

By nightfall, we'd nearly reached the Pinta Trail.

We were about to stop to make camp when the lead

Comanche escort pulled up and signaled us to stop. We all heard the jingle of spurs and creaking of saddle leather ahead of us. It stopped abruptly. Silence. I could hear my heart beating. A breeze kicked up and rustled the leaves of the cypress lining the river.

Little George chose the moment to let out a wail. Blue Flower turned and lifted him from the cradleboard, but it was too late. In but moments, we found ourselves facing a couple of dozen Texas Rangers led by none other than my old friendly adversary, Captain Nathan Benton.

Blue Flower, me, and three of our Comanche escorts were exposed. The other two escorts split up and sought cover on the south side of the trail.

Benton pulled up and, upon recognizing me, flashed a big gotcha grin.

"Where are yuh and yer squaw headed, O'Toole?"

I sighed resignedly. Were we going to repeat our past encounters? Benton invariably backed down after he'd decided that discretion was the better part of valor. Yet, I had a sense that this was a tad different. "Heading home, Captain," I responded firmly.

Benton took a long, hard look at my escorts. "Yuh bring the whole tribe with yuh?" He chuckled derisively.

There was no questioning the fact that we were seriously outnumbered. I remained clueless as to what Benton was up to.

"Mind if we palaver a bit in private, O'Toole?" He promptly slid from his saddle.

Now he had my curiosity up, but I was cautious. After all, even a dead snake has a bite. I slid from my saddle and eased on over toward Benton.

We met about equidistant of the two parties—the Texas Rangers and the Comanche—and shook hands.

"We got a problem here, O'Toole," he near whispered. "Injuns are pitchin' fights across the Comancheria. Folks in Austin are getting' frazzled like no tomorrow. Settlers are buzzin' like angry bees."

He had my attention. "What's that to do with me, Captain?" I near whispered.

Benton eyed my Comanche escorts. He leaned in to me and put his hand aside his mouth. "My orders are to kill Injuns. Many as we can."

Whew! He had me there. I glanced beyond him at the two dozen Texas Rangers who seemed to be itching for a fight. "You have something in mind, Captain?"

"I don't want trouble with you," he whispered with a conspiratorial tone. He looked me straight on in my eyes. "I got a proposition. I'll send six of my Texas Rangers with you as escorts to Rising Cross Ranch. They're good men." He took a deep breath. "You send them heathen Comanche back to their village. We won't attack them. You have my word."

I scratched my chin thoughtfully. There was no reason to doubt Benton's words or his offer. It seemed an honest proposition. "Mind if I talk with my wife, Captain?"

Benton shrugged. "I'm waitin'."

I strode over to Blue Flower.

She had one of the twins in her arms. He was hungry and sucking away like no tomorrow. The way the boys nursed, I figured they'd be full-grown in a year.

I looked around at our Comanche escorts. I was confident that none of them understood a word of English. "The Captain made a proposal. Says he's been ordered to kill Indians. All Indians. He's offered to escort us to Rising Cross and promises not to harm our Comanche brothers."

Blue Flower sighed. Was this to be her life in the White man's world? She nodded. "See no one die."

I motioned one of our warrior escorts over to us. "Buffalo Runner and warriors return to Penateka Comanche village. Tell Buffalo Hump to be careful. Tell him that Texas Rangers will kill all Comanche." I said this all in the Comanche tongue so Benton would not hear my warning. I assured them that they could travel safely to the village.

Buffalo Runner looked to Blue Flower for assurance that all was well.

She echoed my instructions. "Tell Mukwooru to be careful," she added.

I urged Buffalo Runner to head out quickly and to watch his back. Somehow, I didn't fully trust the Texas Rangers.

I waited until the Comanche were well out of sight before returning to a now quite clearly impatient Captain Benton. "The Comanche will return to their village. I trust in your word, Captain. I am in your hands." Despite Benton's assurances, doubt as to the safety of the Comanche seeped into my thinking. I hadn't much choice, as the Texas Rangers were primed to attack. I had to trust that Benton could constrain them. In any attack, me and my loved ones would likely be placed in grave danger.

Benton ordered a detail of six Texas Rangers to escort us to Rising Cross Ranch.

I had to admit that the detail appeared to be about as tough as they came. They were very well-armed, resembling fortresses on horseback. A hardened old Texas Ranger named Hardy headed them up. I couldn't tell whether that was his first or last name, and he wouldn't say. Given appearances, I didn't figure to push the issue with Hardy.

As we rode on past Benton, we exchanged glances. I haven't a clue what he was thinking, but I was concerned that he might yield to his men's itching for a fight and pursue the Comanche. I asked myself what I might do if Benton was to lose control of his men. Would I counterattack? Did I have a prayer of escaping our escort to do that? I was at Benton's mercy and could only trust in God that he'd be good to his word.

———

WE FOUND the Pinta Trail and headed southward. I kept my ears peeled for the sound of gunfire for as long as I could.

Hardy and the Texas Rangers performed their duty silently. None seemed inclined to engage with a White man married to an Indian squaw and their two half-breed children. We stopped a couple of times to rest horses, answer nature's call, and give Blue Flower a chance to tend to the needs of George and Isa. They remained aloof, dismounting when we did and chatting among themselves. I wondered whether I could depend on them in a fight?

We found an excellent spot to camp for the night beside a small stream that fed the Guadalupe River. Given the Indian activity in the region, we decided to cold camp. After a dinner of jerky and pemmican, I saw to Blue Flower and our twins. I gave them my buffalo robe as added protection against the winter chill. As if to punctuate the setting, a few snowflakes began to fall. I seized the opportunity to seek out Hardy.

He was sitting quietly alone from his fellow Texas

Rangers. His saddle served as a backrest. He didn't look up as I approached, though I could tell that he was aware of me.

"You're not liking this duty, are you, Hardy?" I reckoned to speak my mind out front.

Hardy gave me a dark, squinty-eyed look appropriate to his name. He had a solid square jaw that accentuated the toughness resident in his expression. I bristly red beard added to his rough outward appearance.

"Can't say as I blame you. Indians been attacking all over the Comancheria." I stood before him, figuring it was up to him to invite me to sit.

Hardy looked up at me and nodded. "Tain't easy," he finally spoke up.

"Trouble's been building for a long time. Went to Wyoming last year and saw the same with Lakota and Cheyenne Indians."

That seemed to grab Hardy. He figured he wasn't talking to some inexperienced do-gooder kid who didn't understand the laws of the frontier...man's laws, at least. "There's two sides, Mr. O'Toole, but my flag's planted with the Rangers. Can't say as I like the savages, but..." he let his words hang.

I was encouraged that he seemed sensitive to the plight of the Indians. "There's talk of war, Hardy. Big war ahead."

"Set a spell," he said with a motion of his hand.

I sat cross-legged opposite him. "Comanche are banding together. Young warriors are full of fight, full of hate."

"Hate never got nobody nowhere," said Hardy with a knowing grunt. "If there's to be war, we'll be ready." He glanced up at the full moon and back to me. I could sense curiosity in him. "So, yuh been up Wyoming way?" he queried.

I was surprised. "Got a friend with a cattle ranch up near Fort Laramie. We herded a passel of longhorns from Bandera and sold a few to the Indian Agency and the Army. We're hoping to build another herd and head them up next year."

Hardy picked up a stick and absent-mindedly drew patterns in the dust. "Been hankerin' to do some cowboyin'," he ventured with a dreamy smile.

It didn't take much to figure that this tough Texas Ranger was more complex than I'd made him out to be. "You cut and rope?" I didn't ask him whether he could shoot, as the arsenal he carried bore testament to that.

"Worked my family's spread a few years back," he said, still smiling. "Captain says yuh lost yer family to them Redskins."

I nodded. "True."

"But yuh don't hate 'em?" he said with a curious expression.

"I found that revenge wasn't satisfying," I responded. "God teaches us to forgive, but sinners must be punished. I've taken an Indian life or two, Hardy. Had to. But I took no pleasure in it. It was me or them, and it didn't bring my family back."

Hardy nodded. "Man of faith are yuh?"

"It's worked for me so far," I said with a smile. "You?"

Hardy avoided answering. "Captain says Injuns call yuh Walks With Wolves."

"No accounting for Indians," I said with a chuckle. I just didn't figure on explaining to Hardy about wolves and *sunipu* and Indians' ways. I paused and looked away.

"You think Captain Benton was true to his promise not to attack my Comanche escorts?"

Hardy blinked and scratched his beard thoughtfully. "Captain's an honest man, Mr. O'Toole. He promises somethin', he keeps his word."

Coming from this tough Texas Ranger, I felt confident that he was being straight with me. "Thanks kindly," I said. I stood. "Think I'll turn in. We should make Rising Cross Ranch before sunset tomorrow. Appreciate getting acquainted, Hardy."

He stood and reached out his hand before I could walk away.

We shook hands. He had an iron grip, but I didn't let on that it hurt like all blazes. I judged that Hardy would be a true asset on a trail drive. As I walked to my bedroll and Blue Flower's waiting arms, I thought more about the conversation with Hardy. He seemed resigned to eventual war with the Indians. We were talking of war, but I hoped and prayed that we were a long way from it...if at all. I had full faith that God was able to heal the brokenness of our world, but I figured we would have to want it healed. There was the challenge if ever there was one.

I wondered what the outcome of any conflict might be? What might it prove? How many lives would be lost? Changed? What indeed might the future hold? The events, the challenges we faced were like a series of stations on the trail of our lives that we were all living life's journey. It occurred to me that every destination opened a doorway to another journey. If war was to occur, what doorway would its outcome open.

EIGHT
FORTRESS RISING CROSS

IF THERE WERE hostiles or bandits watching along the trail, they never made themselves known. With a half-dozen heavily armed, battle-toughened Texas Rangers accompanying the supposedly legendary Walks With Wolves, it was little wonder that potential enemies chose to leave us be. The weather turned increasingly chilly, and a light morning snowfall deposited a thin patina of white across our trail. It was enough that I saw Indian signs from time to time, confirming that we were being watched.

Hardy and I didn't have any further opportunity to have a serious chat. He appeared to have accepted me with some degree of respect. In fact, he was especially impressed on the morning following our talk, when I felled a buck at a pretty fair distance with a single arrow.

I reveled in his "Dang, O'Toole! That be right, fine shootin'!"

I must admit that I was out of practice, so I was nearly as surprised as Hardy. And Blue Flower gave me a *that's my man* sort of look that got me looking forward to getting home and...well, home.

After a short delay to field dress the deer, we continued our travels. I rode beside Blue Flower with Hardy riding point and the Texas Rangers following behind, except when the trail required us to proceed single file.

"Jack good with bow and arrow," said Blue Flower as we walked side by side along the trail. We did this every hour or so to give the horses a slight relief from their human cargo.

"Mukwooru taught me well," I responded.

"Miss brother. *Kuya akatu...*" She struggled with the words.

"Afraid for the future," I suggested.

She nodded.

"*Kuya akatu aitu,*" I urged. "We must have *tu taiboo* in God." Like her, I tended to mix English and Comanche. I tried to assure her that she must trust in God. I dusted some snowflakes from her shoulders and pulled the buffalo robe more tightly around her. Her eyes caught mine. Ah, love. She had been coming around to my Christian beliefs, though I didn't sense full acceptance from her quite yet.

Blue Flower was torn between two cultures, and it was her love for me that caused her to strive to understand the concept of a trilogy, of a Father, Son, and Holy Spirit that was all-powerful as opposed to the animism faith of her Comanche *numunuu* that worshipped nearly everything dead or alive. I knew that her family would be drawn into battle against the Whites. The confederacy of Comanche tribes was such that all were bonded to the common cause of defeating the settlers encroaching on the tribal heritage. I kissed her lightly.

A couple of our Texas Ranger escorts had been watching us and averted their eyes at our public display of love. They were tough, frontier-hardened men, but not equipped to handle such an emotion.

"We're getting close to Rising Cross, men," I said, smiling and giving a friendly nod to the men.

We all mounted up. It was looking like the day would wear on peaceably.

One of the Texas Rangers began to sing to break the boredom of the trail, but Hardy quieted him. "Yuh got a decent voice, Slim, but we can't hear no Injuns with you causin' a ruckus." A bit of a chuckle went up among the other Rangers.

I did appreciate the respect of the Texas Rangers and the seriousness with which they accomplished the decidedly distasteful—to them—duty of escorting a White man acting like a Comanche, an Indian princess, and a couple of half-breed babies. Their attention to duty, despite their prejudices and inclinations, was right civilized.

I reckoned that we were about an hour's ride from Rising Cross when we saw a hunting party of five Kiowa crossed the trail about a quarter mile ahead of us. They were hunting awfully close to the ranch. I reached out and gave Blue Flower's arm a reassuring touch.

She smiled nervously.

I glanced at George and Isa in their cradleboards. They were sleeping with nary a care in the world. I wished it might always be like that for them.

"Just hunters," I assured her. Recalling my past encounters with Kiowa, I felt fairly confident that they had purposefully avoided any contact with the *sunipu* of Walks With Wolves. Our Texas Ranger escorts likely added to any reluctance they might have held.

We made a final turn on the trail just as the sun was beginning its dance on the western horizon. "There's Rising Cross," I called out to Hardy.

He reined in and allowed Blue Flower and me to come alongside. "Guess we'll be heading back to the captain," he stated flatly. He figured his duty was now completed. He'd gotten us home safely as ordered.

I shook my head. "Y'all can't be heading back on a freezing December night, Hardy."

Blue Flower nodded. She wanted to enjoy the kitchen hearth and our warm bed but also felt that the Texas Rangers deserved appreciation.

Hardy had begun to turn his cayuse.

"You can't leave," I insisted. "There's a dinner ahead and a warm place to spend the night. Y'all must accept our invitation."

Hardy looked over at the five men sitting on horses and shivering in the frontier cold.

A hopeful, pleading look swept each man's face. As I've said, they were tough, but fully appreciative of a break from the rigors of the Texas winter and a decent meal. Cold camping and eating pemmican and jerky were not exactly a luxury.

I awaited Hardy's answer.

"Tain't far to the house," he grunted.

I shook my head and urged Big Red forward.

We pulled up about a hundred yards from the house. I had as yet seen no one, and, far as I could tell, no one had seen us.

"Hail the house!" I hollered.

"State your business!" came the reply.

"Dang it, Shorty! It's us!" I hollered back.

"Boss?" he inquired and stepped from behind the

barn door. He did a double take as he saw the heavily armed Texas Rangers surrounding us.

I nudged Big Red forward with Blue Flower riding alongside. "Y'all got some hot grub around for trail-weary folks, Shorty?" I motioned Hardy and the men to join us. "Glad to feel so welcomed," I added sarcastically, though deep inside my bones, I was pleased to have been challenged.

By now, the shouting had alerted everyone. Kate and Buck emerged from the house, Will stood beside Shorty, and even Isaac and Sarah ambled up from their house nearby. There were plenty of smiles, but no one was taking any action.

"Will...Shorty...Buck...y'all tend to all these horses. We have some cold, tired folks. Kate, stoke the fire and get some grub started." I laughed as they all took to their assigned duties. I helped Blue Flower from her pony and grabbed the boys in their cradleboards, then motioned Hardy and the men to follow into the house.

"You sure, Mr. O'Toole?" queried Hardy.

"What do the Mexicans say, Hardy? *Mi casa es su casa*." I chuckled. "We'll find y'all a warm spot in the bunkhouse after dinner," I added and pointed to the addition we'd made to our ranch spread. It was a fair-sized bunkhouse, constructed in anticipation of housing several ranch hands as our cattle business grew.

Hardy shrugged and waved the other Texas Rangers to follow. Upon entering the house, he paused with an awed expression on his face. "My, Mr. O'Toole, but y'all have a right homey place." He was clearly quite taken with the way the women had decorated our humble home. Had he not been so tough, he might have shed a tear. He took another step, then noticed the shutters with their porthole slits designed to permit the muzzle of a rifle to aim through. That brought a curious glance at me.

"Roof is made of tin, Hardy," I assured him. There'd be no setting fire to our roof.

"Chimney?" he asked.

"Can't smoke us out either. The chimney has a side port with a baffle." I'd designed it so that if attackers tried to block the top of the chimney flue, we needed only to open the baffle to permit smoke to escape. We wouldn't be smoked out. I pointed over to a corner that housed a collection of guns and ammunition. "And there's a food storage area under the floorboards," I added.

Hardy nodded with admiration. "By golly, Mr. O'Toole, it's like a fortress."

I really had never thought of this as Fortress Rising Cross, but Hardy had a point. It had been one of my passions to make our house as impregnable as possible. I suppose it was a consequence of the demons I yet carried from when the Comanche burned my home and killed most of my family. I wondered whether I'd ever shake those horrific memories?

Within the hour, Shorty had stoked the cooking fire, and Blue Flower, Kate, and Sarah had a scrumptious meal on the table where a collection of warm and hungry men had settled in. They were about to dig in when I brought everything to a halt. "Folks, I think it's time to show our thanks." I delivered a prayer of thanks to God that was just long enough to keep the Texas Rangers from eating me instead of dinner.

I must admit to being impressed with the feast Kate and Sarah scraped together at the last minute. It was scrumptious, to say the least. They even roasted the venison from the buck I'd killed on the trail.

I took note of my ever-maturing sister Kate making eyes at Will. He must have noticed, because he blushed and near choked on a mouthful of potatoes. "Kate, you have more venison?" was my feeble attempt to distract them.

It was Kate's turn to blush. "Er...it's all here on the table, Jack," she said distractedly.

Hardy was licking his chops and savoring a cup of coffee. The Texas Rangers hadn't eaten so well in months. "Y'all got a good life heah, Mr. O'Toole. I be right serious 'bout joinin' yer next trail drive."

"Me, too," added Slim.

Hardy stifled a belch. "Thanks to y'all fer the great grub," he said with a broad smile. "It's gonna be tough to leave yer hospitality, but we gotta be headin' out in the mornin' to catch up with the captain."

"You still figure there's going to be a fight ahead?" I asked as Hardy nodded to his men and made a move to get up.

He stood looking kindly at Blue Flower and then at me. "Wish it weren't so," he sighed. He nodded toward my wife. "Her people have been killing, burning, stealing, and worse up north of heah. Not all their fault, but that don't matter none to them folk in Austin."

"They asking for soldiers?" I said concernedly.

Hardy shook his head. "Don't think they want Washington. Them folks are worthless as teats on a bull." He blushed. "Scuse me, ladies."

"Texas Rangers?" I asked.

"Likely recruit a passel. Yep. It'll be Rangers, Mr. O'Toole." He grabbed his hat and nodded to the women. "Guess we better grab some shuteye. Thanks agin."

I had really come to like Hardy. "By the way, do you have a last name?"

He gave me a long look. Full name exchanges implied a level of commitment on the frontier. "Sullivan. Hardy Sullivan."

"Make sure you get back this way for my next trail, Mr. Sullivan."

The Texas Rangers filed from the house. By now, a thin blanket of white had begun to cover the ranch.

I watched after them as Shorty led them to the bunkhouse. I wondered how many of the footprints they were making might be made a couple of years from now. Fighting Comanche would be no easy task. With Christmas but a few days off, I rather felt sorry that they'd likely be missing time with families—at least, for those that had them. Duty and responsibility were tough taskmasters. The life of a Texas Ranger was perilous. Around the next turn in the trail, death could be grabbing at his reins.

———

KATE WAS down the path visiting with Sarah, while Buck had joined Shorty and Will with chores in the barn. The twins were napping. It gave Blue Flower and me a few moments to be alone, ostensibly to talk about Christmas. I hadn't celebrated it since my folks passed away.

We were feeling pretty secure so far as worrying about Indian attacks. I sensed that there were Penateka Comanche hunting parties around within a short ride that kept a protective eye on us.

Blue Flower sat across from me. "Will there be war?" she blurted.

This was decidedly not a Christmas question. I slipped my hands over hers and nodded.

"Will be sad," she said, seemingly on the verge of

tears. This had clearly been weighing heavily upon her. "My *numunuu* die," she added.

To be honest, the matter had been weighing on me ever since my private powwow with Buffalo Hump and Spirit Talker. How was I to find a way to live on both sides of the coming hostilities? What impact could my voice have to avoid bloodshed? "Maybe I go to Austin," I ventured.

"Austin?" Blue Flower queried.

Sometimes, I took for granted that she knew of the White man's government. "The Texas White father lives in Austin. It's a city, my love."

She stared at me. I sensed thoughts churning through her mind. "Blue Flower go to Austin." she finally stated. She wasn't asking.

How was I to respond to that? First concern to come to mind was the hostility we'd face if I were to bring her to Austin. The citizens of the Texas capital were undoubtedly swept up in the growing hostilities. Fear bred hatred, and once acted upon, they made for a deadly combination.

Blue Flower read my face. "Danger in Austin?" she asked.

I nodded. "I will think about it," I said, hoping to put off any decision.

She smiled knowingly. "Jack think."

"Shorty plays a mouth harp," I said in an awkward attempt to shift the conversation.

Blue Flower looked quizzically at me.

"He calls it a harmonica. It makes music. We can sing songs on Christmas."

"Christmas songs? Have drums?"

What a relief to not be discussing Indian wars.

"Drums would be good." I reckoned it would make for a nice blend of cultures.

"Jack drum?" she asked.

What was I to say?

"Have plenty buffalo. Jack kill deer?" She was planning the menu. We had buffalo meat stored away, but were plum out of venison.

My eyes lit up. "Antelope!" I'd seen a small herd on my most recent ride around the ranch. The flighty beasts were a challenge, as they didn't take kindly to humans getting very close. Doggone, but those pronghorns were fast. Antelope or not, it seemed as though we'd be having plenty of meat for our celebrating the Lord's birth. However, by the time we'd figured vegetables and desserts, our time alone had vanished. The twins stirred, and Buck came clomping up the gallery from the barn. It wasn't mud on his boots, try as he might to scrape them off.

———

IT WAS THE FIRST AND, thus, the best Christmas I'd celebrated since the attack on my family, an event slowly fading into my distant past. I think it went by in a blur for Blue Flower. Babies George and Isa weren't yet old enough to appreciate the singing and extra candlesaglow about the cabin. Sarah had given us some pine trimmings that greened the place up a bit. I managed to beat a rhythm on a makeshift drum of deerskin stretched over a pie tin while Shorty blew tunes on his harmonica.

I had snuck out to the barn just as the sun rose. I was trying to be quiet, but my feet made a crunching sound in the icy snow cover. Big Red snorted in his stall and acted as if he couldn't wait to ride, though I think it was mares that he had in mind. I gave Big Red a lump of sugar to settle him down. I found my way to the back of Big Red's stall. There, I unlocked and opened a wooden box that I stored in a corner. I had made it crystal clear that no one was to touch that box under penalty of serious consequences. So it was that my gift for Blue Flower had remained untouched. It was still in the red cardboard box it had been shipped in.

I smiled to myself as I shook snow from my boots and stepped through the front door. I hankered to revel in Blue Flower's reaction to the surprise of this special gift. Sigh! Wouldn't you know that I ran smack dab into my beautiful wife. Call it God's will or whatever you might, but the box nearly split open with the impact. "Er... Merry Christmas, my love," was about as quick a reaction as I could come up with.

Her arms hugged the box as I stepped back just a few inches. She quickly finished what the impact of our collision hadn't accomplished. In her hands was a beautiful sky-blue gingham dress. Blue Flower's eyes looked up into mine, and her loving gaze nearly melted me where I stood. She pivoted and ran back to our bedroom.

I was at a momentary loss as to what to do, so I stood just inside the front door as though frozen in place. Frozen? Cold? I shut the door.

Blue Flower emerged from the bedroom with a smile that was brighter than all the candles and lamps in our house combined. "Jack...Jack..." her voice trailed off. She spun in place. "Blue Flower pretty?" she asked.

I shook my head. "No...Blue Flower beautiful." She ran into my arms and pressed her lips against mine with such passion that I was relieved when I heard the twins' hunger cries from the bedroom. And Kate and Buck emerged wondering what the ruckus was about. Blue

Flower and I stood for a moment with sheepish grins plastered across our faces.

"Oh my, your dress is beautiful!" Kate gleefully shrieked at Blue Flower.

Blue Flower laughed joyfully and pirouetted gracefully across to the bedroom to tend to the twins. It was about the happiest I'd seen her, topped only by our wedding day and the birth of our boys. I was so proud I near busted a button. For a brief instant, threats of war and dangers of the frontier had been forgotten.

As Christmas Day wore on with the feasting and celebrating, I got to figuring that Blue Flower might never take off that dress. It was as though I had performed some great magic in our relationship. It was strong *sunipu* indeed.

As we all sat feasting around the great table in the midst of our ever-expanding cabin, Will stood and gave a cough aimed at getting everyone's attention. He shifted awkwardly with his hands on the back of the chair.

I looked over at my dear sister Kate. She was blushing. At thirteen, she'd become a woman by frontier measures and a right pretty woman at that.

Will looked over at me and then back to Kate. A bead of sweat formed on his brow. "Er…Kate and me…er…we reckon to get married," he finally blurted.

Kate got up and eased in beside him. "Do we have your blessing, Jack?"

What was I to do? It wasn't as though I was Kate's pa.

Blue Flower and Sarah looked at me with wide-eyed expressions painted across their faces that hollered, *what are you waiting for?*

I stood and laid a serious gaze at Will and Kate. Mere seconds passed, but the quiet in the room made it seem an eternity. *"Kuhmabai,"* I finally said in the Comanche language. Blue Flower laughed as Will and Kate shared befuddled looks. "If I must...yes, *kuhmabai* by all means. Get married. You have all of our blessings."

A collective sigh of relief swept the room.

Blue Flower arose and tiptoed over to the cupboard. She smiled at me over her shoulder as she pulled out a platter piled with what appeared to be biscuits. She placed them gently on the table just within my reach. They were not biscuits. This was a heap of round baked delicacies with a hole in the middle and featured a sugary coating. "Bear sign," said Blue Flower. It seemed that Isaac and Sarah had gone to Bandera and learned of the treats from Stella Klappenbach. Some folks apparently called them donuts.

I laughed. They sure looked like bear sign, but this bear sign turned out to be deliciously edible. I devoured one. As I went to reach for another, my hand found air. The bear signs were gone.

Blue Flower and Sarah smiled broadly with their culinary success.

We were cleaning up after the Christmas feast, and we men were readying to tend to the livestock when there was a knock at the door.

It immediately occurred to me that we had let our guard down in these threatening times. The men had chipped in and gifted me with a .44 caliber Colt New Model revolving rifle. I stroked it admiringly. I hadn't even had a chance to load it, but I instinctively grabbed it and headed to the door in response to the knocking. "Who goes?" I called out.

"Hardy Sullivan. Dang, but it's cold out here!"

I swung the door open. "What the?" I spouted as I

beheld the tough Texas Ranger dragging a saddle and draped in a bloodied bedroll blanket.

Hardy dropped the saddle and staggered into the room. "Nokoni," he managed to spit out. He dropped the blanket, revealing a seriously bloodied shoulder. He collapsed into a chair.

Blue Flower rushed to a kitchen cabinet where she stored Comanche medicinal poultices while Kate and Sarah heated water and grabbed cloth strips for bandages.

"Where's the Captain?" I had to ask.

"They be chasin' them savages. They winged me, an' my cayuse slipped and busted a leg. Had to put her down. Only a couple miles from here, so here I be."

Hardy gritted his teeth as the women went to work tending to his bloody but not-too-serious bullet wound. They quickly had him cleaned up and bandaged with his left arm in a proper sling to support his wounded shoulder.

Hardy finally looked around the room and noticed the remains of our Christmas feast. "Sorry to crash in on yer party."

I couldn't hold back a laugh despite the seriousness of Hardy's condition. "Well, isn't this your lucky day, Hardy."

He flashed a quizzical look.

"Merry Christmas."

By now, the women had cleared the bandages and poultices and begun placing a Christmas feast on the table in front of the wounded Texas Ranger.

Hardy appeared rightly bewildered.

"Merry Christmas," offered Blue Flower as she placed what little remained of a pronghorn steak before our unexpected guest. Yes, I had managed to stalk and dispatch one of those graceful critters of the Texas frontier.

Hardy looked up at Blue Flower helplessly for a moment, then broke into a smile as she sliced the meat into bite-sized pieces for him. His shoulder wouldn't be letting him do any cutlery work for so long as he needed the sling.

Shorty and Will were curious, but there was live-stock to tend to. They bid thanks to the women and headed out to the barn. They would be getting hay together to take out to our herds of cattle and horses roaming our pastures. With luck and God's will, we'd not be losing any stock to the vagaries of the Texas winter.

It occurred to me that Captain Benton would eventu-ally backtrack to find Hardy. There would likely be more wounded Texas Rangers, too.

Blue Flower and I locked eyes. The edge had been taken from our Christmas idyll. I shook my head resignedly. Come the new year, I reckoned to be heading to Austin to see what I could learn.

With darkness creeping over the landscape, Isaac and Sarah wrapped little Jack warmly and headed home. Buck had gotten over his embarrassment at his sister being in love and decided to sleep in the bunkhouse with the men.

"You know where the bunkhouse is, Hardy," I said by way of excusing myself and a yawning Blue Flower. "Just leave the dishes over there in the basin."

Hardy paused between chews on the last piece of antelope. "Can't thank y'all 'nuf, Mr. O'Toole."

"I expect Captain Benton will come asking about you tomorrow. We'll get some horseflesh under you, though I expect you won't be doing any fighting for a spell." I half chuckled at that. "Blow out the lamps before you head to the bunkhouse. Good night, Hardy."

The Texas Ranger shifted in his seat, winced at a stab of pain, and nodded toward me. "Night," he mumbled as he took a final bite of Christmas dinner. Afore long, he wiped his mouth with a napkin, nodded his gratitude, and lumbered off to the bunkhouse.

Blue Flower and I heard the door shut and felt a draft as a hint of icy winter breeze snuck into the cabin in the wake of Hardy's departure. I stood behind my beautiful wife, combing out her long black hair at the makeup table I'd brought to her from Bandera. "Did you notice Sarah's eye?"

She shrugged as though not wanting to talk about it.

"It's bruised," I said matter-of-factly.

"Maybe Sarah fall," Blue Flower responded unconvincingly.

"Did Isaac hit her?"

"Sarah no say."

I stepped around to look full-on into Blue Flower's face.

Uncharacteristic tears had formed in the corners of her eyes. "Isaac angry," she grudgingly admitted.

"Never an excuse for a man to strike a woman, especially his wife."

Blue Flower nodded.

I harkened back to my pa's teaching from the Bible about husbands and wives respecting each other. I wished that I still had the New Testament that George had given me. It had literally stopped a bullet and saved my life. I gazed lovingly into Blue Flower's eyes. It was clear that she felt Sarah's pain.

"Comanche men hit slave, no hit wife," she whispered.

I knew that the Comanche women were well-respected in their culture. "I will talk with Isaac," I said as reassuringly as I could. Hopefully, I could muster the words to offer wise counsel without being overly intrusive into the couple's private life. I wrapped my arms lovingly around Blue Flower.

———

MORNING GREETED me with shards of sunlight reflected from ice that coated just about everything in sight. I worked to shake a thick glaze from the fall bar on the corral gate. The news about Isaac having struck Sarah weighed heavily on my mind. I just about had the bar freed and happened to glance up the trail to where Isaac's cabin stood. I had gifted them with a few acres in exchange for occasional help with the Rising Cross Ranch.

The couple had left the Amish country of Pennsylvania as a consequence of Isaac having a serious disagreement with Sarah's father. Isaac had lost his temper and leveled a rifle at his father-in-law. The Amish apparently don't take kindly to such things, so the young couple bade farewell and headed to Texas. They had come upon what appeared to be my abandoned homestead with the burned-out hulk of a cabin. They figured to take possession as squatters. However, I returned after successfully rescuing Buck and Kate from the Comanche. I felt for the young couple plus needed help with the ranch I envisioned, so I had deeded them those few acres. That had been a couple of years back. They even named their first child after me.

Sarah grew vegetables in a thriving garden that she maintained through the warm months until the first frosts came. So, as I looked up the trail, I saw Isaac fixing the fence in front of their cabin. I shrugged and headed his way. Seems God works in strange ways. "Morning, Isaac," I hailed him.

He looked up with a serious expression. "Good morning to you, Jack."

"Looks as though it's fixing to snow again," I observed.

He remained crouched beside the fence and looked up at the gathering dark clouds. "Could be," he responded. Isaac wasn't much of a talker.

"Thanks for your help with the Christmas feast. Y'all sure brought vegetables aplenty from that wonderful garden Sarah keeps. How does she do it?" I knew also that she had stored plenty of preserves for the winter.

Isaac gave me a questioning glance. It was obvious to him how her garden thrived. "You get the gate bar free?" he asked.

I nodded then took a deep breath and said a little prayer to myself. Here I was about to turn eighteen, filled with Bible-taught moral principles, and about to bring fear of the wrath of God to a man a few years my senior. "How did Sarah get that bruised eye?" There...I said it.

Isaac stood. "What are you getting at, Jack?"

"Just curious," I said with a non-threatening shrug.

"Don't know," he responded, though he had deceit writ large in his eyes. He had the good sense to not take offense, but I observed a couple of beads of sweat well up on his brow.

"I hope she didn't get hit," I ventured. "If someone was to hit a woman, I'd find it personally offensive. My pa taught me from the Bible—Ephesians I think it was—how important it was for a husband and wife to love and respect each other. I expect if I found that a person had hit their wife, I'd be sore tempted to lay on a beating they wouldn't soon forget." I paused for effect. "But, I guess no one struck Sarah." My eyes penetrated Isaac's like hot irons.

Guilt and shame were writ large across his face. "I...I was angry."

"Won't happen again?" I pressed him. Anger expressed in violence by husband or wife simply was unacceptable. If Isaac had problems dealing with anger, I'd be right pleased to dissuade him of them.

Isaac shook his head. "I...I'm sorry," he said with all due contriteness.

I reckoned that my calling him out was punishment enough for now. I'd likely thrown a bit of fear into him as to the consequences were he to dare strike Sarah again. "You need help with this fence?" I asked.

He shook my hand. "Bless you, Jack."

NINE
AUSTIN BECKONS

AS I CROSSED from the cabin to the barn a couple of days after Christmas, Texas Ranger Captain Nathan Benton and what remained of his company limped into Rising Cross looking for Hardy. They'd found his dead horse that morning and were able to follow his trail in the melting snow. Dragging a saddle will tend to leave a sign.

"Captain...er..." I almost blurted out a Merry Christmas, and it was painfully obvious that Benton was not in a celebratory mood.

He nodded and tipped a finger to his hat. "Mr. O'Toole, yuh seen one of my Rangers come through here?"

As I was about to respond, Hardy emerged from the bunkhouse with his arm still in a sling. Upon spotting the captain, he strode on over. "Captain, thank God y'all made it out."

It was the first hint I heard of the encounter the Texas Rangers had with the Comanche. Hardy had been close-mouthed about it.

Benton slid from his saddle. "You alright, Hardy?"

"Took a round in my shoulder, Captain. Then my hoss tripped an' busted his leg."

Benton looked at me. There was no love in his heart toward me—me being an Indian lover and all. "Thanks fer takin' care of Hardy here," he said grudgingly.

"Our pleasure, Captain," I said as I scanned the company. "Any of your men need caring for?"

The captain sighed resignedly. "I'd be much obliged, Mr. O'Toole." With that, he dropped to his knees.

It was then that I noticed the dark blood stain spread across his thigh. The broken shaft of an arrow was just visible.

"Shorty...Will!" I hollered. They came running and went to work helping a couple of wounded Rangers. Isaac soon left his cabin and came up to help along with Blue Flower, Sarah, and Kate. We quickly turned the bunkhouse into a field hospital.

I helped Benton to his feet and half-dragged him to the bunkhouse.

"Gotta git to Austin," he mumbled as we entered the bunkhouse. He collapsed on a bed.

Bandages, poultices, and plenty of hot water were the order of the day as we tended to a half-dozen wounded men. Those not wounded were simply cold and were soon helping treat their comrades.

Hot soup and a toasty warm bunkhouse served to rally the company. Even Benton's spirits were lifted.

"What happened, Captain?"

He was propped up with a pillow and glanced at his bandaged leg. "Plain stupid. We was jus' plain stupid. Missed the sign. Rode smack into an ambush. Them savages was on us like paint on a fence. Arrows, bullets...living hell." He shifted his leg and grimaced. "Praise them Colts," he said with true thanks at having the Colt revolvers that were handy in close-quarter fighting.

"You got away?" I said the obvious.

"Don't know how. We took some lead, but gave out more." He scratched his chin. "Jus' when things were lookin' awful hopeless, they quit." Benton shook his head with amazement. "They done broke off the attack. Dang, but they didn't lose but two of them gutless savages." He looked up questioningly at me.

I was at a loss for what might have spooked the Comanche.

Blue Flower had overheard Benton's story. She caught my eyes and smiled as though she knew. She mouthed the word *isa*.

I shook my head. It couldn't possibly have been wolves. I turned back to Benton. "They have a leader?"

"Everything happened fast," he responded. "I think there was one older savage with black warpaint an' a buffler horn headdress. Not big, but meaner than a rattler's fangs."

It sounded very much like Old Owl, the erstwhile shaman that Spirit Talker had chased from the Penateka Comanche village. Maybe a wolf did appear and spooked Old Owl. It would have meant bad medicine for the war party. It began to make sense. However, I couldn't begin to explain it to Benton, as he surely had no interest in the Indian spirit world. "No figuring the Comanche, Captain."

"Gotta git to Austin," he mumbled groggily and lay back. He was asleep in mere seconds.

———

CAPTAIN BENTON AND HIS COMPANY, including Hardy, departed for Austin after resting up at Rising Cross for another couple of days. It had made for an unexpectedly busy holiday season, though it felt gratifying to have been able to offer relief to the battered Texas Ranger company. We were sort of sorry to see them go.

January was about as cold as any we'd experienced during our brief time in Texas. Austin was roughly a four-day ride, if I pushed Big Red hard. With Blue Flower along, it would surely take a tad longer. I tried dissuading, but to no avail. She was determined to see the capital and talk to the Texas White Father herself.

I'd spent the morning doing chores while dodging and ducking hailstones, chunks of ice bigger than .50 caliber slugs that fell from a thick, foreboding sky. The livestock were rattled, especially the horses with their more sensitive hides. Most sought cover wherever it might be found. I kicked the icy nuggets from the gallery as I wrapped my gloved hand on the latch to our front door. I swung it open to find Blue Flower smiling and shoving a hot cup of coffee at me. I gave her a questioning look, and then one of those moments of awakening hit me. Her smile wasn't just any smile. I was becoming wise beyond my years. "You missed your bleeding?" I said less as a question and more as a fact.

She nearly made me spill the coffee as she gripped me in a tight hug. "Yes!" she said with a laugh. "Yes!"

This was happening right quickly. Our twins were but six months old. "You're certain?"

She nodded vigorously.

My mind shifted to my trip to Austin. There was no way I reckoned to take a pregnant wife with two babies through decidedly hostile territory just so she could see the Texas capital. It was sufficient that I was wary of the threats that lurked around Rising Cross, but at least we had our fortress-like cabin and enough defenders to hold off any attack. Besides, I felt as though Spirit Talker's Comanche were keeping a protective watch over our spread.

Blue Flower must have known what I was thinking. Insight to my very innermost soul had been a gift of hers from the time we first met. "No Austin for Blue Flower," she smiled.

I held her at arms-length to more fully take in her beauty. And beautiful she was. Her long dark hair trailed nearly to her waist, and it framed eyes that were brown with a hint of gold. Blue Flower had a straight but delicate nose set atop the fullest lips I'd ever beheld on any woman...not that I'd especially noticed other women. Her frame was what Sarah Fisher and Stella Klappenbach had referred to as petite, but she wasn't soft. No. Hers was the body of a woman of the frontier, more sinewy muscled than plush. And her spirit? Blue Flower was a woman with grit who could shoot a rogue Comanche shaman to death to save her man, yet be the most affectionate and loving woman a man could ever desire. I was blessed, and I reckon the feeling must have been mutual. "*Kamakuna*," I said. Indeed, she was my love.

"When Jack go?" she pressed.

I glanced out the window. The hail storm had passed, and the landscape glittered in the morning son as though God had sprinkled diamonds over everything. Funny thing, it would all melt by dinner. "Maybe a week," I said more as a suggestion than a statement. The Texas winters were fickle. A week from now could bring shirt-sleeve weather. In late January!

She hugged me again and padded barefoot over to the

stove to serve up some breakfast. Gosh, but even her feet were pretty.

———

THE DAY of my departure finally arrived. My hope for mid-winter shirt-sleeve weather was dashed as dark skies portended rain or possibly icy snow. Some folks called it sleet. Big Red must have sensed that we were headed somewhere important, because he was as excited as I'd seen him in quite some time. I wasn't thrilled at having a packhorse along, but Shorty convinced me that it made sense. If I ran into any threat, it wouldn't do to have Big Red carrying any extra weight. I'd need to be mobile and try to make myself an uninviting prey for hostiles.

Blue Flower had packed plenty of pemmican and jerky, but made sure that my first day on the trail would feature tasty home-cooked goodies. Who was I to argue?

I must confess to still being caught up in Blue Flower's pregnancy revelation. Here I was about to turn eighteen, and I'd be father to a third child. It made it all the more imperative that I ensure a secure and promising future. I was driven to build Rising Cross and raise more livestock to drive north to George Freeman's ranch in Wyoming. I felt that made it critically important to learn first-hand of the temperament in the Texas capital toward the Indians. I considered riding down to Bandera and bending August Klappenbach's ear, but that would have been secondhand and I'd had enough of rumors.

I had visited with Sam Collins. In fact, Shorty, Will, Isaac, and I had spent a couple of days helping him with final repairs to the Circle C after the Comanche attack. Collins gave me a contact in Austin and schooled me on Governor Hardin Runnels inclinations. He armed me with more information about the now legendary Texas Ranger Rip Ford. I learned that the US Army wasn't up to the task of stopping the Indian threat partly due to ineffective Indian fighting tactics. They apparently had a habit of pitting infantrymen mounted on sorry excuses for horses against hostiles that fought on fast ponies. In fact, the Comanche had gained a reputation as the best horsemen on the plains. Collins heard that Runnels feared a major invasion. From what I had learned from Spirit Talker and Buffalo Hump, the governor had good reason to harbor such fears. He surely recalled Buffalo Hump's successful raid through central Texas back in 1840. Collins also confirmed Klappenbach's suspicion that Runnels was intent on the Texas Rangers handling the Indian problem.

As if the Indian problem wasn't enough, Collins confided that rumors were flying about concerning slavery. Plantation owners in eastern Texas were fearful of some sort of slave uprising. Collins had heard an estimate that there were better than 175,000 slaves in Texas, and that represented nearly a third of the state population. His descriptions of the slaves got me thinking about my dear friend George Freeman, who had escaped slavery and now owned a thriving ranch on the North Platte River in Wyoming.

Collins's estimate of the slave population naturally made me curious as to the Indian population. Since they were not included in the census and White man's diseases—especially cholera—had decimated many of the tribes over the years, there really was no good estimate of their numbers. Their ability to muster dozens of warriors and form confederations of tribes was admirable, but by my reckoning was that they would eventually succumb to the superior firepower of Texas

Rangers and soldiers, if not more White man's diseases and the near constant onslaught of settlers.

Buck stood holding Big Red's reins as I bid farewell to Blue Flower and our babies. I chuckled just a tad as my little brother blushed upon seeing me kiss my wife's lips and then George's and Isa's foreheads. Kate had already given me a hug, and she stood arm-in-arm with Will. The two figured to marry come spring. Shorty had done his usual fine job with the packhorse and stood by patiently, his mind on the plentiful ranch chores demanding his attention.

I finally mounted up, exchanged loving farewell eyes with Blue Flower, and gently pressed my heels into Big Red's flanks. I didn't look back as we ambled eastward toward Austin. I patted the big stallion's neck as he snorted and nickered his opinion as to the adventure that lay ahead.

TEN
POLITICAL GAMES

MY JOURNEY WAS BLESSEDLY UNEVENTFUL. I even took the risk of building cooking fires, likely a perverse tease to any hostiles lurking about. The fires were as much for warmth as cooking the meager feats of prairie dog and rabbit. I must say that the little critters tested my somewhat rusty skill with my bow and arrows. Spirit Talker would have been proud of me.

I thought about my Comanche brother as Big Red and I plodded along. Spirit Talker's dilemma was hardly different from my own. We desired peace, desired that the White man and Indians lived in harmony together. Could the cultures ever be blended together? The Comanche certainly lacked the resources to withstand the invasion of settlers. They could stick to their ways and be conquered or adapt. Treaties had been made but broken by both sides. It seemed that oaths and promises were made simply to be broken. Most of the Whites who called themselves Christian seemed as hypocritical as the Redmen who made promises in the names of their spirits. How might it all turn out? I decided that I would seek out Spirit Talker as soon as I could after my return from Austin. We needed to strengthen each other's faith in God and in our fellow *numunuu*, our people.

I can't say as to whether Austin lived up to my expectations. It was a sprawling town. Upon arriving, I sought out a blacksmith named Will McGregor, whose name Collins had given me.

It was near dusk when I finally reined up in front of McGregor's shop. I found it curious that its roof extended from a small clapboard church beside it. The smithy was hard at work shoeing a right handsome stallion. I couldn't contain a smile when I saw the sign above the entrance to his shop. It announced:

> ### WILLIAM MCGREGOR
> #### *Smithy and Preacher*
> #### *Sins & Iron Hammered Out Here*

SO, the smithy was also a pastor. Collins hadn't shared that news. I slid from my saddle and shook out a bit of trail dust.

"Kin I help yuh, lad?" asked McGregor with what I'd learn was a Scottish brogue. He paused and looked up from holding the cayuse's hind leg. A couple of quick blows with his hammer affixed a well-formed horseshow to the beast's hoof. He set down the leg and stood upright. He quickly scanned me from head to toe, likely curious as to my buckskins and heavy array of weapons.

Now, I stand about four inches over six feet tall, and I found myself eyeball to eyeball with McGregor. "Name's Jack O'Toole, Mr. McGregor. Sam Collins suggested I look you up."

"Sam?" He laughed. "How's he doing? Got his spread fixed?"

I relaxed a tad. McGregor sported a welcoming grin peeking from a bushy red beard. His was a friendly face by any measure. He was sweating despite the late-January chill. "Sam sends his greetings. Just about finished repairing his cabin."

"Well, come set a spell, Jack. Yuh kin call me Will." He patted the stallion's rump as it fidgeted. "Easy, big fella," he said reassuringly to the cayuse. "This one doesn't like company," he added with a nod to Big Red.

I slipped from Big Red's saddle.

"There be a stall 'round back, Jack. When yer done, come to the back door of God's house here. I expect yer hungry."

I quickly discovered that Will was as friendly and generous as Collins had led me to believe. I skirted wide of the stallion in McGregor's shop and led Big Red and the pack horse to the small horse shed the smithy had pointed out. Once finished, I gave Big Red a loving pat and headed to the back of the church building. The sun had set, so I sort of groped my way along with only a few stars to light the way. I reached the door and was about to knock when it swung open and a right beautiful red-haired woman greeted me with an ear-to-ear smile.

"You must be Jack O'Toole," she cooed with barely a hint of a Scottish accent. "I'm Colleen, Will's wife."

"My pleasure, Mrs. McGregor."

"Oh, do call me Colleen and come in. I've fixed some victuals for you."

I spotted Will behind her as he finished washing off the sweat and grime from shoeing the stallion. An iron stove was centered in the kitchen where it gave off plenty of heat against winter's chill. Colleen motioned me to the table where a steaming plate filled with what turned out to be a venison stew sat awaiting my tastebuds.

"What brung yuh all the way to Austin, Jack?" asked McGregor as he sat opposite me and winked lovingly at his wife.

I paused before stuffing a heaping spoonful of stew into my mouth. I chewed a bit, swallowed hard, and took a swig of coffee. "I aim to learn first-hand what intentions are regarding the Comanche."

McGregor nodded. "Why?"

I explained how I had friends among the Comanche, that my wife was a Comanche princess, and I had two sons by her and another on the way. "I want to keep my family safe and bring peace if I can." As I said the words, they sounded simple enough.

McGregor shook his head. "Yer headin' upstream with no paddle, Jack," he lamented. "That horse done left the barn."

I cocked my head inquisitively. His homey sayings were not encouraging. I was about to ask him to explain when there came a knock at the door.

McGregor's expression had turned grave. The light in his eyes dimmed. "Turns out yer 'bout to learn what's gonna happen, Jack. First-hand."

First-hand was what I was looking for, though I hadn't expected it first off.

Colleen scurried to the door and welcomed a gruff-looking man with a well-cropped red beard but no mustache. He wore a black wide-brimmed hat and long black duster. There was little doubt that he had figured to stealthily blend into the darkness of the night. She motioned him in.

"Oh, y'all got company," the man said with obvious concern.

"It be alright, guvner, this be a friend," assured McGregor with a welcoming motion of his hand.

The man strode cautiously to the table and removed his hat.

"Jack O'Toole, this be the guvner of the great state of Texas, mistuh Hardin Runnels."

I stood and shook Runnels's hand. His handshake was firm, so I gathered he must be a solid citizen. Plus, he was meeting a pastor in a church.

Runnels pulled up a chair as Colleen set a cup of coffee before him. He gave her a forced smile that belied the weighty matters that were apparently on his mind. He glanced at me with just a hint of suspicion.

McGregor tried to ease the governor's concern. "Jack here owns a spread four days ride west of here, guvner." Runnels would know that put me in the treacherous Comancheria. "He's been dealin' with Comanche. Lost his folks couple years back."

Runnels was nodding and appeared a bit more at ease.

"Jack's wife is Comanche, and they have young'uns."

That brought Runnels bolt upright in his chair.

"Which side you on, son?" he asked.

"Side?" I responded. "Why, peace, of course."

"You haven't told him anything?" he queried as he turned to MacGregor.

McGregor shook his head.

Runnels glanced at me. I sensed a bit of compassion in his demeanor and the feeling that he was having to do something he didn't want to do. "Life can be hard. There's so much evil around us." He paused with a nod to McGregor and his wife, then stared resignedly at me. "Defeating evil often requires violence, Jack. It's not a pleasant solution, and I don't take it lightly. People will be hurt...some killed." He sighed deeply. "I'm about to dispatch instructions to John Ford appointing him senior captain of the Texas Rangers with instructions to lead an expedition into the Comancheria and ensure peace."

I wondered why life had to be so hard. It was clear that Runnels didn't relish what he had to do and had come to seek counsel from McGregor. My presence had brought home to the governor just how distasteful his duty was. He was responsible to the citizens of Texas.

Runnels turned to McGregor and then glanced back at me. "Hope you're a man of faith, Jack, because I need plenty of prayer. There are bigger issues than Indians on the horizon, and I fear for us all."

I gave him a curious look.

"Folks across the country getting in a fighting way about slavery. There's fear of an uprising in Texas. I've had to calm my own Blacks back home."

Turned out that the menace on the Comancheria was but one of the problems Runnels faced. I'd later learn that the Blacks he referred to were the nearly three-dozen slaves he owned. It caused me to think a moment about my dear friend and escaped slave, George Freeman. He'd been one of the lucky ones. "You figure to be killing Indians?" I asked.

"They been killing folks. I expect some of them are going to die in turn," lamented Runnels. "Hear tell that the Comanche have joined for a big fight. We need to stop that."

I looked from Runnels to McGregor. The big smithy was shaking his head with obvious sadness. "The Comanche want peace," I blurted. In retrospect, it sounded dreadfully naïve.

McGregor finally spoke up. "The Lord counsels to

forgive. Forgiveness relieves great burdens from folks' souls."

His words caught me, as I had personal experience at forgiving the very Comanche that had massacred part of my family. I nearly forgot about the bowl of stew before me.

"Yet," McGregor paused, "Yet, sins must be punished. Forgiveness must ever linger in the backdrop of punishment for sin. Just as Indians have burned and raped and stolen and murdered, so the Whites have killed and broken promises. Woe to all that have sinned."

It was beginning to sound like McGregor was in every bit as much dilemma as me.

Colleen stepped in and refilled our coffee cups.

I sipped coffee and absentmindedly took another bite of stew, though I'd lost my appetite. "Why does life have to be so hard, pastor?" I finally exclaimed.

Runnels's face seemed to mirror my question. "What of it, Will?"

"It'd be easy to just advise everyone to find peace through prayer, but we know that's not most folks' nature. Tis not enough to pray, we must act. But when all attempts at peaceful solutions have been exhausted, it's not enough to simply pray, no matter how deeply felt. There comes a time to act. Conquering evil demands action. In the midst of overcoming the challenges posed by evil deeds, we develop our mettle to face life. In the fight, we find courage, trustworthiness, resilience, fortitude, steadfastness, resourcefulness, and heroism." McGregor had spouted a mouthful. His words were heavy. He was a preacher, after all. He looked from me to Runnels. "Tain't easy, lads."

Runnels was a man of the land. His plantation was up near the Red River in Bowie County. He was a man of wealth that had been derived from crops tended by slaves. With wealth came power, political power. Nevertheless, it didn't seem to me as though he's ever faced a man in battle. I wondered how he must feel sending men like Ford and the Texas Rangers to face possible death. I gave him a questioning look. "I've fought hand-to-hand against Mexican bandits, Indians, and desperate men, Governor. Indeed, it ain't easy." Here I was, a nearly seventeen-year-old, talking to a leader of our state about the realities of conflict he was sending men to face. I was likely sharing a perspective that even Will McGregor couldn't match. "How do you send men to fight, Governor?" I asked, perhaps a tad impertinently.

Runnels slumped just a bit in his chair. "It's a heavy load, Mr. O'Toole."

I felt relieved that Runnels had not taken offense and appreciated the respect he was showing me, but he hadn't answered my question. Perhaps there was no answer. Sexual immorality, impurity, lust, and greed seemed to thrive among even Christian folks. Add those to those evil sins like anger, vengeance, malice, wrath, and profanity, and it seemed no end to man's troubles. Violence seemed a natural fallout of evil, and yet violence was often necessary to bring peace. I felt guilty of some of those sins myself. Certainly, I had experienced anger and sought vengeance on those whom I considered my enemies. I shook my head. "Answers are tough," I lamented.

Runnels brought himself upright and squared his shoulders. "I must leave, but I'm glad you were here, Mr. O'Toole. I can't say that you've lightened the yoke I bear, but I must strive to conquer the evils of which we speak. I'll pray that Captain Ford is able to bring peace at whatever price must be paid."

There was a pause. I glanced at McGregor, who seemed about to pray, but before he could, Colleen slipped slices of cherry pie in front of us all. Prayer or pie? With apologies to our creator, we ate the pie first. No matter, Runnels would be sending Texas Rangers to bring peace to Texas, even as that peace would likely require killing Indians. What was I to do?

As we ate cherry pie, Runnels shared a bit more about Ford. He'd settled in Texas back in 1836 and practiced medicine and studied law. Turned out that his nickname was Rip. He'd garnered it during the Mexican American War as an adjunct to General Zachary Taylor. Ford wrote letters to the families of soldiers killed in battle and signed them *rest in peace*. Thus, he'd earned the initials RIP Rip Ford signed on as a Texas Ranger captain in 1849 and fought Mexican outlaws, purportedly Juan *Cheno* Cortina's bandits, on the Rio Grande for a couple of years. He soundly defeated Cortina's rabble. He left the Texas Rangers to practice law, get into a bit of politics, and publish a newspaper. He was apparently a soft-spoken man of faith who studied the Bible and taught Sunday school. By contrast, he had battle wounds—a lost finger and a wound from a poisoned arrow that troubled him occasionally. By any measure, Rip Ford was a leader of men.

I hoped that the insights into Ford's background might be handy as I pursued my hugely challenging mission to avoid or at least minimize a violent solution to the threats that swept the Texas frontier. Plus, I'd been introduced to the looming perils of slavery. In the space of but a short time with McGregor and Runnels, I'd filled my addled brain with a crazy quilt of challenges.

McGregor finally got to deliver his prayer, though it

didn't seem to bring any peace to Runnels. The man did carry a mighty heavy load or yoke as he described it.

"I hope we meet again, Mr. O'Toole," said Runnels in parting. "I pray your family is safe."

"And yours, Governor. It was a pleasure to meet you, sir." I was feeling about as grown-up as ever. I'd negotiated a discussion involving deep questions with a pastor and a politician and come out unscathed.

As Runnels departed, I caught McGregor yawning. "The guvner, he drop by now an' agin, Jack. Less 'bout me advice than me jus' listenin'." He gave a nod to a door that led to the chapel. "Yuh kin park yer bones in the chapel fer the night," he said as he took Colleen's hand and led her away to a room adjoining the kitchen. She gave a smile and a little wave over her shoulder, as she followed her husband.

I sat collecting my thoughts for a moment before grabbing my tack and saddle bag. I thought a moment about carrying my weapons into the chapel, but shrugged and carried them anyway. Guess it was a form of putting on the armor of God.

I AWAKENED to a veritable cacophony of kitchen sounds as pots and pans were being rattled about. Colleen was of a mind to fix a fine breakfast for her guest, though I figured that her husband ate right well. I threw on my buckskins and found my way through snow flurries to the privy out back. Splashing my face with cold water from the basin behind the chapel door had the effect of rousing me from any lingering sleepiness. I looked over at the blacksmith shop and saw that McGregor was already stoking his furnace for the day's work.

Colleen poked her head out the door. "Come eat afore it all gets cold," she invited.

I needed no persuading as I took a seat and took in the aroma and warm goodness of eggs, bacon, and gravy. I had just taken a sip of coffee when McGregor entered and sat opposite me.

"A bonnie good morning to yuh, Jack. Sleep well?"

I nodded as I swallowed the coffee.

Colleen wiped her hands and sat beside her husband.

"Let us pray," offered McGregor, and he proceeded to bless our meal.

"Amen," I said. "And thanks kindly."

"The guvner gave us a lot to think on," said McGregor with a wry smile. Seemed he wasn't in full agreement with Runnels, but reckoned to at least offer the man some solace in talking out his dilemmas.

After meeting Runnels, I right quickly figured I wasn't cut out for politics. "Seems war with the Indians is inevitable," I responded.

McGregor nodded. "Seems you've had some Bible teachin', Jack."

"My pa was strong on teaching us from the Good Book. Guess some of it stuck." I proceeded to share a brief version of my story, including how the Testament had stopped a bullet and saved my life and how I'd brought Spirit Talker to faith in God. I even told him about Zeb and how the Comanche called me Walks With Wolves.

McGregor swallowed a mouthful, then got up and walked over to a cabinet. He returned with a Bible in hand, sat, and pushed it to me. "Sounds like yuh might find this handy, Jack. Try to keep bullets from it," he added with a laugh.

"Thanks, Will. Thanks very much," I said with as

much gratitude as I could muster. I paused for another bite of eggs and thoughtfully sipped more coffee. I cleared my throat. "Er...what are my chances of meeting this Rip Ford fellow?"

A broad grin creased McGregor's face. "Stay fer Sunday service," he advised. "Ford's a believin' man."

I quickly calculated that this day was Friday. "Can I impose on y'all another couple of days? Happy to help with your smithing."

Colleen laughed. "I can put you to work." She laughed harder. "Woodbin needs filling, privy needs cleaning, and I saw a rattlesnake back of the chapel this morning."

I got the message. "It would be my pleasure to help," I assured my hosts. Of course, it got me thinking about how I'd headed out to the privy, oblivious to any snake. Then, it hit me. This was winter. The snakes were hibernating, the privy was clean, and the woodbin was full. Colleen had been funning with me.

McGregor joined in with a hearty laugh followed by a belch that might have brought down the building. "Aye, yer a good sport, Jack!" he exclaimed. He arose and grabbed his smithy apron. "Why don't yuh walk around Austin?"

McGregor's suggestion made sense. It was an opportunity to get a sense of folks' feelings. Out on the Comancheria, we were isolated from most of the goings on of the world. Even nearby Bandera offered second-hand news at best.

I decided to dress less as a cowboy on the Comancheria and more like a local citizen, though I figured even that would be a stretch for me. I pulled out my boots and a cotton shirt. I decided to leave my bow and arrows along with my rifle at the church but strapped on my gun. It had gotten such that I felt naked without it. I did go out to curry Big Red and let him enjoy an apple Colleen had given me. I reckoned that where I was headed, I wouldn't be riding, so I patted my big four-legged friend and headed out. Colleen had given me some suggested places to visit, so my day figured to be a full one. Had I hung around the smithy shop and church, I'd have likely felt at loose ends. I had become so used to doing the endless chores around Rising Cross Ranch.

IT WAS midday as I walked down what I figured was the main street. The day had started out with a slight chill in the air. By now, hunger was gnawing at my belly. The weather had taken a sudden turn with a cold breeze and darkening clouds. I was glad that I'd taken McGregor's advice and grabbed my coat before heading out. I found myself standing in the middle of the street, dodging horses and wagons with a saloon on one side and a hotel restaurant on the opposite side. Folks in the saloon would likely offer up the sort of information I was looking for, but it could wait. My belly took a higher priority.

I dodged another cayuse, strode up the hotel steps, and entered the dining room. The place was finely appointed with velvet-cushioned chairs around mahogany tables with fancy place settings. The walls were paneled with more mahogany and featured framed paintings of scenes from the frontier. I felt totally out of my element until a young woman approached me.

She looked me up and down, pausing her eyes at the mountain lion claw necklace with its cross. "We have a table for you right over here, sir," she said as though I were some visiting royalty. She even pulled out a chair for me. She was a right-pretty woman with golden curls done up atop her pretty face with its welcoming smile. "We'll help you shortly," she said as she poured a cup of coffee for me. "My name is Annie," she added with a smile I couldn't quite figure out. It seemed a tad more than friendly.

Well, I must say that my opinion of Austin was getting off to a good start. I looked around at the restaurant patrons. This wasn't nearly like Bandera with cowboys sporting shirts coated with dust and dung-covered boots. Nope. The folks here were right well dressed. Suits, ties, and fine boots were topped off with what I'd learn were bowler hats. I stood out like a skunk at a fancy party.

I wound up enjoying a fine meal, though it lacked the woodsmoke flavor I was used to. As I finished, the young woman who had greeted me stopped by the table. "Was your meal satisfactory, sir?" she asked. "Are you staying with us?"

I wasn't sure that I liked her fetching smile, as it had a certain quality that I found arousing. I figured to put the kibosh on any less-than-Godly thoughts she might be having. "It was mighty fine, ma'am. Nearly as good as my wife's cooking."

"Oh…er…thank you, sir."

I guess I flustered her just a tad. I smiled, arose, and paid for the meal. I was grateful that I had successfully resisted my first big-city temptation. With that, I headed across the street to the saloon. I remained intent on learning what I could about how folks felt about the Indian threat.

THE FIRST THINGS that struck me about the saloon were the boot scraper and the sign at the front door. The boot scraper made sense, as the previous night's sleety snow had turned the streets a tad muddy. The sign? Well, it directed folks who entered the saloon to park their weapons with the bartender. I expect it was in recognition of how minds could get a tad addled after a few drinks, and gunplay wasn't especially welcome. I scraped a bit of mud from my boots and stepped inside. Naturally, I did as the sign directed. I slipped the Colt from my holster and handed it to a smiling bartender who gave me a quick once-over, shrugged, and stuck my revolver in a cubbyhole behind the bar.

"What'll you have, friend?" asked the bartender.

I glanced around the dimly lit room and spotted an unoccupied table along the far wall. I was tempted to ask for water, but figured that might not be sociable in a saloon. "A beer," I responded.

He plunked a foam-laden mug before me.

I left a couple of coins on the bar and strode over to the table.

"Whoa, pardner! Not that table!" the bartender shouted out. "That's Land Jeffries's table."

I turned and looked incredulously at the bartender. "I don't see anyone?" I asked quite naturally.

"Mr. Jeffries owns this place, and he expects his table to be clean and unoccupied whenever he shows up," I was advised.

There seemed no point in putting up any argument. I nodded and made my way to another table. All I wanted to do was listen to what folks might be saying about Indians or Blacks.

A trio of cowboys who had smiled and nodded at me upon my entry sat close by and were chattering about sending Mexicans back to Mexico. Seemed there was no love lost for the perceived enemies of the Texas War for Independence.

The table beside the trio hosted four men who looked as tough as stewed skunk. They were a tad older and trail-hardened. They were upset about a Comanche raid on a ranch a day's ride north of Austin. I pretended to take a sip of beer. Doggone, but it was a foul-tasting brew. I guess I had become a tad careless as I tilted my head toward the men, and one of them noticed.

"Kin I help yuh?" leered one of the men as he laid squinty eyes on me and finished off the last drops from a whiskey bottle.

I gulped. I was clearly physically bigger than any of them, but would as soon not cause any sort of ruckus. "Sorry, Just curious about Indians."

"Yuh ain't no Injun lover?" the man challenged. He appeared to have me tagged as too young to have dealt with Indians.

I gave him as tough a stare as I dared. "Killed as few," I responded.

"Squaws?" he chided.

I shook my head. "Comanche, Kiowa, Lakota…"

"Yer a regler Injun killer," laughed a companion.

By now, the chatter had grabbed the attention of the trio that had been talking about Mexicans. One turned to me. "You be mighty curious, son."

I leaned back a little to appear more relaxed and confident in my skin. "Wondered what Texas was going to do about the Indians?"

The squinty-eyed man smiled. "Gonna kill 'em all.

Hear tell Rip Ford's gonna lead them Texas Rangers." He gave me a tougher look. "You agin' Injuns?"

"There are good and bad. Bad ones should be punished. I know some good ones."

"Tough to sort 'em out, son. Many will die."

I nodded.

The bartender walked over. His expression said he wasn't pleased with the conversation and where it might lead. He looked at me dead on. "You might leave while the getting's good, cowboy."

I curled my six-foot-plus frame from my chair. If the men hadn't noticed me before, they did now. A fight would have been a messy affair. I left the beer behind, took my gun back from the bartender, and headed back to McGregor's place. I'd learned enough of the sentiments in Austin, as the handful of men I had met in the saloon likely had plenty that thought as most folks of their stripe did.

————

I SAT on the back bench in McGregor's little church. Given that there were eight rows of benches, I was seated pretty close to the action. I wore my best buckskin shirt, the one decorated with beadwork and fringe. Colleen led a trio of ladies who sang a hymn, the words of which I was unable to recall, so I sat back and listened. She nodded toward a gentleman seated on the bench closest to the small pulpit over which Will McGregor towered. It was none other than John Salmon *Rip* Ford. He was well-dressed and clean-shaven, likely as befitting a newspaperman. He sure didn't look as though he was a Texas Ranger officer about to raise a few companies of Texas Rangers and begin hunting down Comanche.

McGregor preached for about an hour, and I had to admit he was a charming, if not occasionally overly dramatic, evangelizer of God's word. As he ended his sermon with a rousing amen, I stood to try to intercept Ford before he departed. I needn't have. Colleen had grabbed his elbow and motioned toward me.

I nervously made my way over to Ford. I'd faced Indians, ferocious wild animals, bandits, and desperadoes, but nothing had prepared me for being in the presence of the legendary Texas Ranger. I was physically bigger, but that hardly mattered in the presence of a man of Ford's reputation.

"You must be Jack O'Toole," queried Ford, giving me a quick once-over and extending his hand.

"Er...yes. Pleased to meet you, sir," I said as I shook hands with him. I was impressed with his handshake. My pa had taught me that you could learn a lot about a man by their handshake. A firm but not crushing handshake was a sign of a person with confidence. Pa laughed when he described folks with weak, fingers-only handshakes as shaking hands with a fish. Ford was no fish.

"Hear tell you have a spread a few days west of here and are familiar with the ways of the Redman."

I was taken aback by what he already seemed to know about me. "Yes, Captain Ford. My wife is a Penateka Comanche, and a good friend of mine is of that tribe."

Ford nodded. "Ah, the Honey Eaters."

I was impressed that he knew that Penateka translated to honey eater. Then again, I shouldn't have been surprised.

"Is she of Buffalo Hump's band?"

"His daughter, sir."

That news seemed to impress Ford as his eyes

widened slightly. He smiled. "I'll bet your friend is Buffalo Hump's son," he guessed.

I nodded. "Long story, sir." I could see that Ford's brain was on high alert. He clearly was conjuring up an idea or two.

About this time, McGregor came up behind me. He'd finished saying goodbye to his parishioners. "Good tuh see yuh, Captain. I see you've met Jack," he said while simultaneously placing a huge paw on my shoulder. He turned to Ford. "Got time to set a spell?"

"Thanks, pastor, but I must mosey along. I've got Texas Rangers to recruit," he said with a smile that said he relished the task. He seemed to want to ask me something but hadn't yet figured out how to phrase it.

Ford seemed as easy-going as I'd been told. There was nothing the least bit threatening about this man who'd cleaned up the Rio Grande and was admired across Texas and beyond. I reached out my hand. "Pleased to make your acquaintance, sir."

Ford turned and was about to bid farewell when he paused in mid-stride. His eyes locked onto mine like magnets. "Any chance you'd be interested in the Texas Rangers, Mr. O'Toole. I've begun talking with Tonkawas, Caddos, and Shawnees as scouts, but I sure could use a White man who knew the Indians' ways." His expression turned serious. "You have any interest in scouting for me?"

I glanced at McGregor and then at Colleen. I wasn't exactly in a comfortable spot. "To be straight, sir, if it was up to me, there would be no fighting between the Redman and Whites. Can't say as I'd want either side killed." I caught Ford's eyes straight on. "Thanks for the offer, but no thank you, sir."

Ford smiled. "I appreciate honesty, Mr. O'Toole. My

offer stands." He shook hands with all of us and slipped from the church.

"Yuh jus' made a strong friend, Jack," advised McGregor. "Aye, a strong friend he be," he reinforced with a laugh.

I smiled somewhat in wonderment. I'd just turned down an offer from a famous Texas Ranger, and I apparently was now his friend? I shifted my feet a tad uncomfortably. "I expect I ought to be headed home tomorrow, Will. I rightly appreciate your hospitality."

Next morning, I found myself headed westward on Big Red with a few surprise purchases added to the load on my packhorse. Blue Flower would be mighty pleased. And I had a surprise for Buck and a wedding gift for Kate and Will.

ELEVEN

HOLDING THE HOME FORT

AS I RODE, I found myself wondering what had become of Captain Benton. I thought there might be a chance of encountering him in Austin, but I suspected he was off helping Ford recruit men for the campaign to bring the Comanche under control. My flirtations with the Texas Rangers had made a strong impression on me. They were tough, honest, and courageous, yet they could be downright hard to figure out. By my reckoning, they were tougher fighters man for man than the US Army and didn't answer to so vast a bureaucracy as Federal soldiers. The Texas Rangers answered to the Texas governor. Perhaps that was where my concerns grew from.

I was arriving at the opinion that politicians were driven by money and the power that it could bring. Maintaining that power demanded more money. Since the government was not a business that turned a profit like I was trying to do at Rising Cross Ranch, the government depended on taxes. The bigger enterprises logically paid a greater share of taxes and thus were blessed with greater influence by virtue of that contribution. I suspected there was other money involved that was what folks might call bribery, whereby monies flowed to politicians outside of legal means such that they might do the bidding of the person with the most money.

I thought of Governor Runnels running a plantation with thirty or so slaves. He was likely well off financially, but not nearly so much as the large plantations. The fertile farms of East Texas seemed to be from where the money and influence flowed. If those folks felt threatened, whether by Comanche attacks or a slave uprising, they would be intent on pressing their financial advantage to demand solutions. In this case, it meant raising enough Texas Rangers to put a stop to Comanche predations.

Of course, my thinking drifted to my Comanche brother, Spirit Talker. I prayed that no harm would come to him or his family from the soon-to-be all-too-real hostilities. I still searched for some way to avoid the impending violence.

———

I ENJOYED NEARLY four days of bone-chilling but uneventful travel with plenty of time to think about the present situation and what it portended for the future. I actually thought that—God willing—if I was successful with my livestock enterprise at Rising Cross Ranch, I might eventually have the resources to enjoy outsized influence in Austin. However, reality is a tough master. I wasn't even old enough to vote, much less influence anyone in the Texas capital. My influence resided in my faith and will to persevere.

It occurred to me that scouting with Ford's Texas Rangers could bring me close to the action and that I might even be able to influence tactics and strategies. That would entail getting close to Ford and earning his trust.

I was mulling these thoughts around in my brain when I found myself emerging from a motte of live oaks to see Rising Cross off in the distance. A half-dozen javelinas scattered up an arroyo and on into the grasses. Normally, I would have shot some of the nasty, stench-ridden critters. In the late afternoon light, I could see smoke spiraling from the main cabin's chimney. My stomach grumbled, so it had my undivided attention. However, as I drew closer, there was more, much more. I couldn't believe my eyes. Curious. A makeshift addition had sprouted from the side of the barn, and I could make out some activity near it. I pressed my heels into Big Red's sides, and he leaped forward at a near gallop. I was surprised that the big stallion had it in him after nearly four days of travel in mid-winter. Maybe the lure of the mares had caught his attention and helped him find the energy.

I reined in at the cabin to see none other than Spirit Talker standing with Shorty over near the makeshift lean-to alongside the barn. "Mukwooru!" I shouted.

Upon hearing the Comanche name of her brother, Blue Flower emerged from the cabin. I slipped from my saddle expecting to rush over to Spirit Talker but stopped in mid-stride upon seeing my beautiful wife. She threw herself into my arms before I could take even a single step toward her.

"Isa Pohya!" called Spirit Talker with a laugh at my being waylaid by Blue Flower. He knew that my priorities were in order. Calling me by my Comanche name for Walks With Wolves was simply his way of teasing.

Blue Flower released me and led me over to where Spirit Talker was standing with Shorty.

I grasped his hand, but he pulled me in for a brotherly hug. "What brings you here, my brother?" I asked.

Spirit Talker locked onto my eyes. "Heard call."

"Mukwooru wise. Hear Isa Pohya *sunipu*." I was not surprised that he had sensed the medicine of Walks With Wolves.

Blue Flower moved beside me and hooked her arm through mine. She looked up at me. "*Ana o'a hi'it*," she said, inviting us to eat. I suddenly realized that the sun was sinking fast on the western horizon. I'd arrived in time for dinner.

Spirit Talker followed us to the cabin. Upon entering, his eyes quickly took in his surroundings. He couldn't miss the shutters with the gunports. "Is like fort, Jack," he observed.

"Pray it never must be one," I responded.

We sat at the table and blessed the meal Blue Flower served us. Spirit Talker smiled and made funny noises at George and Isa who were strapped in their cradleboards propped against the chairs. I made a mental note to fashion some sort of seats that would accommodate their growing bodies.

I shared with Blue Flower and Spirit Talker all I had learned from my journey to Austin. My Comanche brother was especially interested in my meeting with Rip Ford. He was impressed with what he heard, but troubled by the man's apparent focus on using a veritable army of Texas Rangers to end the attacks on settlers.

"It's sad," I intoned. "Austin is filled with Whites that fear Indians, Blacks, and Mexicans."

"What do they fear?" asked Blue Flower.

"They are afraid to lose control. With loss of control,

they fear losing their lives." It was about as straightforward an answer as I could muster.

"Control?" echoed Spirit Talker. "God is in control," he said firmly as his teeth tore away a delicious chunk of meat from a beef rib.

I nodded my agreement. It was reassuring to hear Spirit Talker invoke our God after having spent several months among his people. Now, he was a shaman. I found it a tad humorous and perhaps ironic that he was in a position to gradually insert biblical beliefs among his Comanche *numunuu*. "Captain Ford invited me to scout for his Texas Rangers. I told him that I had a family to care for and a ranch to run." I saw a devious sort of look creep into Spirit Talker's eyes.

"Jack scout," he pondered aloud.

"No!" I said emphatically.

Blue Flower glanced from me to her brother and back to me. "Mukwooru does not know," she said with a glance down at her still-flat belly.

Spirit Talker caught her intimation. "Child?" he asked.

Blue Flower and I nodded in unison.

Obviously, this brought a changed perspective to the situation. Was I free to wander off to scout for the Texas Rangers? That was a heavy question. "You traveled alone to Rising Cross Ranch?" I asked by way of diverting the conversation away from Rip Ford.

Spirit Talker nodded. "Was easy." He was right, as bringing along a contingent of warriors could have brought unwanted attention. There was no telling what threats lurked among the hills and prairies of the Comancheria, that even went for the very Comanche warriors that contributed to making it so treacherous. But my Comanche brother was not to be so easily diverted from considering the threat to his people posed by the Texas Rangers. He was deep in thought. If his brain was a fire, I'd be smelling smoke. "Nokoni... Tenawa...Kotsoteka," he paused. He was about to say more when his eyes widened. He knocked his chair over as he dashed to a window and slammed its shutter closed. There was a crash and a thud as an arrow broke the glass and embedded in the wood.

It didn't take me but a split second to close another shutter. Blue Flower grabbed rifles and ammunition and handed them to Spirit Talker and me. I saw Will and Shorty heading our way on the dead run, weaving this way and that to avoid arrows and bullets. I perfectly timed swinging the door open to let them inside our fortress cabin. Somehow, they'd avoided being hit. Bullets whined through the air and arrows struck shutters. Blessedly, nothing had yet made it through the portholes. We had taken defensive positions faster than a prairie fire with a tailwind. The cabin was now bristling with rifle muzzles. I drew a bead on an attacker, fired, and watched the poor soul fall from his pony.

"Tenawa!" shouted Spirit Talker.

The savages were Comanche who either didn't know of our ties to the Penateka or didn't care.

A warrior rode close with a torch and was about to throw it on our roof when he realized that it wouldn't burn. His hesitation cost him, as Shorty's aim was true.

Spirit Talker and I hollered, "Tabu!" as loudly as we could. Calling the attackers cowards in their own tongue should have given them reason to reconsider their attack.

One warrior on a rearing, beautifully-decorated pony motioned to retreat. Three warriors and a pony lay dead or dying in front of the cabin, and there might have been a couple of more wounded Tenawa.

"How many?" I asked Spirit Talker.

"*Wahamaru,*" he responded, holding up ten fingers twice. In the excitement, he hadn't been able to come up with the translation: twenty.

We were outnumbered but not outgunned, and our cabin was pretty much an impenetrable fortress. There was no point in wasting ammunition, so we held our fire as we waited to see whether they would attack again. Blue Flower and Kate had stayed busy reloading our rifles. About this time, I saw the war party leader ride up beside the barn. His pony pranced back and forth a bit. I must admit that he appeared quite regal as Indians go. His face was nearly covered with broad black stripes, and his shirt featured ornate beadwork I'd normally not expect to see in battle. He gripped a Pattern 1853 Enfield rifle-musket that he'd likely acquired on a raid. Blessedly, it looked as though he was the only savage with a rifle. The single-shot Enfield didn't hold a candle to my revolving cylinder Colt rifle. The warrior apparently was puzzled by our defenses and by the taunts he'd heard in his own language.

I looked over to my right toward Spirit Talker. He gave me a confident, almost-devious smile and swung open the window shutter. He peered out. "Mukwooru... Penateka Comanche," he shouted toward the Tenawa Comanche leader. Any Comanche in the region would know that Spirit Talker was the son of Buffalo Hump and a respected shaman of his *numunuu.*

The warrior cocked his head and widened his eyes in recognition. He had made a grievous mistake and had already paid a deadly price. He had talked with the Nokoni Comanche warrior White Knife but had not believed his stories of the *sunipu* at the Rising Cross Ranch. He had now come around to the belief that the

Nokoni warrior had been right. He nodded toward Spirit Talker and brought his hands together in front of his chest as a sign of peace.

Spirit Talker and I nodded knowingly to each other. It appeared that the Tenawa leader was quite ready to parley. It was time for my Comanche brother to fully take charge of the situation. One Indian to another seemed logical. He opened the front door, stepped onto the gallery, and returned the warrior's peace sign. "Mukwooru," he repeated, pointing at himself.

Not to be outdone, I joined him on the gallery. I delivered a riveting gaze on the mounted warrior. I pointed to my chest, "Isa Pohya!" I prayed that he'd heard of the exploits and strong *sunipu* of Walks With Wolves. It didn't hurt that the muzzles of a couple of rifles still stuck out from the windows.

The warrior raised his hand as a sign for his war party to stay back. With that, he dismounted and walked to a spot equidistant between us and his pony.

Throwing caution to the winds and relying on the code of the warrior, Spirit Talker and I walked toward him. I said a little silent prayer and figured Spirit Talker was doing the same. We halted roughly four paces from the Tenawa leader.

"Aruka Hoikwa," he said, pointing to himself. His name translated to Deer Hunter.

There's no accounting for God's timing, as it was just at this time that my old companion Zeb appeared. The big wolf ambled up beside me and sat with his crystal blue eyes staring menacingly at the Deer Hunter.

Deer Hunter's eyes went wide at the sight of Zeb. The Comanche was quite clearly unsettled. He had to be asking himself just what the full power of the *sunipu* displayed before him was?

Zeb punctuated his presence with a low growl.

Spirit Talker knew that the Tenawa war party had ranged far to the south of their normal territory. He quickly advised Deer Hunter that he should never come close to Rising Cross Ranch again except in peace. From what I could understand of the Comanche tongue, Spirit Talker told the war party leader of an upcoming council of Comanche chiefs. In closing, he told them that I was working to help the Comanche. That was true, though I was actually intending to help both sides in the anticipated confrontation in an attempt to avoid violence. It was likely wishful thinking, but I held hope.

Normally, an encounter like this would have called for smoking the pipe. Deer Hunter glanced over his shoulder at his warriors as they sat aboard their nervously prancing ponies in the pasture beyond the barn. Even from a distance, I could sense a blood-lust lingering in the savages despite their losses.

Spirit Talker and Deer Hunter finished their brief parley. The Tenawa warrior looked at me with newfound respect. He looked again at Zeb but averted his eyes when my wolf companion growled. "Isa Pohya *sunipu natsuitu*," said Deer Hunter. Strong medicine indeed. As with the Nokoni Comanche White Knife, I had apparently made a strong impression on the Tenawa leader.

"Aruka Hoikwa *kahni natsuitu*," I told him to live a strong life.

With that, Deer Hunter nodded respectfully to Spirit Talker, took another quick glance at Zeb, and headed back to his horse.

"They go," said Spirit Talker. "No more fight."

Shorty, Will, and the ladies emerged from the cabin in time to see the Tenawa warriors riding off.

We had come out of the scuffle unscathed but for

some bullet holes and arrows in the walls of the cabin. I was about to advise everyone to get back to our normal activities when it occurred to me to check on Isaac and Sarah. I strode to the side of our cabin and peered down the trail at their cabin. All was silent.

Kate walked over arm in arm with Will. "They went to Bandera, Jack," she said reassuringly.

I breathed a sigh of relief. The Comanche had been so intent on attacking us that the Fisher's cabin was left unscathed. They could have burned our barn but hadn't. I looked down at Zeb. It was unusual for him to show up, though his timing had once again been pretty near perfect. I'd never forget the expression on Deer Hunter's face at the presence of my wolf companion.

"Where's your family?" I asked.

Zeb cocked his head, gave a wag of his tail, and trotted away. I began to wonder whether there might be enough dog in his ancestry to domesticate him just a bit. On the other hand, I appreciated his independence and the times when he unexpectedly showed up to strengthen my own *sunipu*. Maybe one day, I'd figure him out. For now, I thought of him as my aptly-named gift from God.

Blue Flower walked over just as Zeb trotted off. "Zeb *kamakuna*," she said, ascribing a love bond to the wolf.

I shrugged. Perhaps she had something there.

As if on cue, Isaac and Sarah, with baby Jack, came rolling in, seated on their rickety old buckboard. The blankets wrapped around them got us to realize that we were standing around shivering in the Texas winter's grip.

"We miss something?" asked Isaac with a glance at the arrows sticking from our cabin wall.

"Just a few Comanche," I replied with a matter-of-fact grin. "Come on up to our cabin once y'all get unloaded."

Isaac nodded. "Sure 'nuf. I learned a few things in Bandera." He looked around. "Hear tell that the governor ordered up a passel of brand-new Colt revolvers for the Texas Rangers from General Twiggs but got turned down." He nickered to the mules, and they lurched on down the trail toward their cabin.

I reckoned Isaac would have more to share, but I realized they'd been on a long wagon ride and were as dead tired as their dusty clothes and facial expressions evidenced. I'd heard that patience was a virtue. Well, we had time and would have to exercise patience. Besides, Spirit Talker and I had yet to decide our next steps.

TWELVE
WAITING GAME

PATIENCE IS NOT EASY. The sun had yet to make its presence known on the eastern horizon. I slugged down a quick cup of coffee and a buttered biscuit. I admit to peeking into the kitchen cabinet on the off chance that Blue Flower had hidden away some of those bear sign delicacies. Nope. There were a couple of sugar cubes, which I stuffed in my shirt pocket with Big Red in mind.

I opened the shutter to the window that had been shattered in the Comanche attack. Frost covered about everything in sight, but a rising mist told me that the day would warm up right quickly. I put on my wolf vest and grabbed my gun belt. From our bedroom, I could hear Blue Flower responding to George's and Isa's early-morning needs. I strapped on the gun, opened the door as silently as possible, and strode out toward the barn. A bit of alone time with Big Red to curry the big stallion while I thought things out and prayed a tad was foremost in my mind.

"Hey, big fella," I whispered as I eased up beside Big Red. I gave him a sugar cube. Horse eyes are very expressive, and love exuded from Big Red's. I picked up a brush and began stroking him. Now, I could think. Here I was, nearly eighteen years old and charged with running a growing ranch. Hmmm. I asked myself why? I had the responsibility of a wife and children and another on the way. I loved them dearly.

My younger brother Buck and sister Kate still lived under our roof, though I expected that Will would establish his own place to share with her once they were wed. There was no question, but the cabin had to be added to. However, bigger life issues were swirling through my mind. Sure, I was answering God's command in Genesis 1:28 to be fruitful and multiply, fill the earth, and subdue it. Well, I sure was trying to do that.

My faith was strong, and that pretty much helped me keep my emotions under control. I mean, I had tried to forgive that Toliver fellow on the journey back from Wyoming and had even held myself in check over Isaac, having struck his wife in anger. Yet, there were far too many folks who'd lost sight of their Maker such that they were ready to resort to violence to solve the problems with Indian attacks. To my thinking, resorting to violence imprisoned the soul. It removed freedom of choice by forcing a decision. To me, it seemed far better to be enslaved to righteousness than a slave to sin.

As I stroked Big Red, it occurred to me that the path free of sin was unencumbered. It was free. I recalled that biblical line about the truth setting us free. I intuitively knew there had to be more than what I was doing with Rising Cross Ranch, but what would it be. Certainly, a successful ranch would increase the influence I might have in Austin, but how much impact might I have over men on a broader scale. I sighed. Here I was oblivious to all around me save currying Big Red and being lost in my reflections on God and life, when I heard the scrape of moccasins approaching. "Mukwooru?" I ventured.

"Isa Pohya. Good morning," responded Spirit Talker.

Then, I heard the telltale panting before I saw Zeb appear in the doorway. He was beginning to act more like a dog than a wolf. I wondered where his family was, surely not far off. I caught Spirit Talker's eyes. It was obvious that he sensed the strong spirit, the strong *sunipu* or medicine, that filled the air with the big wolf present. Zeb's presence portended something. God hadn't put him in my life to simply scare away hostile Indians.

There was still another six weeks of winter remaining. It wouldn't be long before we'd be tending to the many chores associated with spring, though Shorty and Will made those decidedly easier. "You thinking what I'm thinking?" I asked Spirit Talker.

He nodded. He was troubled with the routine of patience, too. Worse for him, he did not have his wife with him.

I could endure the waiting game a tad better, given that I had Blue Flower and the boys to turn to. "Austin?" I suggested.

Spirit Talker nodded. He turned and began caring for his pony. I slipped him the remaining sugar cube, though Big Red saw me do it and gave me a look as though I had betrayed him. I couldn't help but laugh at how animals sometimes took on human emotions.

WE HAD DEBATED about bringing a packhorse. Now, as we camped in freezing temperatures the first night away from the warm folds of Rising Cross Ranch, it turned out to have made sense to bring one. We simply had too much winter gear to be loading our cayuses with so much extra weight.

I must say that Spirit Talker and I were deeply blessed to have married women who understood the demands the frontier placed upon their men. It wasn't about some grand call of the wild drawing us to seek adventure on the vast prairies and majestic mountains of the frontier. No. The travels we undertook were purposeful and fraught with risk. There was the real possibility that one or both of us would not return. We were young and strong and had, by necessity, quickly learned how to survive the untamed frontier. And the perils were undeniable.

We pointed our mounts toward Austin, yet neither of us expected to get there. No, we looked to do a bit of visiting around the city's outskirts to find out what the Texas Rangers were up to. They would need to train. I figured that Captain Ford was a leader who took few chances, so he would strive to have his Texas Rangers as fully prepared for Comanche tactics as possible. We didn't as yet need to be concerned with where Ford's force might head, as Spirit Talker only had a vague idea as to where the Comanche might gather. The tribes had yet to agree on that.

To say that we cold-camped our first night from Rising Cross Ranch is an understatement. The temperature plummeted. A wind kicked up, and it gusted raw against our faces. Cold has the effect of enhancing exhaustion for man and beast, so it was always wise not to over-exert. I yearned for a cup of hot coffee. However, with roaming hostiles, patrolling Texas Rangers, and occasional vigilantes, we sought a low profile. Did I say vigilantes? These were folks fed up with the slow processes of justice. They would gather and take the law into their own hands, at least, the law as they saw it. They conducted sham trials, if at all, often delivering their justice by hanging the accused.

So, we hobbled our horses and huddled in buffalo robes. We took turns sleeping so as to keep watchful eyes on our cayuses and supplies. There were plenty of Indians about that would love to steal horses and acquire White man's provisions, even on cold nights. Perhaps we were over-cautious, but this was 1858, and emotions were tense to the point of needing to be on guard against the unexpected.

We had found a little hollow and cut some live oak branches to form a shield against the wind. About the time we were feeling grateful for the absence of snow, it began. The wind whipped icy flakes forcefully against our crude cover. We exchanged glances and considered building a small fire. We were still a couple of days from the Austin area, so taking the risk could be rationalized. We hoped. I had laid out the kindling and was about to strike a match when a furry face appeared among the live oak branches. It was followed by three more. Zeb and his pack moved in. Our semi-protected little hollow became warm as biscuits fresh from the oven.

———

BY MORNING, the snow had stopped. Spirit Talker nudged me. "Isa go," he said.

I opened one eye. No wonder my toes had grown cold. Zeb had decided to leave early, likely to hunt.

Texas weather could be strange. The crisp chill of the morning and a blanket of a couple of inches of snow had greeted us, but the wind had ceased, and the temperature was rising fast as we saddled up. It was getting warm enough that we could no longer see those tell-tale cloudy puffs from our breath. We even tied the buffalo robes to our saddle cantles, though I kept my wolf vest on.

We rode on. We passed through Sam Collins's Circle C ranch but saw no one. This journey was part of a waiting game of sorts, as we felt pretty much powerless to have any major impact on what seemed all too inevitable. If we could save a few lives by our efforts, we could likely deem our worthy endeavors a success.

Spirit Talker rode alongside. The packhorse was on a long lead behind Big Red. "Wonder what God thinking?" he asked.

"I would like to think He is worried," I responded.

"Why God let men kill?"

That was a heavy question, and I found myself groping for an answer. "He punishes sinners," I ventured.

"Good people die," he observed.

"Maybe He needs them in heaven." I was groping for answers.

Spirit Talker gave me a curious look. What I was saying hadn't resonated with him.

"I think that God tests us. We grow strong by over-coming. tough challenges." I figured that Spirit Talker would understand that in the context of the threats we had already met. Meeting tests was an essential part of tribal cultures as boys grew to be warriors. "Remember that day George was baptizing us in the North Platte and that Cheyenne attacked us?"

Spirit Talker smiled. How could he forget? He had pushed George away from the warrior's coup stick in the nick of time, and I had managed to kill the savage. Now, that was a test. Courage and steadfastness in the face of an enemy was a serious trial by fire.

"We must have faith that good will come of God's power," I counseled.

———

"KIOWA," said Spirit Talker, straining to look off across the nearly flat terrain of the prairie.

If indeed they were Kiowa, they were a long way off. We didn't need company. I hoped they were of the band led by the subchief Kwihnai, translated as Eagle, that we had encountered a couple of years back. If so, they wouldn't dare come near except in peace. I suspected that the Kiowa were raiding ranches, and clueless victims were blaming the Comanche. Folks seemed unable to distinguish one tribe from another. "I think they'll stay away," I said resolutely. "They may be friends of Kwihnai."

Spirit Talker nodded, and we ignored them.

Real troubles now loomed ahead. Half a dozen rough-looking riders had crossed the trail about a quarter mile ahead of us. Worse, they'd seen us. What they saw were two well-armed riders dressed in buckskins with a pack-horse in tow and headed their way.

"They're waiting," I said with a resigned sigh.

Spirit Talker nodded.

It wouldn't do to change direction. They'd likely take that as a threat to avoid a confrontation. It didn't take long to reach the men. They were a decidedly rough-looking bunch. One rode a few steps toward us as we approached. With the sun behind him, I could barely make out his features. I couldn't miss that he looked straight at me through dark, squinty eyes. "Where you an yer Injun headed?" he challenged.

I sat tall in my saddle. I was at least a head taller than my questioner. "My name's Jack O'Toole. We're joining the Texas Rangers. Captain Ford asked us to be scouts." It was a partial lie, as we had no intention of joining the Texas Rangers, and Ford hadn't asked Spirit Talker to scout. I reckoned God would forgive me for truth-stretching.

The man nodded, then smiled. "My handle's Brick Whelan. We're headed to Austin to join up." Then his smile faded. He seemed on the verge of inviting us to join them but had a second thought. "A couple of my friends don't cotton to Injuns," he said with a regretful shake of his head. "Maybe you should just head on yer way."

I scanned the men ahead of us. While I might have welcomed the challenge of trying to turn their minds from prejudice, I was well aware that emotions against the Redman were running high. Whelan was quite correct in his advice. "Much obliged, Mr. Whelan. See you in Austin." It was another untruth, as we would avoid Austin entirely.

We paused to permit the riders to get some distance on us. We were in no hurry, and there was no point in stirring embedded ill feelings. Once they were out of sight, we resumed our travels. We decided to alter our route by turning slightly to the northeast. It wasn't long before we reached the banks of the Pedernales River. By the way, folks pronounce that perd-na-less. Go figure. Anyway, we reckoned to follow it to where it joined with the Colorado River just northwest of Austin. There would likely be more Texas Ranger recruits lingering about, so it would be well that we steer clear of the city.

"*Tenahpu tosaabitu kuya akatu* Comanche," mumbled Spirit Talker. When he spoke in the Comanche tongue instead of English, I could be confident that he was especially serious. In this case, he was absolutely correct.

I nodded. Indeed, the White men we'd just encountered feared the Comanche. Fear was a tough taskmaster. Fear could rule men's souls and drive them to unspeakable actions. "They have reason to have *tosaabitu*," I responded. "But, there are paths to peace."

"Words in air and on paper no matter," observed Spirit Talker.

He was right about that. Nevertheless, both sides broke the treaties with impunity. The Whites wanted the Indians to either accept their way of living or confine themselves to reservations that were in ungodly locations and happened to be located far from their traditional hunting grounds. The Indians resisted, wreaking havoc on homesteads, stealing livestock, and killing whom they saw as invaders. I was actually one of the lucky few who had a reasonably peaceful coexistence with the Redman owing to my ties with the Penateka Comanche and reputation as a tough but fair opponent. I liked to think that they respected me and what they saw as my strong *sunipu*.

Around mid-afternoon, we spotted smoke about a mile off to the north. We decided to investigate.

We reined in at the smoldering remains of a homesteader cabin. The arrow-riddled and scalped bodies of two adults and one small child lay in the yard. Anything of value to the attackers had likely been taken. There were no horses or cattle to be seen.

Spirit Talker scanned the area. He dismounted and examined the arrows. "Kiowa," he stated flatly.

"Humph!" I retorted with a shake of my head.

"They'll blame the Comanche." I dismounted and grabbed a shovel from our packhorse. The bodies already smelled of death, but I managed to find a half-burned Bible that identified the family. The man had a rifle, but it had jammed. He never got off a shot against the savages. I suppose it was a blessing that it had been quick, as there was no evidence of torture. I wondered whether the Kiowa had taken prisoners. Like the Comanche, they might take young victims to raise within the tribe or trade as slaves to other tribes or to Whites for ransom. I thought back on my younger brother and sister, whom we'd managed to save from such a fate among the Comanche.

Spirit Talker spelled me with the grave digging while I fashioned a cross and carved the family name into it. I even added the date, February 14, 1858.

———

NOW, we cold-camped in earnest. We had no desire to be found by anyone. The cold weather seemed to have pretty much broken for the present, so we were reasonably comfortable with no fire. Even Zeb found no need to add his furry family to our midst.

I lay under the stars, unable to sleep. Spirit Talker was keeping the first watch, but I stared up into the starry night sly. Winter would be drawing to a close in a few weeks, and there would be plenty to do around Rising Cross Ranch, though priorities for Spirit Talker and I would be elsewhere.

I got to thinking about my conversations with Governor Runnels and Rip Ford. Who was I to be even pretending to match wits with the likes of Rip Ford? There was no question that a military-style campaign against the Comanche was foremost in their thinking. I wondered what a battle might be like. Oh, I'd fought little skirmishes with bandits and Indians. I had killed in self-defense. But, I had also forgiven and freed enemies.

A pitched battle seemed an entirely different breed. It entailed malice aforethought. This was to be war. It occurred to me that fighting at any level was personal. Nerves quaked in anticipation of battle as punctuated by crude jokes, laughter, prayer, and vomit. Leaders boasted and harangued to boost courage. Rallying cries were shouted on high. Then: engagement. Grim-faced combatants clashed.

Even within the lines of dozens or hundreds of fighters, it was hand to hand, man against man, gun against warclub, arrows against spears. Horses screamed, men shouted insults and threats, and deep in men's guts all shivered with fear. Hearts beat fast, fear ruled, stumbling yet charging on, the battle goes on seemingly without end. Blood and gore, strutting heroes and weeping cowards, cries of the wounded mixed with death wails. Men fought the urge to run, to escape.

For all the supposed glory of battle, the reality was inglorious. Men yearned to be home, to be away from the savagery. The battle raged to what end. Were the victors truly victorious? Was there the remotest hope that Spirit Talker and I could stop the impending doom? Could its momentum be overcome? Would God let this happen? Just about the time sleep finally overtook me, I felt Spirit Talker's hand on my shoulder, waking me for my turn on watch.

I sat with my back against the trunk of a live oak, my rifle in my lap. The nearby horses nicked and whinnied just a bit. I saw long ears prick up but paid no attention. My eyes yearned to close. I shut them for just a moment.

A wet tongue stroked my cheek. My eyes went wide! Yep, it was Zeb, along with his family. I stroked his head, then closed my eyes and quickly succumbed to slumber. I had the best night watch that could be asked for.

Spirit Talker nudged me and placed a cup of hot coffee in my hand. There was an ever-brightening glow across the eastern horizon.

"Fire?" I asked while still in a half-daze.

"No smoke, is good," responded my Comanche brother.

He was right. I looked over at the coffeepot sitting atop burning coals. My head finally came around to the memory that oak tended to not give off much smoke when it burned. "Coffee good," I chortled as a swallow burned its way down my throat.

Spirit Talker pointed southward. "Many gather," he observed.

I found the strength to stand. I saw the impression in the ground beside my bedroll where Zeb had sat and kept guard. I dug my hand into my saddlebag and pulled out a telescope. It had been one of my purchases during my trip to Austin. I sighted it in the direction Spirit Talker had pointed. From what I could make out, better than a hundred men were busily preparing for what was apparently some sort of training.

I handed the telescope to Spirit Talker, and his jaw dropped as he peered through the lens.

"It's called a telescope," I advised.

He nodded and handed it back. "Maybe a hundred men?" he ventured.

"Looks like. They must be Captain Ford's Texas Ranger recruits. I see Indians among them."

Spirit Talker shook his head ruefully. "They learn how Comanche fight," he observed. If this were so, and given the firepower of the Texas Rangers, brutal massacres lay ahead. Fighting would be decidedly one-sided.

We decided to try to get closer. What tribes were helping Ford's army of Texas Rangers?

"Let's ride around and approach from the east with the sun behind us. Less likely they'll see us," I suggested.

Spirit Talker nodded.

We broke camp and saddled up.

As we cut a wide berth around the encampment, Spirit Talker rode beside me. "Maybe Jack scout for Texas Rangers."

It was the first time he'd brought up the idea since I'd mentioned it back at Rising Cross Ranch. And he'd heard me refer to it when we'd encountered that bunch of Texas Ranger recruits. I suppose it had been gnawing at him ever since. Ford had offered the opportunity to me. I wondered whether he might accept Spirit Talker? "Maybe," I echoed.

We'd been playing a waiting game. Perhaps it was time for action.

THIRTEEN

FIRST ENCOUNTER

WE RODE to within what I judged to be a quarter mile east of the Texas Ranger encampment. Surprisingly, there were no sentries. That sure seemed a tad over-confident, even arrogant to me. Then again, they were spitting distance from Austin and likely felt that no Comanche war party in its right mind would come near.

We dismounted and hitched our cayuses to a nearby live oak. I wasn't figuring to spend a lot of time scouting. I pretty much simply wanted to get a better feel for what the Texas Rangers were up to.

We hunkered down, and I took a gander through the telescope. The camp had finished breakfast and was saddling up, likely in preparation for some sort of training drills.

Now stupidity came into play. Mine. The sun reflected from the polished brass housing of the tele-scope. Three riders stopped and looked our way.

Spirit Talker pushed the telescope down into the grass, but it was too late. We'd been discovered. There was no point in hiding and making matters worse. If we ran to our horses and tried to ride away, we'd be asking for even bigger trouble. I collapsed the telescope and slid it into its sheath as surreptitiously as possible. We stood up, and I waved as friendly as I could.

The three riders drew near. "Who are you, and what do you think you're doing?" commanded the lead rider. He was a big, tough-looking hulk and armed to the teeth.

My mind was racing. "Er…looking for Captain Ford," I responded. "I'm Jack O'Toole. I met the Captain in Austin."

"What's your business?"

"He invited me to scout. I brought my friend here… also to scout."

The rider scowled. "We got plenty Indians here. Tonkawa…Caddo…Waco…yep, plenty." He appeared to be thinking about whether he wanted to drag us into camp, perhaps to confront Ford.

The rider beside him mumbled something I couldn't quite hear.

Spirit Talker was standing beside me. He'd heard the names of the tribes that the rider had mentioned, and he was clearly disturbed. We were already learning facts that were a tad scary.

The lead rider gave us another hard once-over. "How about y'all retrieve your horses and follow us in. Don't be doing anything foolish."

We dutifully got our mounts and followed the three to the encampment. We walked, they rode. As we pulled close and walked past tents, we began to receive attention from others. Soon, we were passing through a gathering gauntlet of Texas Rangers and Indians. The rider led us to a larger tent that was apparently the headquarters.

I honestly didn't know quite what to expect. Last

time I had seen Captain Ford, he was all suited up for church. The hatless man who now stood before me was dressed in buckskins. I couldn't miss the huge .44 caliber Walker Colt revolver in the holster hanging from his waist. His clean-shaven face framed a pair of intense eyes that took but a moment to recognize me. "Why, Mr. O'Toole, how good to see you again."

"Found 'em up yonder," said our escort, pointing to where I'd been viewing the encampment with my telescope.

"You doing a bit of scouting already?" asked Ford with a grin.

I shuffled nervously for a moment but then stood upright. "Just passing through, sir. Figured we might run into you."

He paused and took a gander at Spirit Talker. "This a friend of yours?"

Spirit Talker didn't miss a beat. He extended his hand to Ford. "Me Mukwooru, Penateka Comanche." Well, he was upfront about his affiliation.

Ford's eyes widened a tad. "Comanche?"

"My friend is a Christian. He seeks peace with Whites."

Ford nodded. He looked over at the three Texas Rangers that had escorted us. "These men are no threat, men. Thank you. You're dismissed." He turned back to us. "You interested in scouting, Mr. O'Toole?"

I nodded. "Yes, but I must tie up loose ends back at the ranch, sir."

"And your friend? Mukwooru is it?" he asked.

Spirit Talker smiled. He respected Ford for using his Comanche name. "I return to my people, my *numunuu*. We no attack Whites."

"I have a scout name Keechi that lived with the

Nokoni Comanche," shared Ford. "I hold no grudge against peaceful Comanche. If you wish to scout for us, we'd be pleased to have you join us."

This was turning out far better than I could have imagined. Maybe, just maybe, there was yet an answer to our prayers for peace.

"We're headed north to Fort Belknap to finish training. Come join us when you're ready. I expect we'll be looking for hostile Comanche come late April," said Ford. I was surprised at his trust in revealing the timing of his campaign. "If you'd like a bite of breakfast, you're welcome to visit the chow tent. You might still get there before they tear it down."

"Thanks kindly, Captain Ford, but I think we'll mosey home. As I said, we have loose ends to tie up." With that, I nodded to Spirit Talker and half saluted Ford. In but moments, we were mounted up and headed home. We'd found what we needed to know and more straight from the proverbial horse's mouth. We knew roughly the size of the force and the timing of the campaign. There were better than a hundred Texas Rangers and what appeared to be a number of Indians of various tribes. Given their firepower, they would be a formidable force to be reckoned with.

———

I WAS IMPRESSED with Captain Ford. In my young life, I'd observed that a man's religious beliefs tend to shape their character. I likely wouldn't agree with Ford on everything, but he was a Christian man and seemed to be an honest man who could be trusted. I had heard that he supported slavery but hoped he might eventually be dissuaded from that.

In the three days it took us to return to Rising Cross Ranch, Spirit Talker and I mulled over the outline of a plan. And we prayed. A lot of emotion was feeding the movement to rid Texas of the threat of marauding Indians. Powerful folks were at work influencing the political decision-makers. We realistically hadn't a prayer of overcoming the impetus behind that force. We figured that the best we might do was minimize the damage.

Through it all, something was gnawing at me. I felt as though I was missing a piece of a greater puzzle. What had I overlooked?

I also noticed that Zeb and his new pack were traveling with us. Every now and then, I'd spot them off in the distance, moving parallel with our path. His presence drove home my conviction that I had neglected to notice some key elements of our plan.

As it was, we'd decided to head to Fort Belknap toward mid-April and sign on as scouts with Ford. Spirit Talker and I discussed it over and over. Could he first influence the Penateka Comanche to steer clear of any fighting? The last thing we wanted was Texas Rangers descending on the Comanche encampments dotting the Comancheria. But what was I missing?

It hit me like double-struck lightning. We were only a couple of miles from Rising Cross Ranch and riding single file through an old, dried-up wash. I turned to Spirit Talker. "We have a problem," I stated flatly. I wasn't giving enough credence to how high emotions were running against the Comanche and Indians in general. By protecting the Indians, we were running the risk of being labeled Indian lovers. It would make us highly vulnerable to folks who didn't take kindly to that point of view. Our families could be in serious danger.

Spirit Talker gave me a questioning look.

I explained the perceived danger we were putting our families in, but especially my family. I already had a Comanche wife and what were labeled half-breed children. Folks who knew us paid no attention and accepted us, but there were likely plenty of strangers who wouldn't take too kindly to my family situation. For too many folks, the only good Indian was a dead Indian.

"What we do?" asked Spirit Talker.

I reined in and gazed off toward the horizon. "We need to prepare our families in case we must leave."

My Comanche brother nodded resignedly.

FOURTEEN
SEW UP LOOSE ENDS

WE PULLED up at the ranch house in the late afternoon. It had been a surprisingly warm day for late February, but we were trail-weary and looking forward to a hot meal. Shorty, Will, and Buck greeted us and took care of the horses. Of course, I gave Big Red a loving hug before he ambled off. The big stallion let out an excited whinny as he spotted one of his favorite mares. Spring was nearing.

Blue Flower came dashing from the house at the sound of our voices and ran into my arms. It sure was great to be home.

"Jack, clean up for dinner," she cooed, then glanced over at Spirit Talker. He wore as much trail dust as me. "Mukwooru, too," she admonished with a smile.

I sure was hungry. It might be said that I was hungrier than a hibernating bear.

Blue Flower and Kate prepared a delectable feast. As we sat around the table enjoying venison and all the fixings, the time came to discuss the reality of our situation. There was no way to put it off and no way to sugarcoat the situation. It simply had to be confronted.

Blue Flower had excused herself to nurse the twins. Upon her return, she refilled our coffee cups and took her seat beside me. She looked over at me and caught the seriousness writ large across my face. "What?" she asked guardedly.

"We might have to leave Rising Cross." There, I'd said it.

Kate's jaw dropped. "But..." she babbled as she thought of her upcoming marriage with Will. They'd already begun building a cabin of their own.

Blue Flower looked questioningly, yearning to hear more so as to better understand. With the twins and another bun in the oven, her concern was understandable.

I looked at Spirit Talker. He gave me one of those looks that said I had opened the door to the subject, and it was up to me to explain.

"This is one of those times when we wonder what to do when we don't know what to do. We prayed for wisdom. We patiently waited for answers to come to us, to find the strength to face this challenge courageously and take the best action. Captain Rip Ford has raised companies of Texas Rangers and gathered more than a hundred Indian allies to make war on the Comanche. Ford asked us to scout for them. We think we might be able to bring peace." I paused. In my heart, I knew that we'd do well to save lives. "But..." and I paused again. "There's a lot of emotion. Emotion driven by fear. Fear drives folks to do crazy things."

Kate's and Blue Flower's jaws had dropped in sheer amazement at the seriousness of what I was talking about. "Neighbors are good," interjected Kate.

I thought of Sam Collins nearby Circle C Ranch. We could count on Collins. But then, there were other folks around, people who didn't truly know us. "True enough, sis. But there are plenty of folks that don't know us, that only see our ties to the feared Comanche. Fear-driven folks who want to be rid of Indians...all Indians."

I saw fear in Blue Flower's eyes for the first time. Out here on the vast reaches of the Comancheria, Rising Cross Ranch served as a protective cocoon. "Mukwooru will return to his *numunuu* and Prairie Flower. He will counsel his people to avoid joining with the Nokoni, Tenawa, and other Comanche, though young warriors may ignore him. Come April, he and I will head to Fort Belknap to join with Ford's Texas Rangers. We will scout but try to warn the *numunuu* of the Texas Rangers. We must be careful so the Texas Rangers think we are on their side. In a way, this is true. We don't want to see them killed either." I had said a mouthful and then some.

Spirit Talker nodded his agreement.

"If there is trouble, we may all need to escape. Our plan would be to journey to George's ranch up on the North Platte. We would need provisions for several days and must do it as quickly as possible."

"What of Rising Cross?" pleaded Blue Flower. "What of our dreams?"

"Kate and Will can stay here with Shorty. No one will bother them. Isaac and Sarah will be safe, too," I assured her. I looked deeply into her tearful eyes. "We would return when it was safe," I whispered.

"Many moons?" She asked.

I shook my head. "Not too many," I said, trying to sound confident.

"I leave at rising of sun," interjected Spirit Talker.

It seemed settled for now, the near future, that is.

———

IT WAS SORT OF sad to see Spirit Talker depart. Blue Flower gave her brother a big farewell hug and a bag of bear sign she'd baked specially for him. She winked at me. I suspected there'd be a stack in the cupboard.

"Go with God, brother," I said as Spirit Talker mounted his pinto.

"We meet at Pinta Trail. Two moons," he reminded me as he tugged at the trailing line to his packhorse.

———

THE WINTER WAS NOW FLYING BY ALL too quickly. March had arrived. Mornings still brought occasional frost, but the days were already growing warmer. Blue Flower and I had even taken advantage of the balmier days to picnic up on the Guadalupe. I'd regularly impress her with my skill at catching bass. Then, I made the mistake of teaching her to fish, and she realized how easy it was. Those fish seemed attracted to a baited hook like they were steel pulled to a magnet. We laughed. These were good times. We laughed a lot. God was blessing us with a third child, and Rising Cross Ranch was thriving. George and Isa were growing and seemed nearly ready to walk. I guess they were overachievers.

The winter hadn't been especially tough here at the southern end of the Comancheria. We felt confident that we'd move another herd northward next year, mostly our own beeves. But that was a few months off.

Now, we realized that we were in need of supplies, and a trip to Klappenbach's store in Bandera was in order. With emotions about Indians and slavery running high, Blue Flower pregnant, and as tough a frontier woman as she was, we decided it was best for her to stay home at Rising Cross Ranch.

I hitched up the wagon. Will would accompany me. He had a special motive, as he wanted to find a wedding gift for Kate. They'd set an April date to get hitched. It was about a week before I planned to depart to meet Spirit Talker at the north end of the Pinta Trail and go join up with Captain Ford. It was early morning and the skies were crystal clear, so reckoned to arrive in Bandera by late afternoon. We were well-armed as appropriate to the heightened threats that might be faced. In fact, I had acquired a shotgun which I leaned against the seat between us. We bade farewell to our ladies and were soon off in a cloud of dust.

———

THE SUN WAS NESTLED JUST above the hills off to the west as we pulled up in front of Klappenbach's store. His wife Stella was sweeping dust from the planking along the front of the building.

"Welcome back, boys," she said with a welcoming smile. She called us boys, as she was at least twice our age.

"Howdy Stella," I called out. "Can we park around back?"

She nodded. "August is inside arranging a fresh shipment of clothing."

That news lit up Will's face.

Stella didn't miss his expression. "You're the young man about to get hitched to Jack's sister?"

Will nodded enthusiastically.

"We'll get you fixed up with some purty unmentionables," she said with an exaggerated wink.

I watched poor Will flush with embarrassment. "Figure to load up and head back in the morning, Stella."

"You best talk to August, Jack."

I drove the wagon around behind the store, and Will and I entered through the back door. August Klappenbach was standing just inside to greet us. "Howdy August! You still dealing with those Camp Verde camel riders?" I said jovially.

Klappenbach wasn't smiling. "Hear tell, Rip Ford's fixing to put a whipping on the Comanche," he blurted with nary a howdy-do.

His grimness brought me up short.

"Set a spell, Jack," he said with a nod to Will.

We grabbed a couple of chairs and sat to await whatever concerns had stirred the normally quite happy store owner.

"Folks around these parts are major stirred up about the Comanche threat. Much as some like and respect you, Jack, they don't cotton to you being married to an Indian...especially having half-breed children."

I shook my head in disbelief.

"If I were you, I wouldn't hang around Bandera. Get your supplies and head out before the ugly folk realize you're here."

"How long has this brew been perking?" I asked.

Klappenbach shrugged. "Been getting more intense around here as news of homesteads being attacked has reached folks. Nothing personal to you, Jack. Some folks don't have all their oars in the water. They're scared near to death and don't figure the soldiers at Camp Verde will help."

I sighed deeply with the realization that my worst fears were being brought to life. "Fear makes folks a tad unpredictable," I observed. "I appreciate your advice, August. You might let folks know that I'm fixing to join up with Captain Ford's Texas Rangers as a scout. Spirit

Talker will be joining me, but I expect that won't matter none."

Klappenbach nodded gravely. "Proud of you, Jack. Not sure it'll make a difference around these parts. Things might ease some if Ford puts a big hurting on the Comanche."

"Worst happens, Blue Flower and I may head to Wyoming for a spell. Rising Cross Ranch should be well cared for by Will and Kate. We'll see how successful the Texas Rangers are. Just maybe, feelings will lighten up."

"I'll help you load your supplies, Jack. The town's quiet right now, so y'all should be able to slip away safely."

"I need to buy something special for Buck, August. You still have any of those Colt Navy revolvers?"

Klappenbach nodded. "Going to teach your young brother to shoot, eh."

"Shucks, he's eight years old already. He can handle a rifle, but I figured it was time he had a handgun."

Klappenbach smiled. Talk of Buck had eased the pressure. "I'll throw in a belt and holster, Jack."

Will and I went to work grabbing supplies and loading the wagon. Stella helped him find some stylish unmentionables for Kate. To be straight, we both blushed. I was grateful that Stella boxed them promptly.

We were finally loaded and ready to leave. Klappenbach threw one more bag of flour into the wagon. "Safe travels, Jack."

"It's going to be a clear moonlit night. I expect we can make a few miles and catch some shuteye before resuming our travels at sunrise." I paused. "We're still planning a trail drive next year, God willing. Reckon to have close to four hundred head of Rising Cross beeves."

Klappenbach smiled. "I'll look forward to that, Jack. Pray the Indian problem eases and folks settle down."

Stella came out and gave each of us a hug while slipping a plate of fresh-baked cornbread to us. "You boys be safe now, you hear?" she said.

———————

WE DROVE the wagon roughly five miles along a moonlit trail. We even forded the Medina River before finding a spot to camp for the night. Given the ominous nature of the environment, we decided to cold camp. There was no point in attracting attention with a campfire. It's amazing how trouble can find folks even in the vastness of the Texas frontier. Will and I took turns at sentry. There was no point in being foolhardy, no point in assuming we couldn't be found.

What did I say about trouble? The eastern sky was just hinting of sunrise. I was trying to keep from dozing off when I heard a jingling sound drawing ever closer. There was a vague familiarity to the sound. The clop of horse hooves and squeak of saddle leather soon accompanied the jingling of what I recognized as sabers. I gave Will a nudge.

We had pulled off the trail, but the darkness had prevented us from fully hiding our wagon. I slid over to where we had picketed the horses and stroked their noses. We didn't need any neighing or whinnying to alert the approaching threat. Soon enough, a patrol of eight mounted soldiers rode ever closer to our position. They maintained a column of twos. Blessedly, they appeared to be nearly asleep in their saddles. The early morning light was still dim, and they were soon close enough that I could have reached out and touched the officer in the lead. I could barely make out the lieutenant bar on his near shoulder. We held our breaths. The patrol jingle-jangled and squeaked on past us. I could have sworn one of the men was snoring. I stifled a chuckle as I thought on how embarrassed the lieutenant might have been had we awakened them. Imagine their surprise?

We waited until they were well out of sight before breaking camp. I could hardly wait to share this close encounter with family at Rising Cross Ranch. Of course, Will and I would embellish it a tad. We'd think of something to make it sound funnier. Lord knows, we could use some levity to break the stress. We were soon hitched up and once again headed toward home.

———

MARCH LITERALLY BLEW BY. The temperatures were mild, but occasional rain and windy days were a regular occurrence. My little brother Buck and I found time to do a bit of target shooting with his new revolver. The recoil nearly knocked him over the first time he fired it. He was a lanky eight-year-old with not much muscle on his bones. Nevertheless, it didn't take long for him to figure the gun out. He was a natural.

We'd made preparations for Will's and Kate's marriage. We invited Sam Collins and his men from Circle C Ranch. Collins had finally found true love, so he was bringing his new wife. All seemed well but for the lingering concerns with Indians and folks' reactions to the threats.

With help from Shorty and me, Will had nearly completed the cabin that he and Kate would make their home in. It was a two-room affair roughly half the size of the one Blue Flower and I lived in. I partitioned off a couple of acres for them up the trail a bit from Isaac's and Sarah's cabin, and Will intended to acquire more acreage. Meanwhile, he'd continue working for me. We had also begun to add an additional room to our house. Accommodating three children was going to be too much for our present space. I hoped and prayed that we'd be able to build a new ranch house in a couple of years, maybe with a shady dog run to relax in.

Will's and Kate's wedding went off without a hitch. The weather was spectacular, with a seemingly endless crystal-blue sky. The buds were beginning to appear on the few trees we had and gave a patina of green to the landscape. We didn't have a pastor out on the wilds of the Comancheria, so I wound up officiating. Kate looked downright beautiful in a white buckskin dress that Blue Flower had made for her.

For years, I'd seen Kate as my scrawny mostly annoying sister. Now, she had flowered into early womanhood, and I realized she was downright pretty. I guess my appreciation of Kate had begun when we rescued her from Comanche captivity three years ago. The experience was sobering and tended to make us grow up quickly. Of course, that was the way of the frontier. Children didn't stay children for long. I felt just a pang of envy as they shared their first kiss as husband and wife.

Spirit Talker had shared with me how a Comanche boy would stay under his mother's wing until he was around twelve years old. He'd then be turned over to the men for training as a hunter and warrior. It likely made for a good life balance for their culture.

I strove to keep the conversation after the wedding focused on a bright future for Will and Kate. I figured it simply wouldn't do to talk of my upcoming venture with

Captain Ford's Texas Rangers. Blue Flower was already worried enough.

I must share one story. I felt duty-bound to tease my sister. To that end, I placed about two dozen rocks under the covers of their bed. Figuring that might not be enough, I rigged a string of tin cans such that any movement in the bed raised a veritable cacophony of noise. I must admit that I was rather pleased with myself. And it was confirmed during the night and then from the nasty look Kate gave me the next morning when she was drawing water from the well.

FIFTEEN
FORT BELKNAP

IT WAS but a week later that I readied to head out on Big Red. I planned to rendezvous with Spirit Talker at the northern reach of the Pinta Trail. From there, we'd head north to Fort Belknap to join Ford's Texas Rangers.

Blue Flower's belly was just beginning to show evidence of her pregnancy. We spent time making talk about children's names and future plans for Rising Cross Ranch. We tended to avoid talking about the risk Spirit Talker and I were about to undertake in an effort to save as many lives as we could.

The night before my departure, we enjoyed a quiet interlude on the gallery.

"Jack, stay safe," she whispered as she pressed her head against my shoulder.

I wanted to tell her that I always delivered on my promises. Hadn't I brought the horses for her dowry? However, words would never be enough. I figured we wouldn't be gone too long. Ford was a no-nonsense field commander and wouldn't waste time waiting for action. He'd press his own strategic initiative. It was like a

Comanche band on the hunt for buffalo. Once the beasts were spotted, they went into action. This would all be lost on Blue Flower. She was still loving and feisty with courage and toughness bred of her Comanche heritage, though motherhood had raised her protective instincts. I looked deeply into her beautiful dark eyes. "Two moons, three at most," I assured her.

We spent a restless night. I held the boys for a while and prayed that I'd return to see them grow up, to guide their travels toward manhood.

The next morning, I mounted Big Red with a sense of purpose. Blue Flower and I had prayed for strength. I felt empowered, as though God was leading me on a quest. I wasn't surprised when Zeb showed up. Apparently, he figured to accompany me. I wasn't about to argue. God had his ways, and Zeb was part of that. It was as though his presence turned me into Walks With Wolves, my Comanche persona. I was thinking this when Blue Flower placed her hand on my leg and looked up at me all dewy-eyed.

"Isa Pohya," she said as though invoking the *sunipu* of *isa*. Strong medicine would be needed.

———

I RODE STRAIGHT to the Pinta Trail and then followed it northward. Despite the Indian threat, it seemed that more travelers were using the trail. I wasn't up to being sociable, so I took cover whenever I heard or saw anyone ahead of me. I didn't worry about travelers behind me, as I was moving a tad quicker than most despite my cautionary stops.

It didn't surprise me when I smelled smoke upon approaching the Pedernales River end of the trail. Sure enough, Spirit Talker was enjoying a venison dinner while awaiting my arrival. I thought about sneaking up on him but decided not to press my luck. Everyone was on edge these days, including my Comanche brother.

"*Ana o'a hi'it,*" said Spirit Talker, inviting me to eat with nary a look over his shoulder at my approach. He laughed and pointed off toward Zeb, semi-hidden alongside some nearby live oak.

I dismounted and led Big Red into the campsite. "Mukwooru, my brother," I greeted him.

"What take so long, Isu Pohya?" he asked with a broad smile that accentuated the lingering scars on his face from a mountain lion attack.

"Two moons, not one," I chided.

We enjoyed the venison and shared our experiences since we'd last been together. I told him of Will's and Kate's wedding and of our progress in growing Rising Cross Ranch. I also shared my learning of the increased fears Will and I had encountered in Bandera. Spirit Talker had striven to influence his Penateka Comanche to not join the fight up north against the Texas Rangers, but to no avail. Buffalo Hump was forced to accede to the demands of his younger warriors. Many sought their first battle experience against the ever-encroaching Whites. It seemed that hatred ran deep on both sides.

We set off first thing in the morning for Fort Belknap. With early April weather, we didn't need the cold weather trappings that required a packhorse. We aimed to move swiftly and counted on Captain Ford to supply us. At that, it took just about twelve days to reach Fort Belknap.

As we rode to the crest of a raised part of an otherwise mostly flat prairie, we saw Ford's encampment, or what remained of it. The place shimmered in the warm, sun-drenched landscape. We had timed our arrival just as the Texas Rangers were breaking camp. Given our Indian-style garb, we were never challenged as we worked our way toward Ford's bivouac.

We reined in about a dozen yards from Ford and watched as he exercised his managerial style. It was quite clear that he took no nonsense but was respected and well-liked. So far as we could see, no one ever challenged his orders. In fact, the breaking of camp was an impressive, orderly exercise.

Finally, Ford happened to glance up and see us. "What are you men…" he began before recognizing me and then Spirit Talker. "Mr. O'Toole, I'm pleased that you could join us. If you both would be kind enough to check in with our quartermaster, he will make sure you are properly outfitted." He pointed to a couple of very busy Texas Rangers off to our left.

Not knowing what protocols were, I gave a sloppy salute and began to turn Big Red.

"We will be heading north in about an hour. I'll fill you in on your assignment." Ford was waiting for his chief scout, Keechi. I would later learn that Keechi had spent time living with the Comanche, so Ford relied on him.

I received a rapid education on moving a large body of men over long distances. The level of support, especially food and medical care were critical ingredients. So far as I could see, all of the Texas Rangers were exceptionally well-armed with repeating firearms and the ubiquitous Bowie knife made famous by Jim Bowie of Alamo fame. The Bowie knife was worth every ounce of its weight in any hand-to-hand fight. I also noted that Ford had a chaplain along, though he too was well-armed. Many men of the cloth tended to carry firearms on the frontier, so I wasn't surprised.

We huddled every morning and evening with Ford's scouts, often going out on our own. Scouts performed their duty in pairs as a precaution.

As we traveled, we passed several burned-out homesteads with accompanying cross-marked graves. One time, we saw two graves along with a half-dozen smaller graves. If there were graves, it signified that some folks had come along and buried the victims. However, we did pass one homestead where the skeletal remains of a man and two women were hanging on corral posts. Arrows still protruded from the half-clothed bodies. Of course, they'd been scalped. Little wonder that folks feared the Comanche and other tribes enough to have run emotions to a fever-pitch of anger and intolerance.

———

IT TOOK NEARLY two weeks to reach the Red River. I happened to be with the main body of Texas Rangers and was able to watch as Captain Ford hesitated. He was concerned about leaving Texas but had little choice. Marching north into Indian territory was politically undesirable. However, he had his orders to eradicate the Indian threat, so we waded across.

I expect I should share a fascinating part of our involvement. Zeb and his family joined us every evening. Where they were during the day, I have no idea. The Texas Rangers took note. Apparently, a rumor was floating around that I had some sort of connection with wolves. One of the Shawnee Indians had heard of a White man called Walks With Wolves. One evening, as we laid out our bedrolls, two Texas Rangers stopped by along with the Shawnee and a couple of Tonkawa.

One of the Rangers stepped toward me with his hat in hand. "Are you the fella they call Walks With Wolves?"

I was impressed that he got right to his purpose. I smiled. "I've been called that," I responded.

Spirit Talker stood nearby with his rifle handy, just in case.

The Shawnee stepped forward. "Me say true," he declared proudly. He pointed to me, "Isa Pohya," he confirmed.

God can work in strange ways, and timing is one of them. I was about to respond when Zeb chose the moment to amble into our campsite with his family. The huge wolf with his blue eyes and massive head just about made our visitors jump from their skins. Mouths opened aghast, nearly dropping low enough to collect prairie dust.

I smiled confidently and stroked Zeb's head.

To say our visitors were impressed would be a gross understatement. One thing was for certain, we would never have any worries of threat from the Texas Ranger's Indian allies.

Spirit Talker and I slept especially easy that night. In the morning, Zeb and his family were off doing whatever they did when not with us.

After another ten days of our march, Spirit Talker and I managed to locate the encampment of a couple of hundred Tenawa Comanche close to the Canadian River. It turned out that Keechi had already found them, so our news served as a confirmation.

We reckoned that Buffalo Hump's Penateka Comanche would travel to our west and not be far behind the Tenawa. I thought about how strong a force the Comanche could be if they joined together rather than camp separately. Ford would have been hard-pressed to defeat them even with his superior weaponry.

On May 9, Spirit Talker and I spotted smoke to the northeast, right about where the Canadian River was supposed to be. The Canadian fed into the Arkansas River, so it was an important landmark and water supply. Eventually, it would be part of an important route for trail drives out of Texas.

SIXTEEN

LITTLE ROBE CREEK

WE TRAVELED NORTHWARD with Ford's Texas Rangers. We ate right well, as we passed through great herds of buffalo. The meat was quite tasty. One day, a Texas Ranger shot and killed a buffalo and found fresh wounds around embedded Comanche arrowheads. That was a sign that the Comanche were encamped close by. It was May 10, by my reckoning.

Flowers were beginning to bloom. Mid-May was arriving in all its spring glory. The scouts had led the Texas Rangers to a place that was actually in Indian territory well north of the Red River. In fact, we'd reached the Canadian River, winding its way from the Texas Panhandle and through the Indian territories. The place we encamped was among the Antelope Hills or Little Robe Creek. Ford knowingly broke the Federal protections afforded the tribes of the territory. He had little choice, as the Comanche were leading him on a merry chase. Ford's Texas Rangers were roughly a hundred strong and were supplemented with better than a hundred allies drawn from various tribes, including Tonkawa, Caddo, Anadarko, Waco, Shawnee, Delaware, and Tahaucano. Technically, he had also a Comanche ally by virtue of Spirit Talker's presence as a scout.

The next day, we came upon a Nokoni Comanche hunting party preying on buffalo and followed them to within a half mile of their encampment. The scouting party turned back to report to Ford. He was inclined to attack right away but was concerned that he would be tactically blind. His lead scout, Keechi couldn't be found.

Spirit Talker and I had urged Ford to head southward, but Tonkawa scouts arrived with news of a Comanche encampment nearby. We watched helplessly as a battle unfolded. It would ultimately turn out to be three very decisive engagements. Our position on the crest of a low-lying hill overlooking the creek gave us a panoramic view of all that unfolded before us.

The first attack came on the morning of May 12, as Ford personally led his Texas Rangers with a surprise attack on a Comanche camp of five lodges. Ford's Indian allies all wore white cloths around their heads to distinguish them from the Comanche and not be shot by Texas Rangers. We watched in horror as the Comanches were caught completely off guard. We'd been helpless to warn them. It turned out to be nothing short of a massacre. The Texas Rangers held a decided advantage with rapid-fire weapons, and the results were devastating. Ford had studied Comanche tactics and had trained his Texas Rangers to not be lured into man-to-man confrontations or be led into ambushes. Worse, the Tonkawa stopped to loot, kill the wounded, and take horses. Ford's Texas Rangers moved on quickly from the initial battle as they gathered their forces to attack a second encampment.

We saw our opportunity, descended from our hilltop perch, and rode hard toward the Tenawa encampment that we knew was further south. The Tenawa were just beginning to be awakened by the distant sound of gunfire. As we neared the village, we were challenged by a sentry.

"Many Texas Rangers come," warned Spirit Talker.

The sentry laughed it off. The encampment held upward of three hundred warriors. He showed no concern but nocked an arrow and launched it our way as a warning. We spurred our mounts, but the warning arrow found its way into Spirit Talker's upper arm. The shaft penetrated through the fleshy part of the shoulder muscle. We had no choice but to ignore the wound, as there was no time to waste. We bolted back to our ridgeline vantage point. Quickly dismounting, I began to tend to Spirit Talker's wound. I fetched a poultice from my possibles bag.

"Grit your teeth, brother," I commanded.

Spirit Talker set his jaw. I gripped the shaft firmly and broke the arrow in two, then carefully pulled the two ends free while Spirit Talker grimaced. My Comanche brother was tough indeed. There was little bleeding, and I quickly layered on the poultice and wrapped the wound with strips of cotton cloth. "Mukwooru strong," I chided.

There was no time for idle conversation. Spirit Talker seemed none the worse for the wound. The wound paled in comparison to the deep cuts of a mountain lion attack a couple of years back. With the wound treated, we now watched helplessly as the Texas Rangers prepared to attack the second Comanche encampment of Tenawa. As they descended upon the camp, we saw that the Rangers had been spotted by Comanche warriors. We took some comfort in having warned the Tenawa of the lurking danger despite the reaction by the sentry. Unfortunately, we saw the sentry that had challenged us and shot Spirit Talker fall among the first casualties. The Tenawa warriors poured from their lodges to take defensive positions, and Ford pulled up. He considered the situation and figured to send his Indian allies into battle first rather than risk Texas Rangers.

I tapped Spirit Talker and pointed to a lone rider emerging from the Comanche encampment.

"Po-bish e-quash-o," observed Spirit Talker.

This was a Tenawa chief whose name translated to Iron Jacket. He'd earned the name for the scaled-metal-mail jacket he wore, likely a throwback armament from ancient Spanish conquistadors. The Comanche believed it would ward off both bullets and arrows. Poor Iron Jacket had no idea that he was facing Ford's Indian allies armed with large-bore Mississippi rifles and Colt revolvers. Iron Jacket charged. His pony was near-instantly shot out from under him, and he arose only to be gunned down in a hail of bullets. The Tenawa defenders were stunned.

The Texas Rangers charged the village. Though the Comanche were able to mount a solid defense this time, they suffered heavy casualties. By now, other Comanche encampments had become well aware of Ford's offensive.

I turned to Spirit Talker. "We must leave soon," I counseled.

Spirit Talker seemed in shock as we helplessly watched the carnage unfold.

The fighting was intense. Texas Ranger horses were beginning to tire, so Ford pulled his forces back to the first encampment. It made me realize that we'd been watching for several hours. Yet, there was no way we figured to enter the fray. The battle had stretched over several miles and it was often hard to tell friend from foe. It was simply too risky, and, but for trying to save Comanche lives, there was no incentive for us to undertake so great a risk.

About this time, we looked over to our left and saw a band of mounted Comanche approaching. Responding to the sounds of battle, they now brought the hills alive with battle-ready warriors carrying fourteen-foot lances. A handful of headstrong Rangers took on the new threat and were promptly run off, one being savagely lanced to death.

"Chief is Peter Nocona," observed Spirit Talker. "Strong warrior."

Nocona held wooded high ground and avoided being lured to fight the larger body of Texas Rangers with their superior weapons. I pointed to their superior position just as Comanche warriors began taking on Ford's Indian allies in mostly hand-to-hand combat. Most of the allies had removed their white head wraps, fearing it made them easy targets for the Comanche, so the Texas Rangers were forced to hold their fire for fear of killing friendlies. I felt that I was a skilled bowman and could shoot arrows with the best, but I was amazed at how the Comanche fired off arrows with blazing speed and accuracy from galloping horses. Might the Comanche carry the day after all?

We watched helplessly as Ford detached a force to circle behind Nocona's Comanche and cut off any retreat. We heard a bugle sound to recall the Indian allies while Texas Rangers mounted a charge. This would be their third engagement of the day, and it would exact a price. They were joined by a band of Tonkawas. Nocona realized he was trapped, and we watched him lead his warriors away at a desperate gallop.

From what we could make out, the Texas Rangers were tiring, or at least their horses were beat. We later learned that they were running low on ammunition. Ford had his bugler sound recall.

It had not been until this third and final engagement that Comanche warriors had been able to take what amounted to an offensive stance against the Texas Rangers. With Texas Rangers pulled back, Spirit Talker and I left the safety of our perch and rode into Ford's camp. We tried to appear as though we'd participated in the battle. No one seemed ready to challenge that ruse, though Spirit Talker's bandaged arm gave us some credibility. About now, Spirit Talker was feeling fortunate that the large Comanche encampment headed by his father Buffalo Hump sat unscathed. From what I could figure, Ford had decided that it would be far too risky to attack the Penateka Comanche with his tired forces. Besides, Ford reckoned he'd won this day. He ordered both the Nokoni and Tenawa villages be burned.

We were able to ride up close to Ford as he ventured out to make a final inspection of the battlefield. I appreciated being able to observe him close up. I nudged Spirit Talker as we realized that the Tonkawas had mutilated the bodies of the dead Comanche. It was small solace that Ford was horrified at such savagery. I had heard of Indian torture, but something about this left me struggling to keep from throwing up. Spirit Talker shook his head in disgust. Christian mercy wasn't in play.

Ford figured to turn his forces southward, withdrawing back into Texas proper. We had traveled close to five hundred miles to put down the Comanche threat. Had Ford truly succeeded? Time will tell. We had no idea what losses the Comanche had sustained. From the vantage point we'd had of the battle, it appeared that nearly a hundred warriors had been killed and more than three hundred horses captured. By my count, there were at least sixteen Comanche captives. We heard later that Ford's Texas Rangers lost only two killed and five wounded.

By battle standards around the world, the size of the forces at Little Robe Creek may not have seemed huge, but the significance of the defeat suffered by the Comanche was far greater than mere numbers could measure.

IT SEEMED pointless to hang around since it didn't appear that Ford would be engaging the Comanche this day. Given some of the emotion-laden ill feelings we'd encountered in Bandera, it seemed to me that folks would now be going after Indians with a greater boldness.

We entered the Texas Ranger camp and rode to Ford's headquarters tent. We reckoned to do him the courtesy of telling him of our intentions.

We dismounted and were promptly challenged by a Texas Ranger guarding Ford's tent. "State yer business," he challenged. He looked tired and haggard from the battle, and we might have appeared just a tad too unsullied for his tastes.

"We're here to bid farewell to Captain Ford," I said straightforwardly.

"Captain don't wanna be bothered..." he was cut off in mid-sentence.

Ford emerged from the tent. "Did I hear Jack

O'Toole?" How he could distinguish my voice was beyond my figuring.

"Yes, sir, Captain Ford. Figured we'd stop by and bid farewell. Livestock back home needs tending."

Ford nodded. "Can't say as I blame you. I'm grateful for your service." He looked at Spirit Talker. "I expect Mukwooru here will rejoin his people."

Spirit Talker was once again impressed that Ford addressed him by his Comanche name. He nodded. "You did not fight Penateka Comanche," he observed. "Maybe six hundred warriors in Penateka camp." He purposefully exaggerated the number of warriors, knowing the Texas Rangers were tired and not likely to be enthused about taking on a large Comanche force.

Ford nodded and then smiled. "Your father is strong. The Comanche have suffered enough," he said. "And we were low on ammunition," he added with a wink.

That brought a smile to Spirit Talker's lips. He appreciated the mutual respect embedded in the humor. "Penateka wish peace," he said with an emphatic tone.

"I hope so," advised Ford. "I'm much obliged for your help, Mr. O'Toole," he enjoined. "You're welcome to draw some supplies for your travels."

"Thank you, Captain Ford," I responded.

Unbeknownst to us, there would be no further Texas Ranger battle initiatives. Ford had already learned that the Texas legislature wasn't willing to come up with the funds to support an ongoing military-style effort. So it was that he shook our hands. "*Vaya con Dios*," he said, wishing us godspeed. "Be pleased to have you back should the need arise." With that, he nodded and returned to his tent.

We mounted up and headed out. We soon found ourselves about a quarter mile from the Penateka encampment. It appeared that they were breaking camp as a precaution. They couldn't yet know that Ford had no further plans to fight but were taking no chances.

"That went well," I said to Spirit Talker.

He nodded. "Captain say I rejoin my people. This good," he observed. He smiled broadly. "I think God protect Penateka Comanche," he added.

I thought about that. God and a little lie about the number of warriors in the encampment. Many Nokoni and Tenawa had died. The Texas Rangers had plumb worn themselves out, massacring warriors, women, and children in those encampments. It was a heavy price to have paid. "God is good," I said by way of reinforcement.

We resumed our ride. Three Texas Rangers on a distant hill were watching our trail. They were an advance party from Ford's force. They likely didn't appreciate me, a White man, fraternizing with the enemy. They soon turned away, but their anti-Indian emotions had undoubtedly been well-fed. I guess I would unknowingly become a marked man.

We rode unchallenged into the Penateka encampment and quickly found Buffalo Hump's teepee just as it was being disassembled.

We dismounted, and Spirit Talker strode confidently over to his father with me a couple of steps behind. "No hurry. Texas Rangers no fight," he advised. "Mukwooru tell them too many Penateka," he said with a broad grin.

Buffalo Hump smiled with relief. Many young Penateka Comanche warriors were itching to engage in battle, but it wouldn't be this day. "Good to see Mukwooru," he said and then noted the bandage. He offered a questioning look.

"Tenawa sentry. Lucky shot," he said with an embarrassed grin.

Buffalo Hump shook his head. How was he ever to understand young people? He turned his gaze to me. "Blue Flower happy?"

I nodded and held up three fingers. "One more O'Toole," I said with a smile.

"Where Prairie Flower?" asked Spirit Talker.

Buffalo Hump pointed to the southwest. "Mukwooru come with us?"

Spirit Talker and I had yet to speak of our future plans other than the possibility of our families escaping to Wyoming if feelings ran poorly around home.

Buffalo Hump noted our uncertainty. He offered a mischievous smile. "Prairie Flower have surprise."

Spirit Talker lit up like a sky full of stars. "When go?" he pressed impatiently.

I reckoned there was no point in hanging around, as the Comanche had nearly broken camp and would soon be on the move. Spirit Talker and I had already discussed a rendezvous in a month or so. I was about to pay farewell respects to Buffalo Hump when he grabbed my arm and pulled me aside.

"Buffalo Hump grateful. Jack good *tosa*. *Onaa* to Buffalo Hump."

I felt honored that this legendary Comanche chief considered me his son. My eyes locked on his. "*Ap*," I said. He was now the father I had lost. My true father only lived in my memory. I embraced him and Spirit Talker, then mounted up. We all had long journeys home ahead. I was intent on moving considerably faster than a couple of hundred warriors with travois and packhorses. I could ride better than thirty miles a day, while they'd do well to make twenty or so. We shared farewell hugs. I mounted Big Red and soon disappeared from their view.

Now, I could focus on getting home. I hoped to avoid

Ford's Texas Rangers or any of the tribal allies. I was unaware at the time that a trio of Texas Rangers were watching me. About this time, Zeb had taken to spending more daylight hours with me. He was acting more like a dog than a wolf. I reckoned that the presence of him and his pack would tend to dissuade Texas Rangers from coming too near.

SEVENTEEN
TOUGH DECISION

I TRAVELED MOSTLY at night to avoid any escaping Comanche, stragglers from Ford's Indian allies, and the Texas Rangers themselves. I figured that word of Ford's victory would travel quickly across Texas, but not necessarily fast enough to suit me. I prayed regularly for safe passage.

The Red River was soon behind me. Big Red seemed up to the task of picking up our pace. The stallion was a warrior by virtue of being under my saddle, and I was rightly proud of him. I barely paused to catch shuteye. Sleep was necessary, but I was impatient. I checked myself more than once, as impatience can breed carelessness.

Zeb and his pack trailed along just close enough that I was aware of his presence. I was certain that God was ensuring my safety by keeping the wolves nearby. As I reckoned, my strong medicine, fighting prowess, and connections with wolves had established my near-legendary reputation across the prairies of the Comancheria and even northward toward Lakota country. Indians were especially reluctant to challenge Walks With Wolves. I wish I could say the same for Whites.

I treasured the respect that Captain Ford had shown me. I didn't necessarily agree with all of his views—especially about slavery—but the respect was mutual. Men like him, a man named Sam Houston, and Governor Runnels held strong sway over the future of Texas and the western frontier in general.

It took close to three weeks to reach the Guadalupe River at the northern boundary of Rising Cross Ranch. I paused astride Big Red on the northern bank and watched the river flow by before lifting my gaze to take in the vast majesty of the landscape stretched before me. The mid-morning sun's rays cast a patina of gold across the grasses and trees. It struck me that this was land that I owned. Acre upon acre spread far as the eye could see. Cattle and horses grazed freely. God had sure blessed me as I followed his command from Genesis to build upon His creation, to be fruitful and multiply His bounty.

I guided Big Red down the north bank of the river, and we waded and swam across. We were about two miles from the cabin. Big Red was beginning to get a tad feisty as he sensed the readiness of his mares. We forged ahead. Big Red pranced with new energy, his ears erect, eyes wide open, and whinnying and nickering most of the way. Zeb followed along with his pack. He'd become a ubiquitous addition to my travels. He still hunted on his own, but he had started acting more like a pet dog than a leader of a pack.

All was quiet as we approached the cabin. While I was away, Will, Shorty, and Isaac had completed the addition. It had become a very accommodating edifice. June had arrived, and I figured the place should be jumping with activity. As I drew closer, I saw that some of the window shutters had been closed. There was no evidence of any attack, so I was unable to figure out why. Then, I noticed that our front door was new and the old one leaned against the front wall. What I saw scared me to my very bones. Writ large in black paint were the words *INDIAN LOVER.*

Just as I began to dismount, Blue Flower emerged.

The expression on her face said everything. Fear. Anger. She ran into my arms.

As I held her tightly, I noted the place in front of the cabin where there'd been a large bonfire. I quickly read that as part of whatever warning had been visited upon us.

"*Tosa kohtu,*" she said between sobs. White men had set the fire.

I was holding her when Will and Shorty appeared from the barn. "We chased 'em off, Jack, but not before them crazies set the fire an' painted the door," said Shorty. "Nearly got to shootin'!" he added.

"When? How many? Who?" My questions came in rapid succession.

"Two nights ago," said Will. "Must have been six far as I could tell in the dark. They stayed away from my place and Isaac's."

"Any idea who they were?" I repeated.

"Wore masks," said Shorty.

"*Tabu,*" I stated emphatically in Comanche so Blue Flower fully understood. "Cowards," I added for Will's and Shorty's benefit. I looked down at Blue Flower as she strove to collect herself. I surmised that her tears were mostly from relief that I was now home. "Are George and Isa alright?" I asked.

She nodded. "We scared, Jack."

The very idea that supposedly civilized folks would

perpetrate such a deed on my innocent wife and our children. How inhuman, how utterly uncivilized. "Let's gather in the cabin. Will, fetch Isaac to join us." I led Blue Flower back into the cabin. As we passed the old door leaning against the cabin wall, I glanced back at Shorty. "Stick that abomination in the back of the barn, Shorty. I've got plans for it." I ushered Blue Flower to a chair at the kitchen table. Once she was comfortable, I rustled up some coffee.

"How Mukwooru," she asked.

"All Penateka are safe," I assured her. "The Texas Rangers did not attack them." I spared her the details of the other engagements, especially the mutilations by the Tonkawa. It was enough that many Comanche had died. "Mukwooru traveled home with your father. I learned that Prairie Flower is with child." At that news, I was finally treated to a smile. I was about to kiss her when Shorty, Will, and Isaac entered after a perfunctory knock on the door. Kate, Sarah, and even young Buck trailed in after them. I glanced down and was surprised to see Zeb stroll on in as though he owned the place.

"I took care of Big Red," said Buck. "He's in the north pasture and very happy."

My little brother knew full well what the stallion would be up to, and I couldn't help but laugh. That tended to break the tension a tad. "I fear for our safety. Even though the Texas Rangers won up north, not everyone has heard about it, and they remain fearful. Folks that are afraid can be dangerous. So long as Blue Flower and I are here, y'all are in danger. It's what folks call guilt by association." I scanned the faces surrounding me. There were no smiles.

"What Jack do?" ventured Blue Flower. "We escape?"

"That pretty much describes it," I responded. "I

talked about this possibility before leaving to join up with Captain Ford. Mukwooru knows my plan and will join us with Prairie Flower first chance."

"When you headed out, Jack?" asked Shorty.

I sighed. "Day or so. We can't dally. Every day we're here is dangerous for y'all. We will head to George's ranch. It's a long journey through rough country, but I'm familiar with it. George is likely dealing with Lakota and Cheyenne, but better them than unruly Whites with guns and torches. We'll travel light. Just a couple of packhorses with essentials."

Shorty nodded. "We'll do all we can to get yuh ready, Jack."

I sensed a peacefulness had come over Blue Flower. We had a plan to escape to the relative safety of the north country. In fact, she had never seen the mountains with their rugged grandeur. Our escape would be as much an adventure as a flight to safety. "That's the plan," I concluded.

Everyone looked disconcertedly at each other until Isaac first realized that I was ready to be alone with my wife and children after a long adventure. "Let's go get those packhorses trail-ready," Isaac suggested.

We'd be gathering necessary supplies, oiling tack, cleaning weapons, and generally preparing for a month-long journey. It had been a decidedly tough decision. With any luck at all, we figured to return by April of next year to saner, more peaceful conditions. Meanwhile, Shorty, Will, and Isaac would continue our efforts at building Rising Cross Ranch in hopes of a future cattle drive. To that end, I scribbled a note to August Klappen-bach, assuring him that our plans for next year were very much alive.

WITH OUR CABIN emptied of all but Blue Flower, me, and our twins, I finally felt at peace. "I've missed you," I said softly, wrapping an arm around my beautiful wife's shoulders. Just as we kissed, a wail emanated from the new bedroom that had become a nursery. George and Isa were hungry. Our personal feelings would have to wait.

It wasn't long before we were able to enjoy the passions that were made all the more emotion-laden by my prolonged absence. We lolled around the cabin, kissing and hugging as though reconfirming our love. Blue Flower prepared a delicious dinner topped off with sugar-frosted bear sign. As the sun crept to the western hills, we moseyed out to the gallery, sipped coffee, and took in the glorious splendor of the sunset. Blue Flower slipped her arm around mine and leaned against me. "We visit Penateka?" she whispered.

I hadn't planned on any side trips, but she was obviously longing to see her family before we headed north. It would take us out of our way and add a few days to our journey, but I wasn't going to deprive my loving wife of her heartfelt need. I nodded. "We will visit them," I assured her. Actually, the couple of days it would take to reach the Penateka Comanche village would give us a chance to establish our travel routine. Routine was an important part of travel on the frontier. We had to be alert, as carelessness could hold deadly consequences.

EIGHTEEN

NORTHWARD BOUND

EVERYONE GATHERED in front of our cabin to see us off on our long journey. It was both sad and joyful. Sad to leave even for a brief time, but joyful that we'd likely all be safer by virtue of Blue Flower and me heading north.

As I helped Blue Flower into her saddle and handed her the leads for the two packhorses, my sister Kate sidled up to me. "I'm pregnant, Jack," she whispered in my ear with a broad, very happy smile. It nearly brought tears of joy to my eyes. I gave her a hug and nodded at Will. They would likely make fine parents.

I shook hands with Shorty, Will, Isaac, and Buck in turn and mounted Big Red. I'd swear the stallion was giving an all-too-wistful gaze out at his mares. I took a final scan of the cabin and outbuildings before turning to lead us out in a westward direction toward the Pinta Trail. We'd visit Blue Flower's family for a couple of days and then be fully northward bound. With a final wave, we put Rising Cross Ranch behind us for the present. Zeb followed.

Stealth was foremost in my mind. We didn't want to

tempt hostile Indians or bandits we might encounter on the trail. Consequently, we chose not to wear our Sunday best buckskins. We sure did our utmost to be unattractive targets. Then again, having a small pack of wolves accompanying would likely dissuade potential threats. I figured that no attacker with any sense would desire the powerful jaws of a wolf biting down on an arm or leg. If my guns or bow and arrows failed, Zeb would be a reckoning.

———

WE FOUND ourselves about halfway up the Pinta Trail when we had our first suspicious encounter. Three men appeared at first glance to be cowboys were heading our way. The trail at this place tended to be narrow and a bit convoluted as it wound around boulders. There was barely space for folks approaching from opposite directions to pass.

I was in the lead of our little caravan and pulled as far right as I could to enable the trio to pass. Blue Flower pulled her pony in tightly behind Big Red and kept her head down. The packhorses followed her pinto's lead.

The lead cowboy halted as he pulled abreast of me. "Where yuh headed, pard," he said with a gruff voice that spoke of too many cantinas. He stunk to high heaven, likely not having bathed for some time. His travel companions pulled up tightly behind him, and I heard the click of a revolver hammer being drawn back. The cowboy gave me a cold, hard stare and snuck an evil glance at Blue Flower.

I sat fully upright in my saddle. I was physically larger by a long way, but three against one would be a serious challenge. I didn't respond.

"I politely asked where yuh headed?" he repeated, a bit more gravel in his tone.

There was a rocky outcropping to my right that reached just above my head. With Blue Flower and the packhorses behind me, there was no escape. I sighed. "Y'all might be on your way, gents," I finally responded.

"Hear that, boys. He called us gents," he said with a forced guttural laugh. I envisioned him as a snake with its tongue darting in and out. "Nice squaw yuh have there," he said in an ever-more-threatening voice.

I heard a growl.

The cowboy was about to say something when his eyes went above me to the rocky outcropping. He flinched. His jaw dropped. "Er...let's mosey along, boys," he said with a nod and spurs gently applied to his horse's flanks.

As they passed on by, I looked up to be certain. Yep. A pair of crystal-blue eyes set in that big furry head peered onto the trail below.

We breathed a sigh of relief.

"Jack strong *sunipu*," teased Blue Flower with a smile. This was the first that she had seen of Zeb's impact. "Isa Pohya," she whispered my Comanche name.

We had dodged a situation thanks to Zeb. We rode even more cautiously. Roughly four hours or so later, we finally reached the Pedernales River and the end of the Pinta Trail. We set up a small cold camp well off the trail. It was difficult to shelter four horses, but we did the best we could behind a stand of trees. The Penateka encampment was a half day up the river, and it was highly likely that we'd encounter them.

Fresh water and venison jerky topped off with bear sign actually made for a satisfying meal. We hobbled the horses and spread our bedrolls under some trees along the river. We'd take turns at sentry duty. This would be part of our routine as we headed to George's, so it was important to practice it such that it became a habit. It wasn't very romantic, but it would likely keep us alive. We were blessed this night with a cloudless starry sky. The twins were snug in their cradleboards. They'd nearly outgrown the boards, so I'd fashioned a larger pair of carriers that could straddle across the rump of the pinto pony just behind the saddle cantle and hang on either side. They'd come into play right soon.

I AWAKENED TO A WET NOSE. The true sentry on duty had decided it was time to greet the day. I awakened Blue Flower and shared some of the jerky. I was saving the remaining bear sign to share with Spirit Talker and Prairie Flower. She smiled and gave me a big hug and an all-too-passionate kiss. "We see Mukwooru today!" she said excitedly.

We had saddled up and were preparing to mount, when a rustling a little way up the trail caught my ears. Moments later, a half-dozen Comanche appeared. I stood frozen for a second or so, then made the peace sign across my chest. There was a pause before one of them recognized us. Everyone smiled, mostly with relief.

"Mukwooru?" I asked.

The warriors said that Buffalo Hump was about two days north, still on his return journey from the near-miss encounter with Ford's Texas Rangers. They motioned upriver. They would escort us to the encampment.

It appeared that we would be with the Penateka Comanche for at least a couple of days longer than we had anticipated, but Blue Flower would have time to visit with Prairie Flower and share woman talk.

About this time, Zeb and his pack appeared. I was surprised that the Comanche acted unconcerned. They were apparently well aware of the *sunipu* of Walks With Wolves and trusted that I had the wolves under some sort of control.

Our journey to the encampment was uneventful. What little conversation with our escorts was in the Comanche language, as none of the warriors spoke English. Blue Flower translated some, but I understood most of it.

Upon arrival, to much excitement over our visit, we were escorted to a teepee set up behind that of Buffalo Hump's. The camp was mostly empty, owing to most of the warriors having gone off with Buffalo Hump.

Prairie Flower emerged from the teepee that she and Spirit Talker shared, greeting us with open arms and a great smile. It became quite clear that she was pregnant. That sparked special attention from Blue Flower. There was no telling what special thoughts pregnant women shared with each other, but the two would have plenty to talk about.

––––––––

ON THE SECOND day of our visit, an advance party of Comanche led by Spirit Talker arrived. I was relieved. I suppose that was a tad selfish, as it signified that the journey north would soon resume, and I was anxious to be on our way. It remained to be seen whether Spirit Talker and Prairie Flower might accompany us. I wasn't so sure that they'd join us, as Wyoming's North Platte River country held mixed memories for Prairie Flower.

She'd been enslaved, then rescued from that fate by Spirit Talker, who left her with George and his Pawnee wife, Running Waters. It wasn't until a year later that my Comanche brother returned to wed her.

Spirit Talker led a party of twenty warriors into the encampment. They were tired but proud of having been ready to face the Texas Rangers. They had thirsted for battle up on the Canadian River, but it was not to be. I'm sure Buffalo Hump was relieved. In his wisdom, he knew better than to risk many lives in a battle against tired Texas Rangers who had vastly superior weapons. It simply would not have been worth losing warriors.

Spirit Talker scanned the encampment as he rode in. His eyes quickly came to focus on me standing with Blue Flower and Prairie Flower. The twins played at our feet, playing as only ten-month-olds can. He smiled broadly and slid easily from his pony. He approached, pausing to permit Zeb to give him a careful sniff. A wagging tail signified that he'd passed muster. We all laughed as passersby observed in wonderment at the wolf's behavior. Mouths dropped when Zeb licked my hand.

"Isa Pohya!" he exclaimed, giving me a hug. He then greeted the wives not quite so affectionately. This was Comanche protocol far as I could tell. "Buffalo Hump one...maybe two days back," he advised, pointing to the northeast.

"It is good to see you, brother," I said.

"Visit surprise," he observed. "What happen?"

"*Ana o'a hi'it,*" interrupted Prairie Flower motioning toward their teepee. She rightly figured her husband would be hungry. She ushered us to their nearby teepee while a young boy looked after Spirit Talker's pony.

We made ourselves comfortable around a small fire. With me, Blue Flower, and the twins joining us, the quarters were decidedly close. Prairie Flower, helped by a young slave girl, busied herself with the food.

Spirit Talker looked directly at me. "What happen?" he repeated.

"We are heading to Wyoming," I said. "Bad *numunuu* back home." I proceeded to tell about the personal threats and how we'd prayed on it and decided to head to George's ranch while emotions cooled.

"What about Lakota and Cheyenne?" Spirit Talker queried.

I offered a rueful smile. "Whites more dangerous."

"Will and Kate marry. They care for Rising Cross Ranch," interjected Blue Flower.

"I know you travel far and are tired," I said, sort of thinking out loud.

Spirit Talker gave me a questioning look, as though waiting for some sort of big challenge.

Blue Flower gave me a look that said I was moving too quickly.

I shrugged. "Do you and Prairie Flower want to come with us?" There. I had said it.

Prairie Flower nearly dropped the serving bowl she'd been holding.

"Must think on this," offered Spirit Talker.

I caught Prairie Flower shooting him a glance that said he'd better think, think very long and very carefully. "We have a couple of days," I said nonchalantly.

Blue Flower squeezed my arm...tightly.

Spirit Talker and I began to talk of the battle up at Little Robe Creek. The women quickly tired of the now highly-embellished story-telling and suggested we take our conversation outside. Well, we could have sent the women out, but I wasn't of a mind to clean up after our meal. We headed for the pony remuda. I needed to spend some time with Big Red anyway. Zeb trailed along behind us. I think the warriors, women folks, and especially the children were getting used to a pack of wolves being among them. Do recall that the Comanche, like many Indians, venerated the wolf for its attributes of loyalty, strength, and family.

"Wyoming sound good," Spirit Talker revealed. He looked off toward the low-lying cliffs overlooking the river. "Worry about *numunuu*. Need shaman here. Teach of God and Christ." Concern was writ large on his face that his absence could stop the progress he'd made in trying to bring his *numunuu*, his people, to faith in God.

I nodded. I didn't fancy just me and Blue Flower traveling to Wyoming. Having Spirit Talker and Prairie Flower with us would make us a bit less attractive to folks with hostile intentions.

———

WE COMPRISED AN INTERESTING CARAVAN. Me on Big Red, Blue Flower with the twins, Spirit Talker, and Prairie Flower, all mounted on strong ponies, four pack-horses trailing, and a pack of wolves guarding our flanks. What a motley group!

Yes, Spirit Talker had persuaded Prairie Flower to head north with us. We all had Buffalo Hump's blessing. It didn't hurt that we were armed to the teeth. Both women were capable with our weapons, as many women —like menfolk—had to be able to defend themselves well on the frontier.

It took a mere four days to pick up the path we had used to herd longhorns northward the previous year. It was somewhat comforting to be traveling familiar territory. The rivers and creeks were not so swollen with rain and snowmelt, so fording them was generally easier. It took us better than a week to reach the canyon the locals called Palo Duro, loosely translated from Mexican as hard stick. The mane refers to the plentiful hardwoods—junipers and mesquites—found in the canyon. It had been home to Apache, but they were run off by Comanche, Cheyenne, and Kiowa a couple of hundred years ago.

That old nagging feeling that we were being watched began to work its way inside me. I rather expected it might be Indians, but my intuition told me otherwise. I kept my suspicions to myself rather than alarm Blue Flower and Prairie Flower. I was pretty sure that Spirit Talker sensed the same foreboding.

Hmmm. It didn't take long for our fears to be realized. We were following a wash and had just followed a bend screened by mesquite when five mounted men appeared. They were downright mean-looking rascals. Rifles were aimed our way.

One rider was set a horse length in front of the others. There was something vaguely familiar about him. A craggy face, squinty eyes, and thin lips set between unusually large ears that might have been mistaken for wings, but for his *dare you to say something about my ears* demeanor. "Where you traitors think yer headed?" he demanded.

Calling us traitors set me back. Facing down five rifles was not exactly conducive to smart-alecky responses. I had to buy time to think. "Traitors?" I inquired with a confident tone bordering on sarcasm. I couldn't imagine what he was referring to.

"Saw yuh two up at Little Robe Creek conferrin' with them Comanch' savages just afore the fight. Yuh talked Cap'n Ford into leavin' 'em be."

I strove to look incredulous.

"Don't yuh be lookin' surprised. We done seen yuh."

I realized these were Texas Rangers—or at least had been—and fought in the battle up at Little Robe Creek. Apparently, they'd been hunting for us and lucked onto our trail. "You know we were scouts for Captain Ford?" I began trying to reason with the man.

"Don't be listening to him, Donny," said one of the men behind the leader. "We got rope, an' there be trees yonder."

Here we sat. Me, a Comanche warrior, and two Comanche women looking down the barrels of five rifles. There was no way to shoot our way out. By the time any of us grabbed a rifle or revolver, we'd be shot full of lead. This was a decidedly one-sided standoff until the leader made up his mind. I was sending major prayers to God.

I continued my defense. "We needed to get a count of the Comanche in the encampment. Shucks, my Comanche friend here took an arrow in the arm for our trouble. We reported the information to Captain Ford. The horses were tired, and y'all knew ammunition was low."

I guess I was beginning to make sense as the leader raised the muzzle of his rifle.

"He's workin' on yuh, Donny!" said the man behind him.

Just then, the man's horse let out a terrible scream. Zeb's jaws had clamped down hard on the rear leg of his cayuse. It set the other horses to panic as riders were tossed and rifles went flying. "Wolves!" shouted one of the men as he pried himself from the arms of a prickly cactus.

By the time the dust settled, all five were on foot and struggling to pull themselves together. Four wolves were snarling and growling their displeasure. Four of the horses had run off. The one with the leg wound was hurting badly and looked as though he'd have to be put down.

Now, our foes found themselves staring down the barrels of our rifles. I can assure you that a large caliber rifle can make a mess of most anything its bullets hit, and our attackers were well aware of that. "Keep your hands high!" I demanded.

"Wha...what yuh gonna do?" stammered the leader.

Now, I must say this situation sorely tested my faith. Part of me wanted to put a serious whipping on these men. Such a beating likely would not have changed their attitudes toward the Red man. Nope. Here's where I had to suck it up and rely on my Christian teaching of forgiveness and mercy. That having been said, their actions warranted punishment, memorable punishment. I thought a moment. I glanced at Spirit Talker and our wives. They clearly expected me to do something. Even Zeb sat with his head cocked in a questioning pose. I gave the men an icy stare. Then, a knowing smile found its way across my face. "Slowly unbuckle your gun belts and let them drop." I cautiously watched. They obeyed. "Now back away from those guns real careful-like." They did as they were told, and Spirit Talker gathered their guns and holsters, as well as their knives.

"Now, take off your boots," I commanded.

They hesitated.

"You do know what a bullet from this rifle can do to a man's flesh?" I offered as a macabre reminder.

The boots came off. Zeb sniffed the boots and growled.

"Now, your pants."

They didn't hesitate this time. Whew, but they

revealed a ragtag collection of long johns that likely hadn't been washed in weeks. They smelled rather ripe.

"Mukwooru, unload their guns and gather the ammunition. Tie off a pants leg and fill it with the bullets."

The men were increasingly nervous. Zeb emitted a long, low growl, and one of the men involuntarily answered nature's call.

Blue Flower and Prairie Flower were now trying to suppress laughs.

"What yuh gonna do with us?" asked the leader anxiously.

"We told you men the truth about our scouting duties. You need to rethink your hate for our Red brothers. We're leaving you and your guns here."

"But..." said one of the men.

"Count your luck that I'm a God-fearing man in a forgiving mood. Y'all need to come to peace. Hatred doesn't accomplish anything." That was likely enough sermonizing. I reckoned that I needed to keep it simple for them.

They nodded.

"You might be able to catch your horses. I'm going to drop your boots and pants off a mile or so north. You best stay low and watch for Comanche or Kiowa. I'll drop your ammunition a bit further up the trail. If you try to follow us or threaten us again in any way, we will kill you. Is that clear?"

Now, they all nodded enthusiastically.

With that, I moved Big Red over to the wounded horse and put it out of its misery. Mercy killing a downed horse was a law of the frontier. I hated to do it, but it wouldn't do for an animal to suffer.

I led us away from the scene, leaving our five attackers to their fates. They'd been fortunate to have confronted me. Others likely would have finished them all off and left them for the buzzards and coyotes.

Blue Flower's eyes danced with the admiration that comes from fully appreciating the strength of character of her man.

Spirit Talker simply smiled at me.

Zeb? He longed for the horseflesh, but followed us away after all.

Mostly barren rugged prairie now lay ahead of us. I looked forward to reaching the hills and forests beyond.

IT TOOK another four weeks of hard travel to reach just a bit south of the North Platte River. The verdant landscape was a welcome relief. We encountered no threats other than some bears that ran off. We reckoned Kiowa and Arapaho were watching but dared not challenge the *sunipu* of Walks With Wolves. We ate well, as Spirit Talker and I were adept with bows and arrows. We did some trading with the Pawnee. Even the weather cooperated.

At about the time I figured we were nearing Fort Laramie, we met our next challenge.

NINETEEN
THE NORTH PLATTE

THERE MUST HAVE BEEN NEARLY twenty mounted Oglala Lakota warriors strung out across our trail. I quickly recognized my old nemesis Otaktay and his friend Mato. I saw neither hide nor hair of Tasunke Witko, the wise young warrior whose name translated as Crazy Horse.

Spirit Talker and I made the sign for peace.

Otaktay answered by raising his lance high overhead.

Silence.

A pony nickered. A snort. The tree leaves spoke as a breeze sifted through.

Zeb and his pack joined us. That got Otaktay's attention. The savage warrior's face seemed to transform into a dark, evil apparition. His warpaint added to the illusion of malevolence, of pure hatred.

Twenty to four were not especially attractive odds.

We weren't that that from George's ranch. Would he hear gunfire? Fort Laramie was much too far away.

Slowly, I pulled my rifle from its scabbard. I glanced back, and saw that Blue Flower held her rifle across the saddle horn. Spirit Talker did the same, and a revolver had even found its way into Prairie Flower's hands. We might not survive this, but Oglalas were surely going to die.

I could see that Otaktay was mulling the situation over in his mind. His pony pranced anxiously.

Tension. There was plenty of tension. Big Red's ears were pricked up and he snorted. Spirit Talker's pony turned a full circle out of anticipation. George emitted a hunger cry from his carrier behind Blue Flower.

Otaktay was momentarily disconcerted.

Could we avoid a battle? I looked at Spirit Talker. There was a stand of trees off to our left. It was a poor defensive position but the best we could expect given the situation. Of course, that begged the question of whether we could reach the trees in time.

"*Katá! Kize!*" he shouted with another wave of his lance and drove his heels into the sides of his pony.

I understood enough Lakota to translate to *kill* and *fight*.

The Oglala warriors lunged forward behind Otaktay.

I got off a couple of quick shots as we turned and headed for the trees. Spirit Talker reached the trees first, dove from his pony, and started a cover fire as we charged into the trees. We could almost feel the hot breath of the Oglala ponies as they strove to close upon us.

I dove from my saddle and joined Spirit Talker in spitting as much lead as we could at our attackers.

Blue Flower dropped in beside me. Our twins were still in the carriers on her pony that she had somehow managed to tie to a low-lying limb in among the chaos. She began shooting as fast as she could. The rifle grew too hot, and she began firing her Colt revolver.

By my count, at least four Oglala lay dead or dying in the twenty or so yards between us and the hostiles. A couple of ponies were struggling to get up. The scene was one of sheer terror by which weaker women would have surrendered. Our wives fired, reloaded, and fired some more.

The Oglala retreated.

"Hold fire!" I commanded. It wouldn't do to waste ammunition.

Otaktay and Mato were outgunned, yet still had superior numbers. He gathered his warriors about a hundred yards off.

By now, Spirit Talker had switched to his bow and arrows. Given the range at which we were fighting, they could be as deadly. Plus, he could shoot arrows nearly as fast as I could fire my own Colt revolver. "No *kooitu*," he shouted. We would not die.

Otaktay was mustering his force for a second attack. Zeb appeared, but the wolf's *sunipu* didn't dissuade the Oglala this time.

Blue Flower looked over at her pony with the twins still in the carriers behind the saddle cantle. I reached out to stop her, but she was determined to reach the boys.

Otaktay had chosen the moment to charge again. The Oglala closed the ground quickly.

We laid down as heavy a fire as we could. I saw savages fall. One took a bullet to the chest right in front of me and fell at my feet, a hate-filled grimace across his face. Another fell to one of Spirit Talker's arrows. The Oglala seemed to be all around us. Twice, I felt a coup stick touch me. Otaktay galloped headlong past me with Mato at his heels. I clubbed Mato off his pony with a swing of my rifle butt. He hit the ground with a force that knocked the air from his lungs, and I plunged my Bowie knife deep into his chest.

But Otaktay had sped past close enough that his pony's lather hit my face. He snatched up Blue Flower by her shirt and carried her off as she kicked and screamed with all her might. The carriers holding the twins fell, bouncing among the rocks and grasses. Their cries mixed with the shouts of the battle.

The battle-crazed Oglala warrior let out a blood-curdling scream as he charged back past me and headed away with his prize—Blue Flower. My beautiful, loving, and pregnant wife had become a hostage at best, a slave at worst. Otaktay whooped again loudly as he led his remaining warriors away at a gallop.

I watched helplessly and gasped for breath as the Oglalas disappeared in clouds of dust. I was reflexively reloading my guns.

Spirit Talker, Prairie Flower, and I strove to gather our wits. My Comanche brother was the first to take stock of our situation. Compassion filled his heart as he saw the pain and anger on my face and watched the already distant Oglala Lakota carry away my wife, his sister. "Lakota *tabu*," he seethed. Cowards indeed.

I fought back tears but gathered what inner strength I could muster. I soothed George and Isa as best I could and was grateful for Prairie Flower's help. I had to be a leader, to be strong, to take charge. I stood and leaned against the tree. Big Red appeared to be unharmed. The Oglala had stolen our two packhorses, leaving behind the travois and our personal effects lying about. I staggered out to the battlefield and examined half a dozen Oglala warriors. All were dead. One had a broken neck replete with deep fang marks. Zeb had helped.

There was no point in our trying to follow Otaktay's

band. He would still have the advantage of numbers and knew the terrain all too well. Our only choice was to reach George's place and figure out a way to rescue Blue Flower. Might we muster soldiers from Fort Laramie? Could Spirit Talker, George, me, and the couple of hands that worked for George make up a sufficient force to track down the savage Oglala Lakota kidnappers? We gathered up our belongings, and I placed the twins' carriers behind my own saddle. After mercy killing two ponies, we headed north toward George's ranch. There was still plenty of daylight. Zeb led the way, though I sensed that he was anxious to pursue the Oglala.

I prayed mightily that we'd find a way to rescue Blue Flower unscathed. We dared not do anything rash, yet speed was of the essence while Otaktay's trail was still fresh. Now, the question lingered as to whether we would all survive to return to Rising Cross Ranch? God willing, we would.

———————

THE SHORT REMAINDER of our journey to George's ranch was a test of our patience and endurance. We were tired and had taken a mental and physical beating. Zeb acted as though ready to pursue the Oglala savages. In a way, that was encouraging. His energy and spirit kept us riding forward.

The soft light from lanterns soon could be seen casting their light from the windows of George's cabin. The remaining few yards seemed to take forever. At last, we reined in at the cabin just as the orange glow of dusk settled over the mountain peaks to our west. We were a ragged mess. The empty saddle on Blue Flower's pony served as a constant reminder that she'd been captured by the savage Lakota warriors.

"George!" I shouted as we dismounted. "George!"

Running Waters emerged. She paused for a moment. Her mouth dropped open, aghast at the vision before her.

I was a disheveled mess with my buckskins torn and Mato's blood smeared across my chest and arms. Spirit Talker had suffered a couple of bruises from glancing misses of Oglala clubs. Only Prairie Flower and the twins remained unscathed.

"Jack," gasped Running Waters as she rushed to my side. "Jack...what happened?"

"Lakota," I responded. "Ambushed us a couple of miles back. They took Blue Flower."

"Come...come inside. Do not worry about the horses. George will be home any minute." She hoisted the twins from the carriers and led the way into the cabin.

We collapsed into chairs around the kitchen table. Zeb actually followed me inside and parked himself at my feet. He acted more dog-like day by day. His demeanor spoke of readiness to rescue Blue Flower, or at least, that's what I sensed.

Running Waters began heating up some coffee.

I began to describe the attack when George came crashing through the front door. He'd seen the horses outside and sensed trouble. His eyes made a quick scan of the room. "What the?" he exclaimed.

By this time, we were sipping coffee and generally trying to more fully gather our wits. Running Waters had given me one of George's shirts and was tending to Spirit Talker's cuts and bruises. I explained the ambush to George.

The big Black cowboy shook his head. The broad grin

that so endeared him was absent. "I know where their encampment is, Jack. But I doubt that Otaktay would take Blue Flower there. Crazy Horse is gaining power among the Lakota, and he would not approve of Otaktay's action. He's likely holding her elsewhere."

"What will he do?" I said with a hint of fearful tremor in my voice.

"Doubt he will harm her...at least, not right away. He's likely figuring what she might be worth." George sat and rubbed his chin thoughtfully. "I'd reckon he'll want plenty of ponies, maybe some beeves."

"What about the troops at Fort Laramie?"

George shook his head. "Take too much time. If Otaktay only has a dozen warriors remaining from the war party, he's not anxious to lose more fighters."

Spirit Talker nodded. The Comanche way would be to hunt Otaktay down and kill them all as quickly as possible. "We hunt before he decide ransom," he urged.

George agreed. "It's late, but we dare not wait until morning. I have an idea where he might be. I have two cowboys working for me. We'll bring Hank with us and leave Rowdy here to mind the home front with Running Waters and Prairie Flower. Your boys will be safe." He looked down at Zeb. "He's still hanging around?"

I nodded. "I'm convinced he's a gift from God, George."

George's words filled me with hope. A man without hope is lost. George was more than experienced and a man of deep faith, he was courageous. He could likely charge hell with a bucket of ice water and put out its fires.

What could I say? We sure weren't too tired to hunt down the Oglala Lakota savages. We'd refresh our horses as best we could and pack light.

George gathered us around, and we prayed for success. I especially prayed that Blue Flower would not be harmed.

I donned fresh buckskins and high-topped moccasins. They'd be far preferable to boots if we had to do any stalking. I reloaded my rifle and slipped it into the scabbard hanging on Big Red's saddle. Last but hardly least, I grabbed my bow and quiver of arrows. I felt as though they would be most effective for what we faced.

Running Waters packed some grub. It wasn't much, as we didn't figure to be gone more than a day, two at most. Longer than that wouldn't bode well for the outcome. Off we rode into a darkness and a wilderness of night sounds.

My faith was being tested to its very roots deep within my soul that I'd given to God. The frontier was so unforgiving, and we were venturing out at night. I had necessarily grown to manhood in a mere three years. I was as educated as my ma and pa had managed to instill, but taming the frontier turned to be less about formal book learning and far more about keeping my wits sharp, mind alert, ready to react in a split second, and adaptable to my surroundings. It could be said that I lived on the knife's edge of reality. The Comanche had named me Walks With Wolves. Guess that made me out to be a hero of sorts. Hero? Perhaps I'm overly humble, but hero seems to be a word for storytellers. On the frontier, men must do whatever the situation calls for to preserve their lives and the lives of loved ones, friends, and more.

I knew in the depths of my soul that Blue Flower could endure. She was tough, as evidenced by the time she saved my life by shooting a rogue Comanche shaman and later helping fight off Mexican bandits. She was of strong stock, the daughter of the legendary chief Buffalo Hump and sister to my Comanche brother Spirit Talker.

We soon found ourselves fully wrapped in the darkness. Zeb was in the lead, followed single file by George, Spirit Talker, me, and Hank. George was the lead human, thanks to his knowledge of the area, but it was Zeb that we followed. He followed Blue Flower's scent. The big lobo moved as quickly as we mere mortal humans allowed. He'd run ahead, then pause while we caught up.

Would we—could we—find Blue Flower in time? Would she be unharmed?

EPILOGUE

THE AMERICAN WESTERN frontier was mostly unforgiving, a meeting of savagery and civilization. The Comancheria was wild country. Some folks said it was the very roughest part of our western frontier. What made it so? It was Comanche, Kiowa, and Apache territory, for one thing. The region had long been a virtual no-man's-land for White settlers. *Warpath: Jack's Faith is Tested* offers a peek into the courage, faith, endurance, and pure grit entailed in the conquest of the west. It presages the decades it would take to reap the bounty the region would eventually deliver. Jack must deal with man's inhumanity to man and finds his own faith tested.

Life expectancy on the frontier was nothing like today. A male Indian did well to live beyond age thirty, and women could expect to live a tad less. Little wonder that older tribesmen were highly respected. Life expectancy for Whites wasn't much better. A White man on the frontier tended not to live beyond his late thirties. Notably, the brevity of life generally meant that folks had to mature sooner. By the time a man or woman reached age fifteen or sixteen, he or she was pretty much an adult in terms of others expecting him or her to carry an adult set of responsibilities.

Dangers? Anthropology-minded folks claim there were as many as thirteen tribes of Comanche, from the Quahadi or *antelope eaters* in the north to the Penateka or *honey eaters* in the south. Mix in Kiowa, Apache, and Tonkawa, and settlers had their hands full. The very name Comanche loosely translates in the Ute tribal language as *enemy*. Capture by the Comanche invariably led to terrible outcomes. A fearsome lot these tribes were. Notably, Penateka Comanche Chief Buffalo Hump led more than 600 warriors on a raid through the heart of Texas in August 1840, murdering Texans, looting the city of Victoria, and looting and burning Linnville on their march to the Gulf of Mexico. It was not until 1858 that Texas Ranger John Salmon *Rip* Ford led the force of 102 heavily armed Texas Rangers into the Comancheria and brought the Comanche to their knees at the Battle of Little Robe Creek on the Canadian River as depicted hereinin *Warpath: Jack's Faith is Tested.*

The northwestern plains were peopled by many tribes but especially the Sioux, comprised of three groups: Dakota, Nakota, and Lakota. *Warpath: Jack's Faith is Tested* focuses on the Lakota, in turn made up of seven subgroups: Oglalas (famed for Red Cloud and Crazy Horse), Hunkpapas (famed for Sitting Bull), Miniconjous, Oohenunpas (Two Kettles), Itazipacolas (Sans Arcs), Brulés (Burnt Thighs), and Sihasapas (Blackfeet). The Lakota history was no less combative than Comanche or Cheyenne. Despite the violence of the frontier, it's worthy of note that the Lakota held to a worthy set of virtues: generosity, courage, fortitude, and wisdom.

Oh, I do refer to bison as buffalo. Just for the record,

bison and buffalo are quite different. Visualize the water buffalo and then the shaggy, awkward bulk of the American bison. Seems that *buffalo* came into common usage in America to refer to the bison, so I've chosen to use buffalo in my writings.

In *Warpath: Jack's Faith is Tested*, young Jack O'Toole must deal with the threat to the Comanche family of his wife and best friend as posed by Texas Rangers that have been assembled due to the raging fears of White settlers throughout Texas. It is said the United States' western frontier offered new opportunities for hearty folks willing to endure its rigors. It might also be said that folks who settled certain parts of the frontier, like the Comancheria, were not playing with a full deck. They had to be crazy.

Jack had no modern creature comforts. Invention of cell phones and social media was a century and a half into the future. Transportation? Horses and mules ridden or pulling wagons were the vehicles of choice. Jack had no refrigerator to preserve sweet treats. There were no flush toilets or showers. Folks mostly ate what grazed upon or grew from the land. Learning was squeezed from the few books that might be found, especially the Holy Bible. By way of example, my own great-great-great-grandfather brought his collection of books from Ireland in 1851. As a serious and religious-minded pioneer, he had gathered quite an impressive library for his time, such as three volumes of *Lives of the Saints, Lives of Irish Saints and Martyrs*, Geoffrey Keating's *History of Ireland*, Edward Clarendon's *History of Ireland*, a *History of the Christian Church*, lectures and sermons by Father Burke titled *Instructions for Youth*, and Hume's *History of England, Trials of a Mind*. Sort of makes a head swim, doesn't it?

Can't say that the living of the era was luxurious unless you counted the sheer grandeur of majestic landscapes and of nights so quiet you could hear the stars twinkling. To fully appreciate the place, you simply had to love the beauty of the outdoors. Fishing the meandering Guadalupe River in Texas or the chill waters of Wyoming's North Platte River, hunting deer and antelope, raising cattle and horses, and reaping the bounteous yield of the rich soil was sheer joy for a courageous visionary few. For a teen on the frontier, life could be pretty good...mostly. Otherwise, it was downright dangerous.

Thus far, Jack O'Toole has grown to manhood, conquered fears and prejudices, fought Indians and bandits, taken on prairie fires and storms, defended against wild beasts, traveled the wild country, driven cattle, and found the love of his life. As you have seen, he especially draws upon his faith and what he was taught by his parents. And yet, all of this is tested. He has to learn to trust in instincts forged from his biblical lessons. Yes, Jack is on a frontier adventure and more.

ACKNOWLEDGMENTS

Authoring books doesn't simply happen in a vacuum. The author provides the creative talent and crafts the stories, but there's so much more that demands acknowledgment. There are lots of folks and places that contribute to my authoring endeavors. So it is with *Warpath: Jack's Faith is Tested*. The tale is set in 1858 and shares the trials and tribulations of a teen forced to meet the challenges inherent in the dangerous vastness of the western frontier, but this novel stands apart. At its core, it is also about the taming of the frontier. Step in two teen boys becoming men. The protagonist epitomizes the freedom of America's western frontier and represents a final bastion of honor in America. The tale follows Jack O'Toole's adventures in *Perilous Trails: Jack's Adventure Begins*, *Wyoming Calls: Jack's Risky Quest*, and *Longhorns North: Jack's Great Trail Drive*. Hopefully, readers will find *Warpath: Jack's Faith is Tested* worthy of their time and emotional involvement.

I've been blessed with many friends and family who have supported my writings. My wife Carolyn's reviews and encouragement were a huge help, along with very important tech support from our sons Mike and Matt. Thanks to my nephew Shawn for his faith insights. Many more friends and family have contributed support at some level to the creation and publication of *Warpath: Jack's Faith is Tested*, be it encouragement or advice.

Naturally, I am major grateful to the great folks at

Wise Wolf Books. The team they bring to publishing is first-rate in editing, cover design, and the myriad tasks that lead to successful book sales.

It's only right to acknowledge my ancestors who were actual settlers of the south Texas frontier. In addition to inspiring me, they provided a quite helpful true-to-life framework as to the life and times on the Texas Nueces Strip. It has been appropriate to weave them into the tapestry of my western novels. Matthew Dunn (1815-1855) immigrated to Corpus Christi from County Kildare in 1845, established a homestead on Upriver Road, and served as a sutler to General Zachary Taylor's Army in the Mexican-American War. Peter Dunn (1807-1890) immigrated from Ireland in 1850 and established a blacksmith shop in Corpus Christi, John Dunn (1803-1889), my great great great grandfather, raised cattle and grew thousands of acres of cotton, Lawrence Dunn (1837-1864) fought and died with Captain Ware's Confederate cavalry, and my great great grandfather Nicholas Dunn (1835-1912) was a rancher, drover, livestock speculator, and Comanche fighter of some repute. My cousin John Beamond *Red John* Dunn (1851-1940) served as a Texas Ranger in the 1870s under Captain Bland Chamberlain (Company H), subsequently joined a *vigilance committee*, became a farmer and merchant, and curated a museum of military weapons displayed to this day in the Corpus Christi Museum of Science & History. Red John Dunn's brother Matthew Dunn also served as a Texas Ranger, and another cousin, Rut Evans, served as a Texas Ranger in the 1890s (Company E, Frontier Battalion, Alice, TX). My cousin Patrick Dunn was quite successful at raising longhorns on North Padre Island just east of Corpus Christi from 1883 to 1937. John Hillard Dunn (1883-1958), whose personal narrative about his family and his own adventures drove my pursuit of my Texas family legacy, inspired my own writings and led me to write his yet-to-be-published biography *Tough Hombre—Recollections of a True Texan*. Finally, my grandfather, Horace Charles Greathouse, served as a Texas Ranger in 1920 (Company C, Austin, TX). Such real-life characters, coupled with actual events, have served to reinforce the historical settings for my writings.

Most of my authoring has occurred in my office as decorated to channel my inner Texan, but my creative juices have often been inspired and my imagination stoked in cafés and coffee houses across America. My favorites were Hester's Café & Coffee Bar in Corpus Christi, TX, Nueces Café in Robstown, TX, Java Ranch Espresso Bar & Café in Fredericksburg, TX, PAX Coffee & Goods in Kerrville, TX, Ragged Edge Coffee House and Bantam Coffee Roasters in Gettysburg, PA, 1889 Coffee House in Helena, MT, Dunn Brothers Coffee in Rapid City, SD, Postmasters Coffee & Bakery and Brio Coffeehouse in Waynesboro, PA, Birdie's Café and American Ice Co Café in Westminster, MD, Deja Brew Coffee House, New Oxford and Deja Brew at Miney Branch, Carroll Valley, PA, Baltimore Coffee & Tea Co., Frederick Coffee Company & Café, and Dublin Roasters in Frederick, MD, and Qualle Café and Grounded Coffee & Bakery, Cherokee, NC. I must admit to also frequenting a few Dunkin Donuts and Starbucks around our fine nation. The décors and easy-listening music in these fine establishments combined with savory cups of coffee tended to set me in the right creative frame of mind.

Last but not least, I'm especially thankful for the many folks who have read and enjoyed my books.

I do believe it's important to acknowledge how the

old west represents the brave pioneering spirit of settlers who met the challenges and transcended mere survival to enable America to achieve exceptional growth. The settling of the American frontier west is replete with tales of leveraging freedom for individual achievement. I hope you'll agree that reliving our past—even through history-based fiction—often has the effect of pointing the way to an ever-brighter future. Might we be up to it? I hope that the inspiration I've drawn from my having walked the very earth my characters have trodden, coupled with my extensive historical research, will enable readers to fully experience the grit, adventure, and passion of my characters while sensing aromas of gunsmoke, trail dust, leather, and bluebonnets.

Thanks kindly to all of you, and please do enjoy *Warpath: Jack's Faith is Tested.*

IF YOU LIKED THIS, YOU MIGHT LIKE... TWO THOUSAND GRUELING MILES: THE COMPLETE YA WESTERN SERIES
BY L.J. MARTIN

Two Thousand Grueling Miles: The Complete YA Western Series is a true family adventure tale full of can't put it down action!

Two Thousand Grueling Miles: Thrust into the role of family protector, young Jake Zane faces the ultimate test of survival and resilience on the unforgiving Oregon Trail. With a massive mute escaped slave as his ally, Jake must navigate 2,000 miles of harsh terrain, battling wild animals, severe weather, and threats from both settlers and natives. Together with his mother and sisters, Jake's journey is a testament to the enduring human spirit and the bonds of family.

Rugged Trails: With his fields ravaged by locusts, Jake takes a perilous job as a wagon and mule train guard, tasked with transporting precious cargo across treacherous paths. Facing hostile terrain, inclement weather, and dangerous encounters with both wildlife and outlaws, Jake must ensure the safe passage of the train to secure a future for his family.

Stormy Seas: Upon reaching San Francisco, Jake Zane finds himself entangled with the notorious Sydney Duck gang. With the support of his friend, Lord Stanley-Smyth, Jake embarks on a new adventure aboard a coastal lumber schooner and later a freighter bound for the Sandwich Islands. In this coming-of-age journey, Jake learns the harsh realities of life at sea and the treacherous world of gold-seeking adventurers.

The Piccadilly: Tasked with transforming the infamous Bucket of Blood saloon into The Piccadilly, Jake Zane navigates the dangerous underworld of San Francisco. Under the mentorship of Lord Stanley-Smyth, Jake encounters gamblers, city cops, Chinese tong soldiers, and intriguing soiled doves. In this gripping conclusion, Jake's loyalty is tested as he balances the demands of his employer and the complex dynamics of a city teeming with ambition and peril.

TheTwo Thousand Grueling Miles: The Complete YA Western Series is a riveting young adult western series that captures the heart of American pioneering spirit. Join Jake on his epic journey of survival, courage, and adventure. Dive in today and experience the thrill of the untamed West!

AVAILABLE NOW

ABOUT THE AUTHOR

Award-winning author Mark Greathouse's love for the western genre draws upon his deep family roots and love of the outdoors honed from teen years hiking the Appalachian Trail and family travels across America's frontier. Greathouse began writing full time after a successful career as a business executive and later as an entrepreneurial investor and advisor. His service as president of several business and community nonprofits led to their extraordinary growth. He holds a BA in English and MBA in marketing. Greathouse donates time and books annually to support wounded military warriors. He was a Boy Scout leader (Eagle Scout) and served on a local school board.

A member of Western Writers of America and the Wild West History Association, he also contributes articles on the history of America's west to western-themed magazines. Greathouse was recognized as a 2024 Finalist in western genre by the American Literary Book Awards for his sixth Tumbleweed Saga, *Nueces Truth: Texans Face War's Realities*.

His *Frontier Chronicles,* a series of western novels aimed at adventure-minded teens and young adults while weaving a Christian message within their fabric, are aimed at lighting fires of truth, faith, hope, and life purpose in the bellies of today's teen boys and girls. Just as seeds must be sown to reap the harvest, so the seeds of faith must be planted to raise tomorrow's men and women.

GLOSSARY

DEFINITIONS

Bear sign—Cowboy slang for donuts.

Big Father—All-powerful Comanche deity.

Bota bag—A canteen fashioned from leather and popular among Indians, mountain men, and many travelers of the western frontier.

Cold Camp—Camp without a campfire, generally done to avoid the smoke that might alert threats.

Dog run—The sheltered space or breezeway between two sections of some southern ranch houses. Living quarters were usually on one side, and sleeping quarters on the other.

Fletch—The fin-shaped bird feathers on an arrow that help stabilize its flight.

Gallery—A synonym for porch. Folks in the west often called them galleries.

Life debt—A cultural phenomenon in which someone whose life is saved or spared by another becomes indebted or in some way connected to their savior.

Pemmican—Lean dried strips of meat pounded into a paste, mixed with fat and berries, and then pressed into small cakes.

Possibles bag—A leather or canvas sack carried by cowboys and containing essentials like soap, matches, bandages, extra spur, smoke makings, and playing cards

Remuda—A herd of horses frequently used on trail drives and by Plains Indians.

Shaman—Comanche medicine man.

Teepee—An enclosed conical transportable shelter constructed of long poles and buffalo hides with a vent at the top to permit smoke to escape.

Travois—A wedge-shaped structure constructed of two poles and a cross-beam lashed together and dragged behind horses, mules, or dogs by Plains Indians.

COMANCHE TRANSLATIONS

Aitu—Not good

Ana o'a hi'it—Phrase for *desire to eat*

Ap—Father

Aruka—Deer

Eetu—Bow

Ekakwitsʉbaitʉ—Lightning

Ekapitu—Red

Eekᶏsahpana paraiboo—Army officer (soldier chief)

Hawokatu—Hollow, loose

Hoikwa—Hunt, look for prey

Isa—Wolf

Isa wasu—Poison

Kaahaniitu—deceive, cheat

Kahni—Life

Kamakuna—Loved one

Kee—No

Kobe—Wild Horse

Kohto—Build a fire

Kooitu—Die

Kutseena—Coyote

Kwakuru—Defeat someone

Nahuu—Knife

Natsuitu—Strong

Numu—Teepee

Numunuu—Referring to the members of the Comanche tribes. Literally: people.

Ohapitu—Yellow

Onaa—Son or daughter

Paa—Water

Paaka—Arrow

Peeka—Kill

Pia—Mother

Pia huutsuu—Bald eagle

Pia wa'óo—Comanche words for mountain lion, puma, or cougar.

Pihi—Heart

Pohya (or poya)—Walk

Puuka—Horse

Sunipu—Medicine (as in strong medicine)

Suumaru—Ten

Taa Narʉmi—Master/God

Tabu—Coward

Tamu—Rabbit

Tasiwoo—Buffalo

Tenahpu—Man

Tomoobi—Sky

Tosa—White man or woman
Tosaabitu—White
Tumah tuyai—After life
Tuhibitu—Black
Tumhyokenu—Believe, trust
Tu Taiboo—Black man
Umaru—Rain
Unha haksi nahniaka—Phrase for *what's your name?*
Wa'ipu—Woman
Wasápe—Bear
Wutsutsuki—Rattlesnake

LAKOTA TRANSLATIONS

Ate – Father
Ayústan – Abandon, retreat, leave
Igmuwatogla – Mountain lion
Isan – Knife
Iya Tate - Wind
Iyaya – Go, leave
Jiji – Light hair
Katá – Kill
Kize - Fight
Maka – The earth and grandmother of all things
Mato - Bear
Mini – Water
Nagi – The spirit that has never been a man
Niya – Ghost
Oyate – The people or nation
Sapa - Black
Scan—Sky
Ska - White
Sunkmanitu tanka - Wolf
Takuwe - Why
Tanka – Wolf
Tatanka – The great beast (patron of health, ceremonies, provision)
Unk – Created by Maka; embodies all evil beings
Unktehi – One who kills
Wakan tanka – God (monotheistic)
Wamaka nagi – Animal spirit
Wanbli – Eagle
Wani – Four winds (weather)
Wasake – Strong

Wash tay – Good
Wasichus – White man
Wasna – Pemmican
Wi – The sun (chief of all gods)
Wica – Complete man
Wicasa – Man (gender)
Wicasa wakan – Shaman
Winyan – Woman
Wowahwa - Peace
Zuzeca – Snake